# WINDLESS PATH

# (A NARROWBOAT STORY)

© 2024

David Blackburne-Kane

# DEDICATED TO

# DEBORAH

Successfully navigating Britain's canals
requires a windlass key

Successfully negotiating life's journey
requires a windless path

## Table of Contents

Prologue — A Wedding ........................................................ 1
1 — A Rude Awakening ....................................................... 4
2 — Kipepeo ........................................................................ 20
3 — Pinkerton Smith ........................................................... 33
4 — Brenda ......................................................................... 45
5 — 'Rumah Saya' ............................................................... 57
6 — Boating Solo ................................................................ 72
7 — Tess the Cockapoo ....................................................... 87
8 — Lockside Cottage ....................................................... 105
9 — Alex Dewhurst ........................................................... 119
10 — Cracker .................................................................... 138
11 — Fiona Fullerton ........................................................ 156
12 — Colonel Parker ......................................................... 171
13 — A Foxy Tale ............................................................. 187
14 — The Old Lady .......................................................... 203
15 — Beneath the Sycamore ............................................. 220
16 — A Voice from the Past ............................................. 239
17 — Cruising the Cut ...................................................... 256

18 — An Inland Port ...................................................... 275
19 — An Uninvited Visitor ............................................ 294
20 — Clifton Squibb...................................................... 313
21 — The Key to A Windless Path ............................... 328
Epilogue — Halcyon Days............................................. 333

## PROLOGUE — A WEDDING

Shafts of warm autumn sunlight dappled the fallen leaves below the mighty oak. Framed by the stately brown sandstone façade of the old King Charles I School registry office, a beaming glow emanated from the newlywed couple.

Dressed in an ivory white knee length lace dress, the woman complimented his midnight blue three-piece suit. The suit was just a fraction too small, and his ivory toned wrists protruded from the cuff. Her dress clung to her middle-aged curves emphasizing the fullness of bust and hips. In her hand was a small bouquet of royal blue calla lilies that matched the groom's attire. Sat perfectly composed at the woman side was an apricot-coloured cockapoo wearing a blue bandana that also matched the man's outfit.

Photographs of the husband, wife and dog taken, the photographer invited the two witnesses to the marriage to join the happy couple and make up a modest group photograph as a keepsake. Just two hours previously, these two individuals who were unacquainted with each other, or indeed the bride and groom, had been sat in the local Starbucks drinking coffee and quietly minding their own business, when a rather debonair man in his late fifties had approach them separately to ask their assistance in witnessing the wedding and signing of the register.

Now, memories for posterity having been completed the two individuals bade goodbye and wished the genial couple lots of happiness for the future. They both collected a wicker hamper from the usher, given by the bride and groom as a 'token appreciation' of their willingness to share in the happy occasion.

As they walked down the gravel path towards the road, the gentleman drew the accompanying woman's attention to a couple of feline animals sat under the great oak. Both adult cats gave an appearance of being the closest of friends. "Why," the woman exclaimed "It is as if they are watching the proceedings just as any bystander might do."

As they passed through the old wooden gate, they wished each other well and headed off in separate directions to continue the activities of the day as if nothing unusual had happened. How wrong they were! This day was the culmination of some unusual occurrences that had begun around two years earlier on the wild moorland of Devon.

# 1 — A RUDE AWAKENING

I woke to the rhythmic sound of tapping against the steel hulled narrowboat 'Rumah Saya'. This was a typical occurrence for a spring morning on the Staffordshire and Worcestershire canal at Kinver. Nevertheless, it was most annoying, I would have been more than happy to continue night-time slumbers well into mid-morning.

The rhythm was moving now, splitting into two distinct sounds travelling up and down the fifty-nine-foot-long boat. I rolled over onto my side, slowly easing my lifeless body into some state of action. From the for'ard cabin Alex appeared looking somewhat dishevelled with tousled hair and wearing bright green pyjamas. He grunted at me as he slipped the two chrome catches on the swan hatch. Pushing both halves fully open onto the outer steel skin of the boat he glanced upon the calm waters of the canal.

"Swans!" he exclaimed, as if this was the first-time he had seen them. "Swans, always waking us up early, too early, ugh, coffee!" and he stomped off to brew coffee in the galley.

I roused myself, and from the vantage point of the small wooden shelf and cupboard that conveniently hid the 15-inch television and DVD player I tentatively poked my head out of the hatch. I immediately received a serious hiss from the mute swan closest to me. It seems swans don't like me very much. I only want to be friends; I only want to watch them as they tap away at the moss that has accumulated on the water line of the steel hull. It seems they do not appreciate my friendly advances.

It was a pleasant morning for an April day. The whole of nature seemed to rejoice in spring, whispering soft voices to a delighted audience. Up and down the waterway, birds were singing, chirping and flitting about their business of courting and nest building. On a rustic wooden stake sticking out of the water a small male robin with a bright redbreast sang contentedly.

Along the towpath side of the canal were moored numerous and varied boats. Some were new, shiny and well cared for, others older, sadder, and neglected. They made for a colourful scene as each boat sported its own livery. Traditional reds and greens were interspersed with dark blue- and fawn-coloured vessels with various designs of coach line and fittings. Names likewise reflected owners' tastes. There was a seventy foot 'Fellows Morton and Clayton Ltd.', an early iron hull built in 1898 at the Tipton Wharf, North-West of Birmingham. Lovingly restored and re-painted with traditional colours of black and white with a red dividing line and matching red cover over the cramped living space. It was a welcome addition to the linear moorings at Kinver. Beyond that a shorter cruiser type boat named 'Kingfisher' was followed further along the towpath by an even smaller boat, some forty-five foot, named 'At Last'. Perhaps the original owner had longed to possess a boat of his own and had struggled for some time to realise the dream.

A low-level sun was illuminating the scene and in doing so drew out the sheer beauty and grace of these magnificent swans. I watched the male cob who, compared with the female displayed a larger black knob on its orange bill as it gracefully drifted towards its mate. The slightly larger male swan rubbed its long S-shaped neck against the pen, the jet-black nostrils, nail and base contrasted with the vibrant orange of the bird's beak. Both swans turned gracefully in the water and moved slowly away to the far bank, as they did so the female pouted her wings, the soft pure-white of her plumage allowing the morning sunlight to shimmer off her back. On the opposing bank there was the beginnings of a new nest, soon to be used in raising this year's cygnets.

I turned my head away from the hatch in time to see Alex emerge from the kitchen with his coffee. In the corner of the saloon Lapsat, the Black Persian, was looking up at me with big orange eyes.

"Morning Lapsat, sleep well?" I queried.

Lapsat replied in her usual predictable way: "Well as can be expected at my age."

I jumped nimbly down from the shelf and sidled up to Alex. As I rubbed my head against the calf of his leg I started to purr loudly.

"I guess you both want feeding?" Alex questioned, even though he knew the answer before he asked the question. I didn't reply, after all, cats cannot speak!

#

Boss-man, Lapsat and I had been living on narrowboat 'Rumah Saya' for over a month now. We had just endured the winter period in the little cottage in Devon when our protector gathered us up, and placing us separately in two cat carriers, installed us in the little Toyota. I do not pretend I was comfortable, but as soon as I realized we were travelling further than the local town's veterinary surgery, I curled up and slept. A pleasant nap considering the movement of the car and the constant whinging of my feline companion who most certainly was not enjoying the experience and was determined that we both should know the fact.

When finally, we pulled up alongside a man-made river and were carried on to Boss-man's spacious new living quarters, it dawned on me that some permanent change of home was upon us. We had left behind the dark cloud that had been hanging over the little cottage on Dartmoor and arrived at a new and sunny point in life. That evening, when alone with Lapsat, I mentioned the journey and the new environment.

"Hey Lapsat," I said to draw her attention from the empty food bowl that she was contemplating, "is this our new home or what?"

The wise old molly looked pensively around the interior of the boat and replied: "Guess so. 'E brought our beds, food dishes 'nd blankets with us, didn't 'e," then looking to the corner of the saloon area she grimaced and added: "'nd litter-tray! 'aven't used one of those since backalong, not since I 'ad fight with Greenbrow's Alsatian 'nd vet-man said I must stay indoors 'til stiches 'ealed."

I put a quizzical look on my face and questioned: "Don't you mean the German Shepherd?"

"Yes, yes, same thing, Greenbrow calls it Alsatian. Certainly, caused me some grief, 'ad to use dirt box for nearly three weeks. So, I figure we be stuck in doors for a while."

"Why?"

"'tis what 'appens when ee are moved to new area far from y'er 'ome, then ee 'ave time to get used to new space 'nd don't get lost moment ee go outside on y'er own."

It was a puzzling time for a young energetic animal. I was about two years old now. The thing I just could not understand, where was Alex's wife? For over a year she nursed and petted me, then the dark cloud descended! I even remember the day, while waiting at the window I saw Alex return home alone. She never did come back! I miss those peaceful, contented evenings curled on her warm lap. Somehow, I just couldn't bring myself to ask Lapsat, and as cats live in the present, the past becomes a dull memory. Dull but happy.

#

Some two weeks later we were allowed out of confinement. Alex had opened the stern doors of the craft and was calling to us from outside. Being an older and more cautious animal, Lapsat chose to roll over and pretend to continue his morning snooze. I on the other hand, a curious soul, crept cautiously towards the familiar voice. To exit the boat involved climbing several wooden steps and I quickly determined this should be done at a hop, skip and a jump. The pale green grass was wet with spring dew and emitted the smell of new young growth. I love springtime. I hardly remember my first spring, being my very formative days, but last year the smells and fragrances of new growth in the cottage garden had left a lasting impression.

Alex was still trying to coax an indifferent Lapsat to venture outside, while I investigated the small, tarmacked lane beside the boat. Slowly, one paw at a time I advanced towards the pathway. Each step carefully trod while constantly surveying the surroundings for potential dangers. I froze! Frozen with my right paw still in mid-air I glanced upon a Jack Russel with its owner approaching briskly. I have always credited myself to be quick on the paw when necessary, and this was a necessary occasion. Safely back in the protection of the boat, panting and with heart rate accelerated, Lapsat looked at me in that worldly-wise way of hers, inclining her head slightly and grunting: "Foolish moggy!"

Somewhat reluctant to venture outside again I waited for Lapsat to make a move, which she did not do until the following day. Being a few years older than myself, it was more of an effort to negotiate the rear steps to the semi-traditional stern. The benefit of a 'semi-trad' narrowboat is the enclosed seating in front of the helmsman's working area beside the tiller arm. Being a more experienced cat, rather than just disembarking from the boat and giving herself up to the machinations of all and sundry, Lapsat jumped up to the seat on the port or tow-path side of the boat and contentedly chose to watch the passers-by from a secure vantage point. I joined her.

In time we came to appreciate that many canines large and small, along with their owners took a stroll in the morning hours, some attached by lead, some not. A youthful girl would walk each weekday morning down the towpath on her way to school carrying a heavy backpack and return mid-afternoon to her home Wayside Cottage several yards further on after the facilities point. She was a brunette with long wavy hair that emphasized her broad shoulders. Her uniform consisted of a pleated navy skirt and black blazer with a heraldic multi-coloured shield on the left pocket. The red, blue and black stripped tie stood out prominently against the pure white of her blouse. In just a few days she had become a firm friend. Each morning, I would sit on my vantage point awaiting her appearance, while she on the other hand would step from the path to caress my head and whisper kindly comments in my ear. In return I told her she was 'too kind' and wished her a happy day at school, although I believe all she heard from me was a loud purring.

#

A commotion occurred a few days after our settling into our boat home that was instigated by Boss-man. Both Lapsat and I had finished breakfast, meaty chunks in gravy, and were both busy with our ablutions, when a van pulled up alongside the narrowboat. A rough looking character with full beard and moustaches stepped out of the van, stretched, groaned, and called out for Alex. Much commotion, swearing, sounds of drilling and cutting later, he got in his van and drove off. The action had all taken place at the front or bow end of the boat, and naturally we had kept well away, cowering behind Alex's armchair.

When we heard Alex calling us from the front of the boat, we both, curious to investigate the results of the noise, made our way forwards. In the bow doors a flap had been inserted. This was just like the flap in our old home, the cottage in Devon. Lapsat pushed forward and in one quick smooth movement slipped through and out to the world beyond. I followed. My traversing the opening was less smooth, I nuzzled the Perspex flap, pushing it gently and letting it click back into closed position, I pushed again, then I scrabbled through catching my paw awkwardly as I trod on the decking.

The new 'cat door' was a lifesaver. Now we were free to come and go as we deemed appropriate rather than waiting for Alex to open the stern doors and let us roam free. For example, if we spied an aggressive looking animal approaching and we had no other place of refuge, because the tall oak tree was too distant, we could make a dash for the flap. This did involve a quick jump over the gunnels at the bow of the boat, landing in the welldeck and rushing headlong at the flap. Conversely, our nocturnal ramblings were no longer restricted, and just as at Wisteria Cottage we were free to explore and return at our pleasure.

Every couple of days Boss-man would haul a large plastic container on wheels out of the boat and pulling it behind him, make his way north along the towpath. Following on one such occasion, I saw him disappear into a small brick building with a tatty wooden door. He emerged some minutes later with a much lighter vessel, of which, obviously the contents had been disposed of. It turned out to be his personal method of dumping toilet waste. Disgusting! Humans can be so crude. Why they don't just find a soft piece of dirt in the adjacent field or Wayside Cottage pristine garden, dig a small hole, get busy and then scratch soil over it, I will never understand.

While spending time becoming familiar with our new surroundings, we were both getting to know the local wildlife. Swans, robin, blackbirds and others were joined in our immediate vicinity by a local heron, two horses and another cat. The grey heron, that lived in a tall tree somewhere below Kinver lock, periodically flew parallel with the canal cut, landing gracefully on the towpath above our mooring. The first time she flew overhead was an amazing sight that had me transfixed. Huge black and white wings flapping slowly with long ungainly legs protruding from behind. From the bank she craned her head, standing motionless, staring into the murky waters. A sudden stab at the water and in one smooth movement she rose triumphant, a small fish caught in the mustard-coloured projecting jaws of her beak.

#

We first became aware of Chalky the ginger and white tomcat one moonless night. That particular night I had stayed indoors keeping Alex company by sleeping on his bed, something I know he did not appreciate, but it is so warm and cosy and after all the bed is huge, why not share? I was woken from a rather pleasant catnap to the sound of blood-curdling screams. They were somewhat distant, and I immediately recognised the fighting talk of a couple of tomcats in the neighbourhood. Lapsat was out that night, so upon her return in the morning I asked: "Any idea what the fuss was about last night?"

The old moggy continued washing her face with the back of her paw, licking and brushing the soft fur. Presently she said: "Chalky!"

"Who is Chalky?" I quizzed.

"Pub cat, ee not met 'im yet? 'e got a temper like a tor-point chicken!"

No, I had not met Chalky yet. That would be rectified the following evening when I felt the urge to explore a little further from the safe surroundings of our mooring. Below the boat was Kinver lock, as I have mentioned. Beyond the lock was a narrow road which took local vehicles into the village of Kinver, facilitating the crossing of the canal by means of a red-brick bridge that was over 250 years old. Beyond this lay the unknown. Unknown to me. I had no desire to pass beyond the road bridge, who knew what terrors would be waiting to lure me into danger.

Adjacent to the bridge was the local canal pub. A rustic sign hanging over the edge of the outdoor seating area and facing the canal said, 'The Lock Inn' and sported a rudimentary painting of a working narrowboat of years gone by. This is where Chalky lived. I was sitting on the opposite side of the canal from the pub watching patrons enjoying the warm evening air while drinking their beers and eating their chips. Before I knew it, Chalky had appeared, and jumping up on to the balance beam of the lock gate nearest the road, he eyed me up and down. I resisted the urge to run.

Chalky was very attractive. Predominantly ginger haired, streaks of white emphasised his full muscular figure. His small pink nose appeared squashed against the white patches on his flat face. The same vibrant white of his face appeared on his paws and front legs giving him a regal and authoritarian demeanour, which was also reflected in his slow steady movements and overbearing personality. For some reason I was unafraid and sat patiently waiting while he traversed the black and white oak balance beam to access the near bank.

He fixed his look upon me, and we stared at each other for some time before I proffered a simple question: "Was that you fighting last night?"

"Ar, it wor me, babbie."

Babbie! Who did he think I was, I'm not a kitten anymore.

"I got the 'hots' for Bella, but she's Shadow's wench, so I had to scrag him last night."

I lay down, stretched full length, thus exposing my soft white underbelly for his consideration.

"Yow don't really interest me babbie, yow've been fixed!"

Does this Chalky speak in riddles or a different language all together? 'Babbie', 'been fixed', 'hots' and what is this 'scrag him'. I would have to ask Lapsat if she understood his language.

"Well can't hang around babbie, gotta keep movin'. Oh yeh, watch yow-self about these parts of a night-time, can get a bit rowday, know what I mean? It's the hoomans you know."

I rolled over into a sitting position and wrapped my long fluffy white tail around my hind legs. "Thanks for the advice."

He responded: "Tararabit," and was gone. It would not be too long before I learned the import of those auspicious words of warning.

#

The only other significant members of the animal community in the area, were two magnificent horses that lived in the field opposite the towpath. I was well acquainted with these animals, and their smaller equivalent, as we had a field with three horses and two ponies close to our Devon cottage. This field was set down lower that the canal and butted up against the River Stour which itself meandered purposefully toward the greater River Severn. Watching these creatures at pasture was a very pleasant and relaxing pastime for a senior cat like Lapsat, but for me, I preferred action and adventure! Such action was soon to disturb my curious life.

What I did discover while investigating the horses one day was a small wooden hut which had seen better days. However, this became a favourite haunt of mine. I could slip through the wooden fence and undergrowth, drop down the embankment and squeeze through a rotten wooden plank that had come loose from the structure. Inside was dark, and foreboding, until I cautiously explored it fully and found it devoid of fear. In the far corner was a small collection of hessian sacks which made a most acceptable bed. Frequently, when looking to sleep outside our narrowboat home, I would come here, curl up with my head pushed deep under my front paws and dream of a past life on Dartmoor.

Being a cat, I am unable to understand the time, but I do understand day and night, the movement of the sun, and have a good sense of timing when Boss-man puts out breakfast and dinner. I can't say exactly what time it was when I heard the raucous voices emanating from the direction of 'The Lock Inn'. I had settled down comfortably on my newly discovered hessian bed to allow my dinner to digest without worry when my slumber was disturbed. Curious the aroma of cooked fish always arouses my senses. Then the sound of breaking glass, a bottle no doubt beings smashed against the bridge stonework. Naturally my inquisitiveness ensured I would investigate. A simple sighting of the trouble would involve exiting the dark surrounds of the hut through the rotten plank, climbing the embankment, pushing through the undergrowth and wooden fence. This accomplished, I cast my eyes on two male youths sitting on the bottom gate's balance beam. Shattered glass from a beer bottle lay strewn at the foot of the bridge while a small pile of discarded rubbish in the form of paper and Styrofoam containers that had contained fish and chips was resting nearby. I crept cautiously closer to the source of the enticing smell.

In the village, just a few minutes' walk by human legs, is a small corner shop selling groceries, a butcher, two barbers, an Indian restaurant and a Chinese take-away. How do I know all this you may wonder as I have never stepped a paw beyond the bridge near the lock. The information about the local area was supplied to me by Nala, a golden Labrador Retriever who would amble confidently passed our boat on frequent walks. When her silver-haired master stopped to speak with Boss-man, Nala and I would sometimes have a quiet word about the big wide world beyond the canal.

It was on one of these amiable chin-wags Nala told me about the village. It seems her owner likes to frequent one of the Turkish barbers in the village main street, and while doing so, Nala sits patiently outside observing the local community coming and going.

Along with the aforementioned businesses, Nala informed me there was a rather good Fish and Chip shop called 'The Frying Plaice'. Now, it must be said I am rather partial to a piece of cooked fish; however, you can keep the chips, too fatty! This information did not come as a big surprise to me, as on occasion Alex would leave the boat and set off on foot towards the village, returning a short while later with a most enticing aroma of fish and chips. He is a kindly old soul and always shares some of the fish with us cats. Sorry, I digress.

A third young man, a tall guy with the hood from his coat obscuring his face, appeared above the parapet of the bridge and upon seeing the two below hastened to join them. The body language and demeanour of the three clearly indicated a tense situation was developing with angry but hushed words being exchanged. The most vocal of the two men was dressed in dark khaki cargo trousers and a thick woollen military green pullover. I crept closer. The scene was well lit as the pub had not yet closed and thus its two powerful arc lights lit the area and cast eerie shadows upon the mown grass. Keeping to the shadows so as not to attract any undue attention, I worked my way close enough to hear the verbal exchange.

"You're a complete scumbag, you stupid great ..." a motorbike revved loudly as it accelerated across the bridge interrupting the remainder of the expletive laced exchange.

"Don't you go at me fish face. I delivered your stinking packet of crack to 'Jumbo Jim' like you said. If he not pay you, that's your problem not mine."

More expletive accusations followed, then it got physical. Hoodie raised a middle finger, which for some reason that I cannot fathom caused an adverse reaction in cargo man. As he lunged forward, his mate shouted for him to stop and 'Let's get the hell out of here Cracker.' Cargo man was not placated by this, choosing to move forward menacingly. The man in the black hoodie jacket took a step backwards and raised an arm in a defensive move, but Cracker swung a clenched fist and punch hoodie in the stomach.

I guess it was unfortunate that the man in the hooded coat was standing so close to the lock, the physical contact from his former partner caused him to unbalance, and in an instant, he disappeared. Almost simultaneously I heard the loud splash of water being driven from under his rotund body. Was it the angle of the light or did it seem he hit his head on the caping stones of the lock's brickwork. I could not be sure.

The second man reiterated his ultimatum: "Let's get the hell out of here Cracker." Without a reply Cracker turned and legged it with his erstwhile mate in hot pursuit.

I waited, fully expecting a very sodden man to emerge from the lock, perhaps by way of climbing the lock ladder. But nothing happened. Moving forwards I peered over the edge. The water level had fallen about two feet since the last boat had passed through some hours earlier. Floating serenely on the water was a dark shape. It was the lifeless body of a young man floating face down, the hood of his coat now separated from his head. There was nothing I could do to save him.

## 2 — KIPEPEO

Please excuse me. Here you are reading my narrative, but thus far I have not introduced myself. My name is Kipepeo. I am a five-year-old black and white Persian long hair. When I look in Boss-man's floor-length mirror in the bathroom I see a reflection of my snowy-white coat, interspersed with black and chocolate patches. The most prominent patch stretches over my head and right eye, giving me a distinguished and regal appearance, at least in my opinion, and being a self-opinionated creature, I must be right.

My first recollections of life were a cosy soft linen towel in the corner of the sitting room of the old cottage. A rather large black cat, also a long-haired Persian was watching over me. Over the course of the next few weeks, I discerned a tall human figure that kept bringing me tuna fish and milk in two small dishes. Perhaps I was unwell, I don't know for sure, but I didn't venture far from the towel for some time. However, I was learning fast. The small room had two doorways and through them the human male and his female companion would enter and exit. Against the opposite wall was an open fireplace, and when the humans lit the wood fire, I happily watched the flames dancing and casting a warm orange glow around the room. The warmth that emanated from the fireplace seeped across the room and made me sleepy.

My feline friend was older and became a mother to me. She also became my mentor. "Ee know where ee came from right?" she questioned in her strong Devonian accent one evening when the human occupants of the cottage had retired for the night.

"Not really," I replied, nonetheless curious to know how I came to be in these pleasant surroundings.

She didn't reply directly. First, she washed a patch of her right foreleg with her rough pink tongue, while I waited eagerly for an answer.

"Ee was found in they old shepherd's 'ut at Dingles farm. Farmer's wife 'eard scratching noises 'nd discovered ee 'nd ee two siblings among pile of straw. They 'umans reckoned you were all about eight days old but very sick 'nd no sign of y'er mother."

"What happened to my siblings?" I promptly asked.

The older cat paused, collecting her thoughts, before she replied: "Well, one, a little bey tomcat, y'er brother was taken to Lady Marchant at Chapel 'ouse, I think 'es aw-right."

"The other?" I queried, already having a premonition the news would not be good.

"Farmer's wife did 'er best, they say, but y'er little sister, a molly, died they same night she was found."

Silence filled the living room at Wisteria Cottage. I did not know my siblings, but they were still part of my life, now I was alone. Only me. 'Where had they buried my sister?' I wondered: 'Was my brother happy now?' 'Where does he live?' 'What was his name?' The only sound among the silence was the grandmother clock hanging on the stone wall, ticking away the time. I felt as if I had just started out on a pathway, a journey. 'Where would it lead?' 'What would I find along the way?'

Interrupting my deliberations my friend spoke again: "Ee be okay? Look a bit pale."

I assured her I was fine, just absorbing what she was telling me.

"Brenda, Boss-man's wife took ee in they night 'nd them 'ave been nursing ee, with my 'elp, naturally."

"Boss-man?" a frown indicated my statement was really a question.

"Oh, I be call 'im Boss-man, I hear people call 'im Alex, but them are good to me, 'nd I respect that, thus I be call 'im Boss-man, 'nd Brenda, 'is wife is Boss-man's wife!"

Without another word, my companion, stood, stretched, and ambled out of the door towards the kitchen. I heard a clicking sound and a small thud, then nothing. She had gone into the garden. I could not decipher the clock on the wall; indeed, I did not even know that it told people the time. What I did know is that it was very dark outside and that indicated night-time. Black Persian would be out most of the night roaming the surround fields and barns. Perhaps, one night she would take me with her. I slept.

#

It was a happy little home; a sense of well-being and calm permeated my young life. During the day there were many comings and goings. During the night Black Persian usually roamed outside unless the weather was inclement.

My name is Kipepeo, I have mentioned this already. I was ashamed to say I did not know my companions name and had not thought to ask. I imagined that Alex or perhaps Brenda had called me Kipepeo. Why? What did it mean? What was my friend's name? How long had she lived here? I was determined to find out tonight when Boss-man and his wife had retired to bed.

The daylight at the small cottage window intensified as Black Persian returned. We greeted each other, and she wandered into the kitchen for breakfast when Alex appeared, and I guzzled my food in the living room as usual. I was developing quite an appetite. Curious, I seemed to be getting bigger each day, not so you would easily notice, but the towel seemed to be shrinking in size, that much I did know. I so much wanted to talk to my feline friend, but she wandered off into the corridor that led to the upstairs bedroom and curled up in a tight ball to sleep the day away.

During the daytime I took to exploring the room I was living in. I have previously mentioned the two doors, one to the kitchen by which there was some means of exiting the cottage, the other to a small corridor and steps leading upstairs. It would be a few months before I could climb the stairs and avail myself of the cosy bed during the daytime. There must have been some other area out of sight as I periodically heard water gushing and occasionally it sounded like rain inside the cottage. On the mantlepiece above the fire were various silver picture frames with people depicted within. Either side of the fireplace were fire irons, a wicker basket with solid pieces of dry hardwood and a strange wooden statue of an Egyptian cat.

Looking up I could see two china plates, painted pictures in vibrant colour adorned the plates. I did as yet not understand what they depicted, however, in time the paintings of narrowboats on a canal in both summer and winter scenes would become an integral part of my new life. In a dark corner mounted on a solid hardwood Indian table was a non-descript flat black object. This aroused my curiosity no end, as in the evening Boss-man would do something to it and it would illuminate with moving images and sound.

The sun was setting, the light coming through the Georgian windowpane became less and the human couple came to both of us, petting and stroking our abundant fur and wishing us goodnight. While I loved having them around and was so grateful to them for their care and kindness, this evening I could not wait for them to ascend the steps to their night-time haunt. I didn't want to seem too impatient, but I was keen to ask more questions.

Sitting up in my towelled bed I watched Black Persian wander the room, restless, alert, keen to stimulate her senses with outdoor smells and sounds.

"Do you have a name?" I blurted out with eagerness.

She stopped pacing the room and looked around at me. Cats don't smile, but I saw a cheeky grin cross her face.

"Huh, ee don't know my name yet do ee! 'tis Lapsat."

"What?"

"Lapsat," she turned away as if ashamed for a moment, then with resolve she continued: "Boss-man gave me name when them first brought me 'ere as a kitt'n. Apparently, it is Chinese for somethin', somethin' not very nice. I don't know what. I can't ask, but 'ave become used to it."

Lapsat was quick to change the focus of the discussion: "Y'er name Kipepeo means butterfly in Swahili, an African language. It seems them like sound of it, but we be call ee Kippy. Much easier to remember 'nd say."

Kipepeo! Curious, I figured my name was unusual for a cat, but to be called a 'butterfly'. Well, I would just have to flit about the house more! Being a young kitten I had a tendency to skittish behaviour, rushing around the room like a spring on legs, and then suddenly collapsing into an inert bundle. Lapsat had rolled on to her side and was making contortions on the hearth rug. She was a wise old cat being some five years old now and still playful, you should see her with Brenda's knitting wool. Quite a mischievous rascal.

Lapsat stopped squirming and stretched her full length, her soft underbelly exposed, paws upper-most pointing to the furthest corners of the room. She was totally relaxed and comfortable in this home environment. I wondered where she had started life, had she been found in a shepherd's hut also? With one smooth easy movement she rolled onto her stomach and reclined in the same manner of the Great Sphinx of Giza in Egypt. On the coffee table rested a beautiful hardbound book, which while I could not read, contained many colourful photographs. On one brief occasion I had seen a picture of the Sphinx and recognised its grandeur. That is when I realized Lapsat had a small white patch of fur in the centre of her forehead in much the same way the Great Sphinx had the representation of an erect cobra head. Why I had thus far failed to notice the white patch against the jet-black fur I knew not, but it certainly afforded Lapsat a regal countenance. A wise old cat indeed.

We sat for some time just staring blankly at each other, then without another word Lapsat stood up and trotted towards the kitchen. The familiar click and soft thud emanated from beyond, and I knew she would not return until daylight chased the night away.

Time to explore. It had been a few days since I had been welcomed into the home, and now I was feeling more restored, my curiosity was driving me forward. I took tentative steps toward the kitchen. Slowly, very slowly, I peered around the doorway. Shiny pots and pans hung from a low oak beam on the ceiling. A large cast-iron Aga cooker, red enamel shining brightly in the moonlight that came through the little window on the far wall was a feature of the small kitchen. The room had a homely and inviting smell of freshly baked products. The floor was covered in buff-tinted flagstones, and on the top of one such stone in the corner behind the door were a food and water bowl. I took a sip of Lapsat's water and sniffed the food bowl. It was empty!

The kitchen had a solid brown door leading presumably to the cottage garden. In the door was a small window like object just inches from the floor. I cautiously approached and looked out. The scene beyond the door was certainly garden for I could see the light of the full-moon casting shadows of the trees and plants. The view was hazy due to the nature of the window, but I figured this was the exit point for Lapsat each evening. I pushed my nose against the plastic window, nothing happened! I pushed a little harder, still nothing. Then I used my hind legs to propel me forward with more determination. The Perspex moved slightly, but something was resisting all attempts I made to open it. Of course, what I did not yet know, the cat-flap had a lock system. It recognized the 'chip' embedded in Lapsat and 'unlocked' the flap so she could enter and exit. I on the other hand would have to wait three weeks and endure a humiliating visit to a man in a white coat in the neighbouring town before I would be allowed out at night or any other time.

#

Time past quickly enough. Contentedly I wandered around the little cottage. It seemed easy enough to attract the attention of the humans, scratch away at the soft furnishings and a hand would appear almost instantly along with a verbal rebuke. I was distressed the time I knocked a china vase off the mantlepiece above the fire. It made a terrific crash which frightened me something rotten. I leapt from the shelf and dived for cover behind the sofa. Just in time, Boss-man's wife appeared wielding a kitchen knife. She was not well pleased, and I admit I was truly sorry, but the damage was done and that was all there was to it. Upon realising the knife was not meant for me, she had been chopping onions, I crept sheepishly from my refuge and rubbed my head against her legs in the same fashion that I had seen Lapsat do. Wow, what an effect. She calmed down immediately and picking me up in one hand looked into my lime green eyes and castigated me with a grin on her face.

"What are we going to tell the Master of the house?"

I didn't comment, just purred softly.

Generally, it was a happy home, two humans and two cats. What was noticeable to both of us were the periodic absences of our human companions. They would leave the cottage for weeks at a time and even the all-wise, all-knowing Black Persian did not know where they went. Each time they left however, a feeding machine would be set up in the kitchen which dispensed food daily at six o'clock in the morning. Every few days Lady Marchant would call. We were convinced these inspection visits were to check if we were entertaining uninvited guests in the form of fieldmice or neighbour tomcats. Upon her departure we would discover some 'treats' in the kitchen and some fresh salmon in our food bowls. Perhaps her visits were not so bad after all.

Hours turned into days and days into weeks. These were joyful times. I was content each evening to curl up on Brenda's lap, purring noisily while Lapsat being more independent availed herself of the hearthrug until such time as the humans took to the bedroom and Lapsat went outside to explore. I remained indoors.

It was while ensconced on Brenda's lap one evening that I heard her comment to Boss-man: "I think little pusskins is old enough to go outside now, don't you?" Although I didn't hear an audible reply, I figured it was in the affirmative as Brenda, directing her words to me, added: "You won't get lost now will you little thing?" It was few days later when I accidentally discovered my exit route was now open to me. I had been pressing my nose against the transparent plastic flap in the kitchen door, as I heard a commotion from without, when much to my surprise it flipped up and allowed me to slip easily through the gap into the world into which I had been born.

At first, I remained close to the cottage, walking around the stone walls and eagerly absorbing the sights and sounds of the immediate neighbourhood. However, in time I gained confidence and ventured further from my secure den. Beyond the kitchen door was a small garden with plants, shrubs and vegetables of various size, shape and colour. To the front of the cottage was a grass lawn and a pathway to a small gate. Beyond the gate was a tarmacadam road which did not excite me, especially as my first encounter was a frightening experience. I had not been prepared for the large grey metal object that propelled itself down the lane at, what to me seemed supersonic speed, and which Lapsat later informed me was a 'sports utility vehicle', whatever that is. I would avoid the front of the house as much as was possible and just concern myself with the rear, which was far more interesting to an exploring animal. At the bottom of the kitchen garden was a good-sized shed which backed onto a hedgerow that encompassed the rear of the property.

It would be some days before I had mustered enough courage to venture through the hedge. I had discovered a roundish gap with scrapped earth forming a hollow that was easy enough for me to pass. Imagine my amazement as I first set eyes on Farmer Graham's land. Fluffy woolly white animals on four legs, like me but much bigger, grazed in the open pasture. I sat watching, and they in turn looked up and started watching me. A solitary black sheep held my stare while the others returned to their chewing.

Standing proud, and towering above another hedge on the far right, was the farmhouse. With an abundance of caution, I traversed the field of sheep with a view to exploring the house. My plan was foiled by two consecutive incidents that occurred while I carried out my plot.

Distracted by a huge wire enclosure with clucking birds inside, I deviated from my path to investigate. The sight of two dozen female Rhode Island Reds clucking and prancing about the straw carpeted pen, was a new novelty experience for me. It appears these birds have a lot to say, constantly gossiping about their life, egg production and grain quality. However, upon my approach they all refused to continue their conversations and silence descended like a dense fog. One particularly forward feathered creature started to squawk at full volume: "Danger! Beware!" This caused the other birds to echo the call of distress.

I had no intention of hurting them, indeed, they were behind a wire prison fence, but the commotion led to the second and more serious reason I was unable to enact my plan to survey the farmhouse. "Go!" barked the border collie sheepdog that had rushed out of the adjacent outhouse. "Get lost moggie!"

I know when I am not wanted, so I promptly got lost.

Safely back in the cottage haven I regaled Lapsat with my adventure and the sudden retreat. "Black and white markings with a pointed and amusing looking face," was how I described my assailant.

"Old Shep! 'armless. 'is bark be worse than 'is bite. Isn't it?"

I don't know if that was supposed to comfort me, but I decided from this day forward I would exercise great caution if venturing onto farmer Graham's land.

#

About a year after my arrival at Wisteria Cottage, Alex and Brenda started to make frequent trips in the silver Toyota

Yaris. There seemed to be a tension within the walls of the cottage that had not existed previously. Brenda still made a fuss of me, perhaps even more so than in the past, I didn't mind; cats live for the moment, so why worry about the future.

Then, one unusually damp day in August the humans left on one of their regular daytrips, and sitting sedately on the windowsill I awaited their return. Instinctively as they returned, I knew something had changed. The way they walked from the car to the cottage door, downcast, gloomy and withdrawn. Instead of walking over to me at the window and picking me up, Brenda walked straight through and upstairs to the bedroom, Alex following closely behind. I looked across at Lapsat, who sat on the rug in front of the vacant fireplace, she returned my gaze.

"Wasson?" she questioned.

"I don't know!" was my simple reply.

A dark cloud had formed over Wisteria Cottage on the wild moorland of Dartmoor.

## 3 — PINKERTON SMITH

Boss-man had very kindly fitted a cat bed or hammock in one of the saloon windows of the narrowboat that both Lapsat and I would share, but not at the same time. It was from this vantage point I lay trembling, restless and unable to sleep, watching blue light pulsing through the narrow gap between the curtains.

The advantages of being a cat are many, we can stealthily investigate and slip unnoticed through dangerous situations, we can curl up, hidden in tight or narrow places. However, there are disadvantages, such as when you observe a lifeless body in a canal lock and are unable to shout for help or use a mobile phone.

I am not sure how long I stood staring at the black hoodie jacket floating serenely in the gloom but there was some relief when I noted Buster, the border collie with his owner Megan the nurse, approaching. As a nurse, Megan works late some days and before retiring, she will take Buster for his night-time constitutional. It was the collie who saw me at the lock-side, and dragging his owner behind him came over with every intention of annoying me. However, he was distracted by the floating object; then Megan took an interest. Three point two seconds after first observing the sodden coat, Megan screamed! The sound pierced the quiet of the night with such ferocity I feel sure the residents of St. Peter's churchyard stirred briefly.

That was all the stimulus I needed to take off like a pyrotechnic rocket. I entered the safety of the boat just a second or two after Alex, who alarmed by the cry, opened the stern hatch, and stepped out onto solid ground.

As I lay still, awaiting my beating heart to steady, I became aware of the local male tawny owl hooting as he frequently did of a night-time. Strangely, the sound of the owl intensified the silence of the night, that in contrast to the violent outburst some time earlier, had now descended upon the sleepy canal. With due deference Lapsat returned home and demanded an explanation to the current flurry of activity at the lock. It appeared she had been mouse hunting at Wayside Cottage and knew nothing of recent events. I told her what I had seen.

"Pushed ee say?" Sitting on the saloon floor she flicked her tail back and forth in an agitated manner.

"Yes, the man in military colours thumped him in the stomach and I guess he lost his footing, slipped, perhaps being so close to the edge of the lock and all, I think he hit his head, and ended face down in the water," I said excitedly.

Black Persian is not a cat of many words. She closed her eyes, flicked her tail, and rotated her ears in a restless way. The sound of hoo-hoo seemed more intense. How I wish that tawny would shut up.

"They other two guys?" Lapsat inquired.

"Disappeared in a hurry, I don't expect we will see them again." How wrong my observation would prove to be. "What's going on outside now?"

"Police, ambulance, men in uniform, onlookers from public 'ouse, oh 'nd Boss-man all 'overing around lock. Mark my words, it will all be back to normal boatin' dreckly, ee wait 'nd see."

#

Lapsat was right of course. Next day around mid-morning the first narrowboat came up through the lock, it was a hire-boat from Stourport. The crew were totally oblivious to the previous night's incident, although they did comment on the small length of blue and white 'police' tape still attached to the paddle winding shaft. In fact, I was putting the nocturnal events down to my over-active imagination when in the late afternoon a young woman approached the lock and quickly laid a simple bunch of red carnations against the 'totem-post' that marked the end of the lock mooring 'mushrooms' and the 'permit holder' moorings, of which our boat was first above the lock.

The bringer of red carnations was a youthful female, tall and slender with rich chestnut brown hair, an air of sophistication and smart casual attire. Without doubt any human would have commented on her striking beauty. It was not her appearance however, that struck me as much as her downcast demeanour and slothful deliberate movements. She was almost dragging her feet as she moved, and as she turned to depart, I couldn't help but notice the white silk handkerchief she was using to dab at her moist eyes.

Cats live for the moment as I have said before. Thus, for us the day was much the same as any other day, eating, sleeping, grooming, catnapping, sniffing and sleeping some more. There was a noticeable change in Alex's attitude during the day. Much time was spent chatting to passers-by about the events of the previous evening. Little time of day was spent with the joggers and cyclists as they rarely stopped, being preoccupied it seems with their health regimen. However, the dog walkers were a different breed altogether.

First to stop and chat was Chip the Sausage dog. Well, he is really a Dachshund, which I have been reliably informed, by Chalky the Pub cat, means 'badger-dog' as they can chase and bring down a badger. I can't pronounce Dachshund, so I call him a Sausage dog. Predominantly black he has some chocolate patches on his legs and paws, and while short in stature he is long in body and has dropped ears. Alex didn't talk to Chip as he doesn't speak dog language, but he did have a long discussion about the man in the canal lock with Chip's owner, a rather feisty looking middle-aged woman, whom I considered would benefit from an exercise routine herself.

Later in the morning I saw Boss-man speak to the mature woman who lives at Lockside Cottage below

Kinver lock. She regularly walks her fractious Cockapoo, the three-year-old fawn coloured menace. When I see this troublemaker coming, I make for my favourite hiding place, stay in the boat, or climb the tree. On a leash she is not such a troublemaker as her owner holds her back, but if set free and she sees Lapsat, Chalky or myself, and is inclined to do so, she chases us at full speed. She just cannot help herself!

Keeping half-an-eye on the Cockapoo, who was patiently waiting on her lead at the auburn-haired owner's side, I saw an olive-green car pull into one of the three parking spaces adjacent to the lock. Three individuals slowly emerged, and gathering a small cloth bag and a large bunch of mixed flowers, ambled very sedately towards the totem-post where the red carnations were already resting. Alex and the woman had stopped speaking, and like me were watching the proceedings in silence.

The man, perhaps in his mid-forties knelt and arranged a framed photograph, cricket bat, a red baseball cap and a small green-elephant plush toy next to the carnations. Watching through moist eyes were the woman, without doubt the black-hoodie's mother, and a young teenage girl who bore a striking resemblance to the older woman. They were locked in each other's arms giving the impression that if they were to let go, certainly the teenage girl might collapse in a heap on the ground, or perhaps even both would do so. The father of the boy stood and took the large bunch of mixed blooms from the mother and placed them alongside the carnations that were already present and added a small card.

The disconsolate threesome moved towards the lock and stood in silence for some time staring blankly at the greywater below. Finally, they returned to the car, climbed in, and drove off. I do not class myself as an emotional feline, but this short episode upset my normally carefree attitude for the rest of the day.

The sun was high in the sky when a small white van with distinctive logo pulled into the parking space. In the following hour or so, a bright young man with an air of suave confidence set about taking still photographs and recording video footage of the area. He walked up and down recording the scene including the lock, canal-side public house and totem-post with its distressingly gaudy adornments. I was at a loss to his intent.

#

Boss-man was chatting to passers-by again. This time he was sat on the gnarled old bench conversing with 'Gentleman Jim' as Alex liked to call him. It was late afternoon and the white van man with the cameras had left the scene. The senior gent most certainly fitted the part of a gentleman, stern and upright in his pin stripe grey trousers and beige sports jacket, a cravat completing the aristocratic allure. At his side was his namesake, Jim the Bassett Hound with his black 'waistcoat' marking across his back, long snout and big, very big, floppy ears. As I was unacquainted with the animal, and thus unsure of his disposition towards the feline community, I kept my distance. This was no problem as 'Gentleman Jim' was a little hard of hearing and spoke in a loud condescending manner as he discussed his favourite subject; the history of Kinver.

"Kinver Light Railway," he was explaining to Alex, had its terminus just behind us, where the pumping station is today. I glanced up to admire the red bricked façade, tall imposing windows and cream coloured 'hat' that formed the roof of the old electric pump house that Gentleman Jim said had been built in 1938 for South Staffordshire Water Company.

"The water pipe was laid along the old tram track at the back of the field where the horses are grazing. The line was built in 1901 by the British Electric Traction Company and ran four and a half miles from the Fish Inn at Amblecote to the depot here at Kinver."

"Was it very popular?" Alex asked.

"Oh, it was popular enough in its time, carrying passengers, mostly families from the Black Country on day trips, along with some freight including fresh milk. On one bank holiday 20,000 people, mainly from Dudley, travelled the route, most to visit Kinver Edge. A great day out for the town dwellers. Its demise came in the form of the motorbus which replaced many tramlines around the early thirties."

I filed this information away in my limited memory for a night-time exploration when I could investigate the route of the tramway at my leisure. It would not be tonight however, as previous events from the day were about to resurface.

"I still haven't visited Kinver Edge," admitted Alex to the suave gentleman.

"You cannot be serious? It's a must-see attraction. The sandstone ridge and hillfort along with the rock houses. Part of the National Trust, don't you know."

"Worth a visit then?"

"Absolutely old boy! From the iron age hillfort you can see three counties, on a clear day you understand. Shropshire, Staffordshire and Worcestershire."

"Makes me think of sauce, Worcester … oh, never mind," Alex interrupted apologetically.

"Now the rock houses," the gentleman continued without being derailed, "are quirky little homes carved into the rockface, and lived in up until the sixties. The Holy Austin Rock Houses have been lovingly restored by the Trust so you can see what life would have been like. Volunteers will even tell you stories of the past residents going all the way back to 1777 when a man called Joseph Heely took refuge from a storm with a family of rock dwellers.

"Wonderful views along with wildlife as far as the eye can see. If you visit on a warm day, you can hear the buzz of insects in the heathland, and in summer there are many butterflies that festoon the grassland. You might even see an adder or a grass snake if you are lucky."

"Sounds fascinating. Now I have more time to myself I will make a point of listening to your advice."

Raising his left arm the gentleman glanced at his wristwatch, "Must detain you no longer, if I am late home the memsahib will have words to say!"

'Poor man, under his wife's thumb,' I thought as I watched him rise and stride off towards the village.

#

Most evenings Alex followed a set routine. He cooked himself food, which he put on a flat plate and ate with a knife and fork; why guzzling from a bowl on the floor is not good enough for him I will never understand. During this feeding time he would press a button on the television remote to activate the black screen hanging on the cabin wall.

Periodically I help him by climbing up on his armchair and stepping on the black button device, which seems to affect the action on the screen. It also causes some consternation from my master, who getting equally annoyed and flustered at the same time, grumbles at me and frequently pushes me to the floor. This rarely deters me if I am in the mood for an affectionate pawing of his lap, and I will attempt the process again.

On this particular evening, Boss-man had finished his beef and ale pie with mash and put the plate on the small occasional table at his side. The smell of the gravy adorning the plate was very appetising, and despite having eaten only half an hour previous, I considered a small addition to my supper was in order. Boss-man obviously did not agree with my intentions, so he got up, grabbed the plate, and took it to the kitchen sink. By the time he had returned I had got the better of him, curling up in the warm dip left in the vacant seat.

After picking me up and depositing me in his lap and checking that Black Persian was happily curled up on the window-bed, he turned up the volume on the television to watch the news. This was a ritual held each evening that I was not much bothered about. Pictures and sounds of mistreated or suffering humans of varying ages along with reports of attacks perpetrated against animals like whales, or even sometimes dogs attacking humans. Not interested!

Following thirty minutes of this, a nice young lady sitting on a cream-coloured sofa appeared up on the screen. It would be nice to try out that sofa, it does look cosy and the young woman in her green-cotton dress would surely want to stroke my head and make a fuss of me. What happened next jolted me out of my stupor.

The nice young lady was saying: "… sudden death of a young man at Kinver."

I looked up with a start, my heart thumped in my chest. Alex who was also glued to the visual display gripped my body with sudden ferocity causing me to emit a loud cry. The sudden exclamation was enough to attract Lapsat's attention, and we all stared at the screen together.

The display was filled with moving pictures of Kinver Lock. The picture panned out revealing in the bottom right corner the totem-post and its enhancements. A second shot from the far side of the lock started with 'The Lock Inn', showing more of the lock from a different angle and including a view of our home moored on the left against the towpath.

While watching the screen we heard the presenter explain: "The young man was discovered by a dog-walker about ten o'clock last night floating in the lock beside 'The Lock Inn' at Kinver. Despite the best efforts of the emergency services, he was pronounced dead at the scene." A large picture of the young man who had drowned filled the screen. "A police spokesman said: 'We are not looking for anyone else in connection with this incident. There were no suspicious circumstances. It appears to have been a tragic accident where, under the influence of alcohol the young man slipped and was unable to climb out of the lock. The local coroner has been informed and a post-mortem will confirm the cause of death.'"

The screen reverted to the presenter who concluded the brief report: "The man has been named locally as Pinkerton Smith, who attended Kidderminster College and was an active member of the Kinver Cricket Club. His parents and young sister are being supported by specially trained police officers at this difficult time."

The story that followed on the local news channel could have been about a volcano erupting in the local housing estate for all we cared. Stunned silence saturated the little boat.

Darkness rolled in as the daylight faded. Boss-man finally took himself off to bed, but we could both hear him tossing and muttering for a long time. In the subdued light of the boat Lapsat voiced what we were both thinking, "ee said 'e was pushed?"

"Unquestionably, there were two men, one pushed or punched him. That is why he slipped or fell into the lock. The police must have found the beer bottles and assumed he was drinking alone."

"Too bad 'umans can't understand us, we will never be able to tell they what ee saw."

## 4 — BRENDA

A wise old tomcat from down the lane once told me that life is like a path. It takes many twists and turns, undulates up and down, and can be overgrown by hedgerows. You do not know when the path will end, or what weather conditions you will encounter along the way. Sometimes the path is calm and straight with warm sun to brighten the trail, alternatively, around the next corner may be unseen trouble, a hill, a boulder, or stormy weather.

The dark cloud that had descended on Wisteria Cottage that April day did not lift despite the arrival of spring which resulted in longer and brighter days. The cottage garden returned to life, with large and small plants alike vying for space in the rich soil. The garden was Brenda's pride and joy. Many happy hours were spent among the pansies, daisies, peonies and other delicate blooms with their soft lines and whimsical nature. Springtime rejoiced with an assortment of smells from the fragrant plants, soft but bright greens augmenting the rich reds and yellows of the tulips along with a veritable assortment of insects, some of which would become moth or butterfly, all busily going about the business of life.

With life comes death! This was a simple fact that as a small kitten I had already become acquainted with. The depth of our grief upon the death of a loved one is commensurate with the length of time we have known or shared our own life with that individual. I mourned the loss of my sibling kitten sister, whom I only knew by information Lapsat provided, a lot less than I would come to mourn the loss of another much closer friend from the human realm.

Brenda was like a soul mate to me. She it was who had nursed me as a very sick weak kitten. Bringing me into her home, providing a small warm bed, regularly feeding very small portions of food and milk until strong enough to climb gingerly onto her lap and enjoy the gentle stroking of her large but comforting hands. She lavished affection on both me and my feline companion, however, Lapsat being an older and more independent animal sought out her ministrations much less than I.

Frequently, on her return home in the little silver Yaris she would give both of us a treat or toy that she had purchased in the local town. As she stepped through the kitchen door calling our names I responded promptly and purred happily as I rubbed my soft furry head against her bare legs. She in turn would open the packet of treats, or extract the toy and bending low, pass one to me and another to my adopted sibling. These treats, according to Brenda, often contained something called catnip, which although I am unaware what it is, or where it comes from, makes me feel relaxed, happy and overly affectionate. She really is my best friend.

One particularly useful addition that was placed on the kitchen floor some weeks ago, was a scratching post. It was brought home by Boss-man's wife the day after I had torn a strip out of the living room sofa. Both of us cats were drawn to the post by the irresistible smell of catnip, and as it had such a lovely rough texture were eager to scratch away.

#

Although the darkness over the cottage remained, in time the initial silence and tension eased to a noticeable degree. Boss-man and his wife spent most evenings quietly sat together in the little living room of the cottage, chatting to each other in low-tones. It became apparent to Lapsat and I, that they would spend increasing amounts of time away from the cottage during the daylight hours. Walks down the country lane towards the village or journeys taken by car to destinations unknown to us animals. Then there were the extra telephone calls. Brenda's mobile phone would purr, she would answer promptly, and on frequent occasions would make for the bedroom for a private, undisturbed conversation.

It had been a rather dull and damp day on Dartmoor. Even though it was late spring, Alex had lit the open fire in the living room, burning a few hard wood logs, as he said: 'to take the chill off the cottage'. A few embers still burned long after the humans had retired for the night. Lapsat and I were both indoors due to the inclement weather and that is when Lapsat expressed her observation: "'ave ee noticed Brenda 'as lost weight?"

I hadn't! After a thoughtful pause I commented: "Yes! Now you come to mention it, I did think her lap seems a little less comfortable of an evening," Black Persian started to paw the hearth rug, "and the cough?" I added.

"The cough, yes, right, that cough. Dry 'nd persistent." Lapsat stopped pawing and sat upright. "Not right 'idden it?"

We didn't have an answer, but somehow subconsciously we shared our innermost feelings of anxiety. We just knew something was not right.

"I expect she will be better soon," I remarked positively. But my hopeful remark was misplaced; before the summer was finished, I would be proved wrong.

Our little moorland home was decorated externally with wisteria floribunda vines, lending their appearance to the name of the cottage. Warm rays of spring' sun warmed the plants on the south and west of the cottage and thus the stems growing clockwise produced large clusters of lavender-purple flowers and the air was filled with a sweet fragrance. In the far corner of the wisteria was a blackbird's nest. I would happily sit for hours listening to the jaunty melody of the adult pair. This springtime they produced three warm-brown spotted juveniles, their antics provided a necessary distraction from the ongoing concerns of our own home life.

Another welcome distraction was the regular visits of the window cleaner. A small white van would pull into the driveway and park next to Boss-man's car. A 'strapping and rather handsome young man,' so Brenda said, would climb out, open the tailgate, and pull a hosepipe and telescopic pole from the rear of the van. Methodically he would work his way around the cottage using the soft black brush on the end of his pole to wash cobwebs and spiders from the window frames and leave the diamond shape leaded panes clean and shiny.

If I were outside when he arrived, I would casually saunter up to his van, sniff at the wheels and then lay underneath the warm engine. On days when I was feeling particularly mischievous, I would deliberately get in the way of his hose pipe or his legs causing him to mildly curse me. This was not something that troubled me as knew he liked me and would always spend time petting me when he had rolled his hose pipe away.

Naturally, I was not outside every time he visited the cottage, and on such occasions when I happened to be indoors, I would rush to a window and chase the brush as it moved up and down and sprayed water. If I sat on my hind legs, I could reach up and paw at the water on the outside of the glass as if it were a new toy. I delighted to see the cleaner's smiling face as he laughed at my antics.

#

The established routine of our guardians making regular day trips away ended abruptly one day in mid-summer. The day started badly and got worse. Calico cat who lived somewhere further down the lane periodically would trespass on our territory. If spotted by either Lapsat or me, a standoff would occur, where we stood facing each other snarling and hissing. Calico, a tri-coloured female with fetching large black and orange markings on top of her predominantly snowy-white fur was a hunter, and we did not like her sojourning on our patch. Recently we had caught her hiding in the beech hedge watching the blackbird nest and the fledgling birds as they learned to fly. On this day the youngest of the birds emerged and rather than fly to the nearby sycamore tree for safety, chose to land on the wooden gate that opened to the lane beyond.

Calico was out of her hideout like the speed of a lightning strike. The little fellow stood no chance and was carried off in triumph, no doubt to be presented as a gift to her owner. It was Lapsat that had witnessed the event followed by the distressed call of the mother bird. When my companion relayed the deplorable events of that morning, we shared our sorrow together, just as we would share our sorrow for events yet in the future.

Alex and Brenda had left the cottage early that morning, in much the same manner as they had done several times over the past weeks. Boss-man was in the driving seat of the little car as usual, but on this occasion before driving off he had placed a small black leather suitcase carefully in the car's boot. Deep within, some intuition told me the little case belonged to Brenda.

Following the blackbird incident along with the departure of my mistress, I was feeling restless and found myself pacing the cottage, sitting, getting up, laying down, pacing some more. Finally, sat on the front room windowsill later that afternoon I waited for them to return home. Alex returned alone!

Over the next few days, Boss-man would spend most of the day away from the cottage, each evening returning alone. I waited loyally from late afternoon every day to welcome Brenda home, but in vain. She never returned.

Black Persian commented on Alex apparent absentmindedness: "No food again tonight," she observed one evening.

"He never forgot before, but he is so absent minded now. I guess we must just fend for ourselves." It didn't trouble us too much as he always made a fuss of us when he remembered we were around, giving us extra treats as if to make up for his distraction.

A few days later, watching from a good distance, I was delighted to see Lapsat, who had been crouching in long grass at the bottom of the cottage garden, pounce on a moving object. It turned out to be a large brown rat with grey-brown fur. We knew he was somewhere in the old coal store but had failed for some time to get him.

"Oo arr. Got 'im!" shouted a triumphant Lapsat. "'bout time too. Must take my trophy to Boss-man, 'e will be pleased."

"Is that the one that has been in our compost?"

"Tis the one. Look at that pointed nose."

"And the long scaly tail, ugh, well done Lapsat," I added with enthusiasm.

We marched with resolve toward the kitchen door. On arrival and before we could make our presence known, Lapsat froze, dropped the dead rat, and hushed me to silence. Alex was closing the door and locking it. Nothing unusual in that, but his clothing? Sharp black suit, black tie, black shoes with a shine you could see your face in, and a black look on his face.

He was gone for some hours, and upon his return he lowered himself into his favourite cosy chair and sat quiet as a church mouse. The rat had long been forgotten, but something inside me desperately wanted to share a gift with him. When the horrible Calico had attacked and carried off the juvenile blackbird, it had lost two feathers. I strutted purposefully out of the cat-flap and sure enough found one of the feathers near the garden gate. Carrying the feather very gently in my mouth I returned to the living room and sat in front of Boss-man willing him to notice me. He did.

"Hello Kippy," he said in a melancholy voice, "is that for me?" He reached down, took the feather, and looked at it carefully, "Oh, it's a young blackbird."

Suddenly I was very afraid. Would he misunderstand my intended kind gesture? Would he think I had killed the bird? Would he be angry with me? How foolish not to think carefully beforehand what I was doing.

I need not have worried. "You and Lapsat don't chase birds do you, so you just found this. Was it a baby from the nest in the wisteria? I wonder what happened? Is the bird okay? Did something kill it?" I told him Calico, the trespassing cat, had done it. But he just looked at me pitifully, all he heard was a long drawn out 'miaow'.

Lapsat came up and sat next to me. Then we both lay on the hearthrug while Alex sat very quiet and meditatively cocooned in his comfy chair. As winter drew on, this is a scene that would be played out each evening. We kept Alex company and enjoyed the warmth of the open fire until he chose to go to bed, when we would explore outside on evenings when the weather was not too inclement.

#

I came home one evening to inspect my food bowl as per usual and having eaten the contents, I casually strode into the living room. After knocking the china vase from the mantlepiece as a kitten, the space had remained empty. I fully expected everything to be the same as previously but quickly became aware of a double silver photograph frame in the space previously occupied by the vase. Looking at the contents of the frame unnerved me at first. On the right was a large smiling face, a portrait of Brenda. On the left a scene of Boss-man and his wife at the helm of a striking blue narrowboat.

That night after Boss-man had retired to bed, Lapsat and I puzzled over the pictures in the frame. Like myself, my older feline companion had no understanding what the photographs could mean. Boss-man's wife had been with us, and we were all happy. Now she was not with us, and Alex was not happy, neither were we.

My confusion was compounded the following day, when while I was inspecting the hedgerow in the farmers field adjacent to the cottage garden, I encountered a very scruffy and unkempt feline by the name of Whiskey.

"Yoo, keep back dude," was his opening gambit.

"Hey, I mean, I don't know you, you not from round these parts?" I stammered unhelpfully.

"Yoo live here?"

"In the cottage, yes."

"Right o. Yes, well I'm Whiskey."

"Whiskey? Is that your name?"

"Yoo bet yer."

"Hello Whiskey. I'm Kipepeo, but you can call me Kippy."

"Yoo got food then?"

"No, sorry, no food. We get fed in doors by Boss-man."

"Boss-man? Huh."

I had the impression the conversation was not going too well, but nonetheless I persevered: "You live around here?"

"Nope, don't live anywhere really. I'm what they call a feral cat." There was a lull in the conversation and then Whiskey continued: "Actually, I'm not a real feral, I lived in a house a long way away with this old, very old lady. She got sick and people took her away, but they forgot all about me. I learned to fend for myself since then."

"You're a stray then."

"Yoo bet yer."

I can't say exactly how the conversation ended, but it seems he just wandered off. I returned home with disturbing thoughts in my head. He had been abandoned and become wild, living with nature, he certainly needed a good grooming.

Could it be, was it just possible? Had Boss-man abandoned Brenda to become a feral human who had to fend for herself?

#

Curiously, over the winter months items started to disappear from the family home. Bedding and furnishings were taken away in degrees by Alex in his little car. Boxes were filled with books, ornaments and kitchen utensils. A tall man in a grey suit called and took measurements, writing them down in a black notebook. Then he produced a camera and went around the cottage inside and out taking pictures. Very strange actions that even Lapsat was at a loss to explain.

As the slightly warmer weather returned, strangers, usually older couples, came to visit the cottage. It was apparent that Alex did not know these people personally, but he enthusiastically welcomed them and made a point of showing them all around the little home. These events we felines found most intrusive and upon sight of an unknown vehicle pulling up next to the Yaris, we both made a quick exit and hid in the coal store at the bottom of the garden.

The black and tan removal van was just too big to pull into the cottage driveway and thus it stood outside the garden gate while boxes, and all the remaining furniture was carried out by two men in checkered brown overalls. Alex spent some time in the lane apologising to the occasional local who, unable to pass the cottage in their vehicle, had to reverse, turn around and take a longer route to the village. Those folks who were thus inconvenienced seemed not to mind, and most stopped to offer soothing words of comfort through the open car windows.

Thorough out all this uncertainty and disruption, one thing remained constant, unmoved; it was the double portrait frame of a smiling Brenda and the happy couple together. Where had she gone? Would she ever come back home? Could we have our happy family again? I so longed for an answer, but it never came.

## 5 — 'RUMAH SAYA'

The six-millimetre steel superstructure of the narrowboat 'Rumah Saya' was painted admiral blue and lacquered to present a reflective finish. A semi-traditional stern allowed visitors and favoured animals to sit in a safe space outside the main cabin but clear of the helmsman's working area. The boat was fitted out as a 'live aboard' and contained a good size galley or kitchen with cooker, fridge, freezer and even a washing machine. Beyond the galley was a reasonable space for the living room or saloon with a small enclosed multi-fuel stove. In the corner was a small office table and upright chair where the more mundane aspects of modern living could be managed. Further along the interior was the bathroom with cassette toilet and shower. Finally, the master bedroom with double bed and ample wardrobe and cupboard space.

It was to this 'second home' Alex and Brenda would visit when they wanted time away from the Devonshire cottage, and it was to this living accommodation that Alex had turned into his new home when Brenda had died.

On the wooden shelf above the television cupboard was displayed the double silver photo frame, Brenda's warm smile beaming out to comfort anyone who choose to notice. I noticed! It was a reminder of a past life that I recognised had gone forever. The boat contained a few other items from the cottage, books, pictures and our beds of course. Otherwise, the past was consigned to history and being a feline, easy to forget.

Lapsat and I settled into our new home easily, most of the first two weeks while we were confined to quarters; we slept, ate and explored the inside of the boat. Alex however was restless and distracted. It would seem reasonable that he was finding it difficult to adjust to the boat as a permanent home. To holiday here for short periods of time, with the one you love is one thing, to make it a permanent residence is quite another. It was springtime when we all arrived in the little Yaris, which looking from the saloon window I could see parked across from the towpath. Periodically, Alex went off either on foot to the local village or in the car to locations further afield, just as he had done in days gone by, to purchase supplies.

#

The morning after the news report about the death of black hoodie, I ventured out of the cat-flap and wandered down to the lock. The weather that day was calm and still, but ominous black clouds were gathering on the horizon. Since the tragedy it had not rained and I was keen to evaluate the scene of the crime, I fancied myself as something of a crime investigator.

Grass alongside the lock had been trampled on, cigarette butts had been carelessly dropped by some of the spectators of that night, and wheel ruts cut into the ground as the body had been dragged away on a trolly to the waiting ambulance. It was a sorry sight that dug up memories I would like to have dismissed. The most difficult part was that the humans did not realise others were involved and it had not just been an accident. If only I could find a method to convey this simple information to Boss-man.

I sauntered slowly down the length of the lock towards the bottom gates. I pictured in my mind the scene, It was here that Cracker, yes, I remembered his name, had pushed Pinkerton Smith. It was here that he had stepped back too far. It was here he had fallen. Did he hit his head? I was sure he had. If so, why had the police not seen the evidence, but even if they did find a bruise or contusion would they recognise the significance? A drunk man might have fallen on his own, but he would have been relaxed and unlikely to smash himself against a stone wall.

The bottom gates were pushed together in a V shape, held closed by pressure of water in the lock. Only when the lock was completely empty and all the pressure released could a person ease the gates open by pushing against the balance beam, even then it could be hard work as I had observed when watching boat crew members straining to open the gates before the water level had equalised. Attached to each gate at upper-ground level was a simple walkway, a solid oak beam bolted in place and covered in non-slip grit. Thus far I had had no reason to cross over to view the lock from the public house side. However, I had seen Chalky cross effortlessly on several occasions.

Tentatively I placed a paw on the rough surface. I looked down. Mistake! It was just over nine feet drop to the water below, and even though the lock sluice paddles were closed a significant amount of water was escaping through cracks in the closed gates. With steely determination I willed myself onward, one paw at a time, until I had reached the far side with no adverse distress.

My sensitive nose immediately detected an odour. Not the most pleasant it has to be said, but it was one I recognised. Fish! Fish that had gone passed its prime. There it was, the paper and plastic wrappings from the fish and chip shop, purchased by Cracker and his mate from 'The Frying Plaice', left in a heap among the broken glass of the beer bottle. Disgusting creatures these humans. I would need to be careful not to step on the glass shards.

I worried the paper a little just in case there was a sliver of fish still edible, but to no avail. However, there was a small piece of paper inside the bag. It was long and narrow with writing and numbers printed, rather than handwritten, upon it. If only I could read human words. I am not sure why, but for some psychic reason I felt compelled to carry the paper back to Alex on the boat.

Pushing my way through the little cat door from the front of the boat I surreptitiously made my way through the master bedroom and bathroom areas to the saloon. Bossman was nowhere to be seen. The car was outside, so I figured he had not gone far, perhaps walking to the village shop for supplies. I carefully placed the scrap of paper behind my food dish in the kitchen where I hoped it would remain safe until I could hand it over in person.

Lapsat was in the cat bed at the window and seemed to be in a deep sleep, but knowing us cats as I do, I knew she was only half-asleep, ready to spring into action at a moment's notice. There was no 'moment' and certainly no need for action, so I found a good location in front of the Squirrel multi-fuel stove in the corner next to the bathroom door and lay down. The fireplace in Wisteria Cottage was open and accepted good sized logs, this small cast-iron stove was enclosed, having a secure door with toughened glass window to view the flames. From our first night on the boat, Alex had lit the little stove each evening 'to take the chill off the boat' as he put it. Most of these spring evenings required two or three small logs to warm the boat successfully. Next to the stove, along with fire irons was a bright green painted coal scuttle beautifully decorated with traditional roses in narrowboat style. I wondered if he would use the coal in colder weather as he previously did in the cottage during the winter.

It was not till much latter, that laden with two large shopping bags and a wonderful smell, Alex returned. The bags contained basic provisions, but the smell came from a third bag with a small logo that I have come to recognise and love; 'The Frying Plaice'.

Black Persian who had hardly moved all day, except for the occasional stretch or change of position, was suddenly by my side fully alert and purring even louder than I was. Fish, chips, peas and bread roll consumed by Alex, and goodly sized pieces of fish without batter consumed by us felines, and we were all in a favourable mood. When Boss-man settled back into his soft armchair I casually retrieved the paper from behind my food bowl. I moved to within leaping distance of his lap and sat on hind legs patiently awaiting his attention. He, however, was engrossed in the newspaper he had brought back with him from the village. I pawed at his leg gently. Absentmindedly, he brushed my paw away. I pawed again more determinedly. He grumbled and pushed me away again. I opened my claws and very gently dug them into his leg. This had a notable effect!

"Kippy!" he exclaimed, "don't do that." Putting his paper on the floor beside him he said: "Come on then, jump up."

For once, my purpose in occupying his lap was to draw attention to the paper, not for a fuss to be made of me. I purred loudly. "Kipepeo, what have you got there." He took the paper gently from my mouth, glanced at it, "Chip shop receipt, ha," and crumpling it into a small ball threw it at the coal scuttle. It missed!

"But that is important, it was from the night the boy was drowned, you must look again, don't throw it away," I ranted on.

"Silly cat, why do you make so much noise miaowing."

I jumped down, rushed to the fire, picked up the paper and returned immediately to his lap, pushing my head and hence the paper up for his inspection. This time it worked, he took the paper and instead of throwing it away, he uncrumpled it slowly and viewed the contents.

"A receipt for two portions of fish and chips from 'The Frying Plaice', but I only bought one portion with peas?" He looked puzzled for a moment then continued: "Oh, but this is not mine Kippy, the date is last Sunday, and it is food for two persons, 6:54 p.m." I could see he was about to dismiss it again; however, something made him stop and think. "They say the young man died sometime between 7:30 and 8:00 p.m. last Sunday. Did you find this among the discarded chip wrappers at the lock." I understood what he said, but he did not understand my reply.

There was nothing more I could do, so I went outside looking for Lapsat who had already started her nocturnal ramblings. Would Boss-man think about the receipt? Would he realise more than one person had been at the tragic incident last Sunday night? What could he do if he did realise? That was now his problem, I was in urgent need of digging a hole in soft soil.

#

The next day started out much as any other. I wandered inside around dawn and found a small amount of food in my dish to set me up for the day ahead. As it looked like a fine day again, I went back outside and worked my way to the boat roof and finding a nice corner of the solar panel I settled down for a serious snooze. Things were going well for some hours until a commotion caught my attention, again at Kinver lock. This time it was a party of hire-boaters trying with difficulty to negotiate the lock.

Yet again more novice boaters who had hired their boat on Monday from Stourport. Despite there being two young couples on the boat it appeared they had taken two whole days to reach 'The Lock Inn' public house and Kinver lock. Matters started well enough with the two women running up the towpath that cut under the bridge to work the lock. There was some loud expostulating of ideas as they reminded themselves of the procedure, followed by raising the lower ground paddles with the windlass keys.

These strong galvanised angle irons had a handle at one end and two different sized square sockets on the other. Slot the key, using the correct size socket of course, on to the spindle of the paddle and rotate to raise the sluice and allow water to flow into or out of the lock. Simple!

I failed to see why they made such a meal of the job as they must have done several other locks already since leaving Stourport basin. My attention was aroused as the woman on the far side of the lock started to wind upwards only for the paddle to crash down almost immediately. "Wrong size socket!" the other woman shouted over. Both started to wind their respective spindles, although not successfully until they had established which way to turn, and whether to engage the safety catch while winding or not. The simple safety mechanism should be easy enough, but how many people I have seen struggle to use it. Winding the paddle up and you leave the catch engaged or push it forwards to engage when the ratchet is fully lifted. To lower, release the catch and lower the paddle. Easy! The boater on the near side raised the paddle without problem but did not engage the safety catch. By a small chance of fate, the paddle stayed raised for a second or two, enough time for the woman to step back. Then, without warning the heavy sluice fell with a violent crash, which caused the spindle to turn with speed. The windlass key that was still loosely attached to the shaft spun at the same speed, then flew off, landing a few feet away on the lock side. The woman swore but was lucky not to have lost her key in the canal, or worse been hit by it in the face by it.

Kinver lock, due to the proximity of the bridge has angled lower gate balance beams made of steel rather than the traditional wood, which present more of a challenge to use than if opening wooden doors. Heaving and straining the two women pushed the gates open and leant heavily on them to recover from their exertions. From my vantage point I could not see the lower side of the lock, but the crash and resultant shout indicated some problem getting the boat into the narrow space between the gates. Once the doors were closed and they had remembered to lower the paddles, the women approached the top gates. Here there are two ground paddles and a gate paddle. The normal safe operation is to raise the ground paddles first and when partially full, raise the gate paddle. The hire boat was about sixty feet long and the young man at the helm had rushed it into the lock so that the bow hit the cill. The woman with the fair hair wound the gate paddle up to its full height in one swift movement and water rushed into the lock chamber as a torrent. Listening to the shouts of alarm it was clear to me they were flooding the front well-deck of the boat with canal water.

Despite the chaotic actions of the crew, the boat rose steadily and finally with the top gates open was ready to exit the lock. Helmsman put full throttle and shot forward. Unfortunately, the lock at Kinver exits on a curve in the canal, and the boat made contact with the canal bank causing it to bounce unceremoniously across the cut to the far side. Now, I know, as I have seen it happen before, that on the tight bend the water flows slower and causes silt to build up, thus, the momentum of the boat drove it onto the sandbar causing it to become stuck.

The helmsman made the first novice mistake in these circumstances, and applied more power, this resulted in the boat becoming even more stuck as the stern being lower in the water pushed further onto the mud. From the towpath, the remaining woman who had waited to close the top gate was shouting at the crew demanding to know why they were not stopping to pick her up. The narrowboat now had the two men and the woman with the fair hair who had already embarked the vessel as it left the lock. They started gesticulating and shouting ideas on how to resolve the problem. Helmsman started to reverse, while the other man climbed onto the flat roof and grabbing the barge pole started pushing the front of the boat away from the vegetation.

At this point I became rather concerned with the plight of our resident swans who had built a nest for their young just opposite our boat. Both birds raised their necks and glared at the offending steel hull. Man on the roof made a valiant effort to push, but all he was doing was pushing the nose of the boat towards the centre of the canal, only for it to swing back when he removed the pole. The woman on the towpath, who turned out to be wiser than first implied, instructed him to push from the stern of the boat and for helmsman to apply medium reverse thrust while rocking the tiller through ninety degrees. Slowly, very slowly their more methodical approach started to yield results and the boat pulled back off the sandbar.

#

Excitement over, I wandered off towards the two horses in the field below the canal towpath. Black Beauty and Dobbin. Alright I don't really know their names, but these are the names I have given them, perhaps you could do better? Black Beauty is a jet-black Friesian, about 15 hands tall. I think his name suits him. Dobbin with his beautiful mane, chestnut brown patches on white is a Galineers or Gypsy Cob and stands around 14 hands tall.

    I stood watching the two equestrian animals for some time, but as they look down on me both in stature and demeanour, I don't speak with them much, other than to pass the time of day. The time of day, being about midday, so it seemed to me from the angle of the sun, I was just considering a short nap when I heard the car pull up next to Alex's silver motor. As previously mentioned, being curious by nature, I wandered back up the grassy bank to the small parking area opposite the boat. Covered in garish squares of alternate yellow and blue the hybrid Volvo dwarfed Boss-man's car.

Over time I have learned from my mentor to take advantage of safe locations when investigating unusual events. Thus, I slipped under the Volvo and lay down, curious to see who had arrived in this flamboyant vehicle. Boss-man appeared in the open hatch at the stern of our boat and raised a hand to the occupant of the car, who by this time was moving away, although it was only his sharp black trousers that were visible to me at first. Both men disappeared inside the boat and as I suspected they would not be making an appearance for some time I settled down for a snooze.

A sixth sense alerted me to a present danger. Opening my eyes, I looked straight into the eyes of a dog. A cockapoo to be more precise. This was the fractious cockapoo who belonged to the auburn-haired woman from the cottage beyond the bridge. Her eyes were wide and reflective as he stared at me in my safe place.

"Hello," she said amiably, as if butter could not melt in her mouth, "I'm Tess."

"Go away," I hissed loudly.

"Aw, I just want to be your friend."

"No you don't, you want me to come out so you can chase me."

She thought about this for a while. "True enough, but I still want to be your friend."

I was rescued by the woman calling 'Tess, come here' and 'oh, what a good girl you are,' and 'alright cuddle buns, mummy loves you,' and other such schmaltzy expressions.

Putting Tess on a leash they walked on, and only just in time as Alex and his visitor reappeared. I moved away from my safe place to avoid any altercation with rubber tyres and lay in the shade of the oak tree watching him drive off in the flashy car.

#

That evening as if drawn by a common inquisitiveness, Alex, Lapsat and I sat around the television at news time. Nothing. Following the main evening news, local events were discussed by the nice young lady on the cream-coloured sofa. 'Travellers had set up camp in a local beauty spot, bingo event at local care-home, and wet and windy storm 'Iris' to affect the area tonight and tomorrow morning.' No drowned man.

Alex turned the television off, and I jumped onto his lap so he could make a fuss of me. Lapsat jumped onto the window-bed. All remained quiet and calm until the campanologists started up. It was Wednesday, and most Wednesday evening was bell-ringing practice for locals at St. Peter's Church. Eight renovated bells, some dating back to 1746 are rung by enthusiastic ringers.

That night storm 'Iris' made its presence felt, and us felines stayed inside the dry cosy enclosure of the narrowboat with Boss-man. Large rain drops battered the steel roof, while the wind caused the boat to rock slightly against its moorings. Strange as it might seem, this was a very pleasant experience, certainly when cosseted in secure surroundings. I wondered how Black Beauty and Dobbin were faring.

As the previous night, when the news started, all three of us were in attendance. Contrary to the previous evening the first item on the local news was 'the drowned man at Kinver lock.' The nice young lady, tonight in a red and black full-length dress, told us that an autopsy had revealed: 'Pinkerton Smith had not eaten anything prior to his death.' Also, 'There was no alcohol or toxic substance presence in his body at the time of his death.' However: 'he had a contusion on his head which had previously gone unnoticed.' So, he did bump his head, he had not been drunk and he had not eaten fish and chips from 'The Frying Plaice' or any other establishment. Interesting I thought.

Next on the screen a policeman appeared. This was the same man I had seen speaking with Alex the previous day. DCI Blackwood was explaining that the police were actively looking for two young men seen in the area around the time Mr. Smith had died. A grainy picture of two mugshots replaced the Inspector while he continued his oratory. I recognised the faces instantly. It seems the receipt from the fish shop had led the police to check local CCTV in the High Street, thus producing the pictures of those who 'might be able to help with their enquiries.' I remember thinking how unlikely it would be to see them again.

The final part of the report was an interview with a very tearful young woman who explained that 'Pinky' was 'a beautiful young man with so much to give in life and so much to look forward to.' It was the same young woman I had seen the day after 'Pinky' drowned, the woman with the red carnations.

The news moved on to flooding in a local primary school due to a burst water pipe. Alex turned the television off. The face of Cracker was etched on my mind. It was not a face I expected to see again in a hurry. How wrong could I be? I did not realise that in due course I would come face-to-face with Cracker himself!

## 6 — BOATING SOLO

Opposite our mooring our neighbour swans had been taking turns to incubate their eggs in the nest made of dried grass and sticks. On fair weather days Alex would leave the 'swan hatch' open and I would jump onto the wooden shelf above the television to observe the progress of the noble pair. I have been given to understand it is now late May and both cob and pen had been sharing their pre-parental duty for some six weeks. I was excited to see a very small brownish head with black beak and a pair of dark eyes protrude from the pen's underbelly one day. As it turned out there were five cygnets in the clutch who would remain with us during the summer months.

We had been living on narrowboat 'Rumah Saya' for about two months when Lapsat and I detected something was about to happen to change our routine. It started when Boss-man returned home one day with two harnesses, one grey, one black, which he proceeded to fit on both Lapsat and I. Lifting me onto his lap he drew the black harness over my head and made some adjustments in the length of the straps. It was a good fit, and when he was satisfied, he took it off me and repeated the procedure with Lapsat's grey harness.

Two days later there was a flurry of activity from Boss-man. It started when he fitted our new harnesses and two leads attached to anchor points he had set at the stern of the boat. We both climbed out onto the stern seating area, and I jumped on to the roof. The lead was just long enough for me to reach the solar panel, my favourite observation point. Here I had a good view of his antics. First, he attached two long ropes to the single cleat at the centre of the boat roof, pulling each rope to the stern, one on either side. Next, walking along the gunwale on the starboard side he lifted each of the rope fenders that protected the boat and laid them on the cream-coloured roof. A chrome tiller arm was attached to the swan neck shaped tiller and a brass kingfisher tiller pin slipped into place. Finally, before starting the engine, Alex produced a windlass key which he laid on the seat next to Lapsat.

Naturally this was not the first time we had heard the engine, as he would run it most days to help charge the batteries and provide some hot water for washing up. The big diesel engine settled into a steady rhythm while Alex cast off the mooring lines, gathering them in neat coils and placing them for'ard and aft. We were moving.

Now this was a sensation neither of us felines had experienced before. The putt-putt sound of the engine increased slightly as Alex gently nudged the throttle forward. As he did so a whirring noise from the bow of the boat caused it to swing slightly towards the centre of the canal. Lapsat let out a cautious miaow. "Wasson?" she queried in her thick Devonshire accent.

"Guess we are in for a boat ride." I replied speculatively.

The initial ride did not last long. We passed the traditional working boat, and narrowboats named 'Kingfisher' and 'At Last', but it appeared that no sooner had we cast off than Alex was drawing into a new mooring space. As it turned out, just north of our permanent mooring was the Elsan disposal and water point. Alex quickly attached a hose to the standpipe and started filling the boat's potable water tank. Previously, most days, he had laboriously wheeled a large water drum to collect the precious necessity, using a small pump to transfer water into the storage tank located at the bow of the boat under the well-deck. While filling, Alex took the opportunity to empty the toilet cassette and dispose of the rubbish.

A few minutes elapsed before water started to run out of a small hole in the front of the boat and Alex emitted a satisfied grunt. Hose coiled, ropes gathered, engine ticking over, and we were on the move again. For about ten minutes we chugged at a very slow pace passed other moored boats that I had not seen before. Lapsat and I were now far from our home hunting ground, an adventure was in the making. I was getting rather curious as to what would happen next and indeed where we were heading, when I foresaw a problem looming large on the horizon.

It was a lock, just like the one at Kinver, but we were approaching from below, an angle I had not experienced previously. The boat drifted silently into the bank on the port side and Alex grabbed a centre rope to attach to a 'mushroom' which someone had kindly painted white so it would be easily seen from a distance. He took hold of his windlass key and marched smartly toward the lock. Water rushed out at the base of the old wooden gates causing a miniature whirlpool that gathered two small pieces of wood and a plastic bottle. Miraculously it appeared to me, the gates opened, and Alex returned to the boat. Now, being a cynical cat, I was puzzling how once in the lock, our lord and master would close the gates and raise the boat. Almost all the boats that had passed 'Rumah Saya' at our mooring had at least two crew members, although I had noticed the occasional solo boater.

Expertly the long boat slipped between the brick lock walls without a bump and Alex brought her to a smooth stop. Now I knew for certain he had done this before! No sooner had he entered the lock than a bright-eyed head appeared above.

"Hey, I got this for you."

"Good on you mate, thanks."

Gates closed, sounds of water rushing and boat rising steadily, followed. Now I would like to point out at this moment in time, both Lapsat and I were about to go into hysterics. Wouldn't you? Well, it was our first time on a boat, being buffeted around by water in a deep chasm, surrounded by moss covered bricks. As it turned out, having Alex on the boat for our first lock experience was a blessing as while he was talking calmingly, he petted both of us. Minutes later, we exited the lock to the cheery waves and salutations from the young guy on the top gate who was waiting to take his boat down the lock. We had survived!

On the south side of Hyde lock was the old lock keeper's cottage. The cottage is old, that is, not the lockkeeper. Actually, the lockkeeper is dead metaphorically speaking! No longer does each lock or flight of locks have a dedicated keeper to watch over them. In our modern era the locks and surroundings are maintained by The Canal and River Trust with its numerous workers and volunteers along with contractors moving around the network as required. In bygone days the cottage would have been home to a worker and his family who maintained the lock and surrounding area, tending the grass verges and flowerbeds and providing solace to working boatmen as they passed through the lock. The keeper's wife might have provided home-made staples for sale and the children would have played happily among the trees and shrubs at the lock side. The industry of the area has long since gone. Furnaces for producing wrought iron that lined the canal have been replaced by vistas of open meadow sweeping down to the canal, and deciduous woodland on the northern bank. Only the managers house remains, keeping quiet sentinel over past industry.

From my vantage point I had a good view of the passing scenery and its resident flora and fauna. Peacefully oblivious to the cares of modern life a flock of ducks gathered on the grassy meadow near the canal edge. Male mallard ducks with their iridescent green head and neck sat calmly among their fawn-coloured female counterparts. A small number were standing and gazing upon the water's edge, as if keeping lookout for unwanted intruders.

Further away from my vantage point a flock of sheep comprising of yews with bold white faces and full fleeces of wool awaiting shearing, grazed alongside this year's brood of lambs.

Before my attention returned to the journey in progress my eyes were drawn to a movement at the edge of the woodland beyond the meadow. Were my eyes deceiving me? I kept my focus on the distant gap in the tall trees, and sure enough, there it was, a solitary muntjac.

From my careful attention to narrative provided by Lapsat, Chalky and humans such as Boss-man, I had learned much about life on this planet, and this beautiful and unusual deer was part of my previous education. To personally see a Reeves' Muntjac deer in real life was undoubtedly a treat for any keen naturalist. Unlike other species of deer, the muntjac has haunches higher than their shoulders, and a wide flat tail. The animal I was gazing upon was a male, as it had small antlers and a pronounced downward black line on its face. I was sure that nearby, deeper into the woods I would have found female does and possibly a young fawn or two.

The canal meandered towards Dunsley tunnel. A large foreboding sign gave instruction and warned of dangers to be had within the tunnel. This didn't bother me or Black Persian at all because we can't read! No sooner than we had entered by way of the western portal than the mouth of the tunnel to the east opened to us. It was just twenty-five yards long! A sharp turn to the port side and we were on course for Stewponey lock.

It seems Alex was having a good day, for as we approached the lock beyond the busy concrete road bridge, I could see the gates opening and a boat exiting the lock. As they passed, they exchanged a jovial greeting along with 'there's one behind us coming down.' Alex applied throttle and the boat aimed perfectly aligned for the lock entrance, but at the last moment the strong undercurrent of water from the overflow culvert pushed the nose sideways and we bounced off the lock wall. In Alex defence it must be said, many boats must have hit the side as the old brickwork had been badly chipped away over years. Once in the lock we were in luck again. A party of enthusiastic hire boaters were eager and willing to help, and in no time at all we had risen ten feet to the higher level. As the boat rose, my vantage point on the roof afforded me a good view of the old wharf, stables for the horses, workshop and cottages. Immediately beside the lock was the octagonal toll house dated 1772. It was from here that the Staffordshire and Worcestershire Canal Navigation Company would exact toll monies from the commercial boats using the waterway in dreamy days of old.

Stewponey behind us, we motored on passed moored boats, the canal passing under a 250-year-old brick bridge, which opened out into Stourton Junction.

"What's up there?" I inquired of Lapsat, as I cast eyes on a couple of locks taking the canal off to the right.

"That be Stourbridge Canal, that be, goes all way to Birming'am, so I be told."

We were not going to Birmingham on the Stourbridge Canal, as became apparent when our boat continued straight ahead. Alongside us on the right, reddish brown sandstone rocks rose above us, to the left wooded shrubland leading to the river and beyond, Stourton Castle. The estate dates back to 12$^{th}$ Century as a hunting lodge. It is not a real castle, nevertheless, today visitors come to view the house, and walled gardens that were redesigned around the 19$^{th}$ Century.

Our journey continued as we rounded a 90-degree bend to the left, crossing over the River Stour which ambled away below us on its way to join the River Severn at Stourport. Immediately after the solid stone aqueduct was 'Devil's Den'. Lapsat told me that not much is known of the strange opening at water level in the sandstone rock, except that it might have been used as a boathouse by a local family in times gone by. The entrance was securely closed with a wooden door and heavy padlock to prevent inquisitive individuals like me, exploring the depths beyond.

High escarpments, festooned with trees, shrubs and bracken caressed the meandering canal. Oak, ash and yew adorned the ancient waterway. Perhaps the most serene was the willow, the 'weeping willow' as Black Persian described it. Golden fronds of gentle green cascaded as a living waterfall from the sky. "Watch out!" Lapsat cried as the branches brushed the roof of the boat and threatened to cast me overboard.

It was about this point in time that Alex announced: "That's it for today girls!" A comment which I took to mean he had gone far enough for his first day solo boating and was about to moor at a rather beautiful rural location. Once the boat was secure, Boss-man lengthened our leads and allowed us to wander onto the towpath and surrounding wilderness. The hedgerow was full of brambles, nettles and bindweed, but it was good to be back on terra firma.

#

The next morning, the late spring sun started its ascent in the sky at an ungodly hour. Being awakened early, Alex opened the stern hatch and attaching harness and leads, allowed us to step outside. I was immediately transfixed by the sight of warm sunlight dancing through the swaying trees and sparkling on the rippling waters. Lapsat and I sat for quite a while at the stern of the boat, taking in the dreamy calmness that the British countryside offered on an undisturbed spring morning.

Suddenly, a small flash of turquoise blue shimmering in the early sunlight skimmed passed me just feet above the water.

"What was that Lapsat?" I quizzed eagerly.

"What was what?" she unhelpfully replied.

I glanced to my side, only to find her busy licking a front paw and totally oblivious to the spectacle I had witnessed. My contemplation was only interrupted by the smell of bacon cooking in the galley!

"Hey, you two, breakfast is ready," Boss-man called up to us as he placed our dishes with dry food and small pieces of bacon on the floor. 'What a guy!'

Alex himself sat down to eagerly devour his bacon bap before he cleared the dishes, attended to his ablutions, and then prepared the boat for an early departure.

There is nothing quite so peaceful as cruising the canal on a warm sun filled spring morning. A gentle breeze ruffled my fur, and my senses were stimulated further by the smells of new saplings slightly moistened with early morning dew and the odour of a nocturnal fox that had passed our way the previous night. This most pleasant interlude was not to last long however, as into view came another set of lock gates. As per usual, Alex drew the boat gently to the lock landing and secured a rope. Taking his windless key, he set off to prepare the lock. Today however, perhaps in part due to the early hour, there were no willing volunteers to assist. How would he manage on his own?

The standard procedure for opening the gates and steering the boat into the lock was employed with one small variation. Just before the stern of the boat entered the lock, Alex flipped the throttle to neutral and he stepped off on to the edge of the canal immediately before the lock gates. He was able to do so at this lock as the ground swept down to the water just before a small footbridge. The boat carried by its own momentum, slipped easily forward until it gently nudged the riser plate at the top of the lock, the front fender cushioning the impact as the narrowboat came to a graceful halt. Bottom gates closed, Alex opened a ground paddle at the top just a couple of notches on the rack and pinion. Water started to lift the middle of the boat and carried it very easily backwards until the button fender at the stern made contact with the lower gates. When Alex was happy the boat was stable, he allowed more water to flow. Steadily in stages he opened the sluice fully on both sides and the boat rose, with us eagerly anticipating a new vista.

Departure from the lock was another Alex speciality. Before the lock was completely full of water, Alex nudged the boat forward until it kissed the steel scuff plate on the top gate, then he activated tick over on the throttle and went to open the gate. Top gate open and paddles closed and with the boat moving slowly forward Alex shut the throttle to tick over reverse just as the boat came level with the gate. 'Going astern' did not take effect immediately, which allowed the boat to be well clear with just enough time for Alex to close the gate and jump back on board as the narrowboat pulled back towards the lock gate. Throttle up, and we were off again.

Our journey, punctuated by locks, took us passed a narrowboat marina, public house, ornate gardens and through a small village. Onwards and upwards, ever upwards. Somewhere would be a summit pound, a stretch of water between locks which was being fed by a pumphouse raising water from the river below.

And thus, we arrived at Botterham! Botterham locks are unusual in that two locks combine, sharing middle gates and creating a 'staircase lock' rising over twenty feet. Alex did his usual thing and moored up at the lock 'mushrooms'. I watched him disappear from view for a few moments as he inspected and prepared the upper lock chamber, ensuring it was full of water. Then he emptied the bottom lock chamber and opened the gates. The long but narrow boat slid gracefully into the lower section of the lock, stopping just short of the massive wall of rock and centre gates. Clambering onto the roof of the boat he walked along, centre rope in hand, and climbed the vertical lock ladder. The gates closed and slowly we rose. We watched the gates open and then Alex standing on the bridge above the lock and with rope in hand, tugged hard to ease the boat forward into the second chamber. The process of closing the gates and raising the boat began a second time.

As we drew level with the grass verge a soft but excited voice shouted " 'at, 'at ..." A tiny grubby hand, index finger extended, pointed directly at me. The boy's mother knelt at the side of the pushchair and corrected her son: "cat, cat," she said, and added "a kitty cat ... no, look Jamie, two cats, see the black and white on the seat."

Calling over to Alex who was opening the top gate she asked: "Do your cats live on the boat with you?"

"Certainly do, but I keep them on leads when we travel so they don't get lost in unfamiliar surroundings."

Our next mooring turned out to be next to the local supermarket, a most fortuitous stop as it turned out. Bossman left us locked up inside while he went to get supplies. On his return with two full carrier bags of human goodies, he produced a rather exciting looking chocolate, fresh cream filled doughnut. He called to Lapsat and I, and then much to my surprise he stuck both index fingers into the cream and offered the dairy treat for us to lick. There followed another treat as he opened a small tin which allowed a mouth-watering aroma to assail our senses. Into both our food bowls Alex placed a small portion of the finest pink salmon. Our lord and master is a kindly soul.

Beyond Botterham and after Bumble hole lies Bratch. This was the most exciting of our lock encounters on this adventure. A set of three locks so close together they appear to be a staircase. However, each lock has its own gates and a side pound acting much like a miniature reservoir. On first sight the locks rose above us like a towering impregnable fortress, how would Alex cope on his own I wondered. Tied up below the lock entrance Bossman went off to investigate. He did not return for some time, in fact it was not until two boats had followed each other out of the lower lock that he returned and powering up the engine, eased us into the first chamber. As it happened there were two volunteer 'lockies' assisting us through the flight.

Above the locks wide open fields greeted us, while looking back was a grand view of Wombourne with its many brick houses and trees combining to make leafy suburbs of Wolverhampton. Beside the top lock the obligatory lockkeepers house, now renovated and whitewashed and just below, the octagonal toll house now used by the volunteers.

It was later the same day when we arrived at Autherley junction. Again, a black and white fingerpost pointed towards Chester, Great Heywood and back the way we had come, Stourport. Here, Alex 'winded' the boat, turning it 180 degrees by pushing the nose of the boat into the bridge hole where the Shropshire Union or 'Shropie', as the locals call it, starts its rather direct line to Chester and Ellesmere Port. Then with deft action on the rudder and throttle, combining to push the stern passed the junction, our boat made its turn. The term 'winding' pronounced as wind, according to all-knowing Chalky, came from the days when working boats had no engine, and would make use of prevailing wind to help them turn at junctions or 'winding holes'. Lapsat did not hold to this view and said 'it comes from the old English word for turn, 'windan' as in 'windlass'. Confusing! But entomology aside, we set off on the return journey to our base at Kinver. The route being the same held no surprises, although the manicured gardens at Ashwood were a joy to revisit.

Below Greensforge I saw it again. A flash of brilliant, turquoise blue skimming the water ahead of the boat. This time Lapsat saw it too. "Ah, they be a kingfisher, they be."

I marvelled at the vibrant shimmer of this tiny bird's wings, as it glided across the water in the warm sunlight, looking for small fish and insects. Presently, it alighted on a small dead branch overhanging the canal, and apparently stayed content to wait while our boat passed. I gazed upon its orange-brown underbelly, its small head and long black and orange beak.

"Them nest in river 'nd canal banks by burrowin' into soil they does," said Lapsat eager to update my knowledge of avian life. "Ee be lucky to see 'im, 'only righteous sees kingfisher', so they say."

On the third day of our return cruising, from my rooftop vantage point I caught sight of our resident swans, and joy of joys, five dusty grey cygnets, tiny bundles of mottled grey fluff, following very close to their parents. As Alex drew the boat into the mooring and tied up, I looked out with pleasure upon robin red breast on his wooden post in the water, and with less pleasure, Tess the cockapoo who was sprawled un-lady-like on the path while her owner, dressed in a striking yellow pullover and blue jeans waved to Alex. Once secured to the bank, Boss-man removed our harnesses and we both happily, although wary of Tess, stretched our legs on the grass verge. The youthful brunette in her navy and black uniform returning from school was delighted to give me a gentle rub of my belly. I repaid her by curling into a ball around her hand and extending my claws to show my appreciation. The young lady didn't seem overly pleased with this sign of affection on my part!

Home sweet home. Well with boating we take our home with us, but for Alex this was the end of his first solo boating experience, and we were back at our home mooring. I couldn't help wondering how many times he had done that very journey with Brenda in happier days?

## 7 — TESS THE COCKAPOO

"Butterfly, you don't look much like a butterfly to me!" I had been quietly minding my own business, sat on the grass verge when Tess wandered up, lay down on her stomach and stretching her neck forward and flat on the ground she stared at me and tried to engage me in conversation.

"No, stupid, I'm a cat. My name means butterfly."

"Yeh, I know, Chalky told me, Kipepeo. Silly name. Now my name, Tess, that's a great name, my mistress called me Tess when I was a little puppy. Really cute I was ..."

"So, what went wrong?" I chipped in.

"Arg, none of your lip you little scamp, or I'll chase you up the towpath. Now, I'm called after Tess of the D'Urbervilles, you know, some book thing, or so she told me. Anyway, my mistress, Fiona, well she needs my protection, so I go everywhere with her even when she goes to the bathroom. I shield her from undesirables. I bark at danger. I stop your feline friends from getting in our garden. We live beyond the road bridge you know. Nice place, proper house, made of solid brick, not some old floating barge."

I yawned.

"When the tall thin man in short trousers and luminous vest puts paper in the metal box at the garden gate, I growl at him. Occasionally when he has a bulky package, he dares to touch the garden gate, and I let out my fiercest bark, until he offers me one of those little brown yummy things, then, well, you know how it is, I just let him in so he can see the mistress. But, if he ever touched her, or forgot to give me a treat, I would be obliged to bite his ankle."

Fiona, had released Tess from her lead while she sought blackberries among the brambles, gathering them one at a time, placing them in a small wicker basket lined with kitchen paper. Curiously I noted that Boss-man had struck up a conversation with the woman, an animated conversation at that. I guess they were too engaged to notice Tess' quiet barking and growling and my miaows in reply. The irritating canine must have noticed my gaze had shifted away from her. "You listening to me Kip?"

"Kippy, names Kippy not Kip."

"Yes, well as I was saying, nice place, big garden, nice view of canal."

The non-stop chatter was starting to annoy me, it wouldn't take much for me to extend a claw or two and swipe!

"Lockside Cottage," she continued without prompting, "a bijou residence; shame about the old lady upstairs."

My ears pricked up. "Old lady …"

"Yip, Fiona's mother, she stays upstairs much of the time. Don't see her often and I am not allowed up the stairs. Gate, you know, blocking access. Not right that. How can I protect the house when I can't go upstairs. What if a burglar came through an upstairs window?"

"He'd need a ladder!" I observed.

"Or a rat?"

"A rat! A burglar needs a rat?"

"No stupid. A rat sneaks upstairs and I can't get it."

"Oh, please shut up, you talk too much."

"Well, I'll say, it's not much of a conversation with you."

"Conversation! Who are you kidding, you don't stop talking, I can't get a word in."

It was at this moment Fiona called out: "Tess, come on then. Walkies!"

I must have given an audible sigh of relief as Tess, giving me one final stare observed: "I'll be back, you wait and see."

Well, he wouldn't be wrong about that. What neither of us knew at the time was that a memorable incident would occur next time we met.

#

As Tess and Fiona disappeared from sight on their walk along the canal bank, I had a strong urge to explore a little further from my comfort zone. I wandered along the canal edge to the lock and after taking careful stock of the area, checking all was safe, I walked the plank that crossed to the public house side of the lock. I had done this before, in fact, this is where I had found the receipt from the chip shop that I had presented to Alex. Now however, I considered a sojourn at 'The Lock Inn', which I knew was Chalky's haunt, to be a valuable use of time.

It was easy to slip between the rotting wooden slats in the fence without breaking my stride. I stepped up onto the dark wooden decking, being careful not to slip on the damp mouldy patches at the edge. The deck contained chrome tables and chairs spaced evenly around the area. Here many patrons would come, weather permitting, to enjoy a drink or some plate of cooked nourishment. At the foot of one table was a smallish 'puddle' of creamy sauce, still fresh; I licked with pleasure. Further on passing the side door to the main building I discovered a collection of beer bottles and glasses in two separate crates, all waiting to be sorted and washed before the evening revellers arrived.

The back of the pub had a closed off section, securely padlocked, but easy for me to limber under the door. Gas bottles, sacks of coal, and logs for the fire stacked in neat piles. I sniffed around for some time, sensing the presence of mice, but as I was not hungry and had no real desire to 'play', I left them in peace, for the time being.

The car park was large and for the most part covered in tarmac. Only two cars were in residence, obviously belonging to landlord and bar staff as the establishment was not due to open for a couple of hours. A large heavy oak door provided access to the bar from the car park by way of a small porch. It was fortuitous that the door was held open by a wooden wedge that had been slipped under the door. Slowly, one paw at a time I crept forward towards the threshold. Cautiously I glanced inside. The lounge was dark and dreary. No lights had been turned on yet, but there was an orange flickering glow coming from the fireplace which held a couple of small wooden logs that had recently been set on fire, more for ambience than heat.

I placed a paw on the grey and brown carpet and immediately withdrew it. The carpet was worn to a thread and sticky from spilt beer. The smell of beer also permeated not just the carpet but the whole establishment. I mused on how Chalky could live in this dreary and pungent smelling institution. Overcoming my initial repulsion, I moved forward, ever checking for signs of life and keeping a clear escape route to the car park in focus.

Large solid wooden benches accompanied thick set tables and chairs covered in tartan patterned cushions. This is a place I would not want to be seen in when filled with clientele. Moving more courageously around the bar I came face to face with Chalky. He was sat upright and staring right into my face; obviously he was fully aware of my presence and just waiting for me to fall into his trap.

"Geet lost yow 'orrible moggie from the cut," he hissed at me.

I stood my ground. Mainly because if I had run, I knew he would have chased me off the premises. "Hi Chalky. Just wanted to see where you live."

"This is my patch, go back to yow boat life, yow have no interest for me molly. Oy like my wenches to be queens then we can 'ave fun together."

"You've got mice in the wood store," I goaded.

"So! Keeping them for later, they don't know what's going to hit them. Now time for yow to move of my patch, and if Oy catch you here again …"

Our high-pitched howling and hissing was interrupted by the pub landlord who, disturbed by two cats growling, shooed us both out of the door to the car park with a sweeping brush. "See you Chalky," I said as I made a hasty retreat to the neutral space beside the canal.

"Not if Oy see yow first!" he countered, but I could see the grin on his face. He liked to make out he was a big and tough tomcat, but I could see through the façade to the soft-hearted persona within.

#

A gentle breeze had begun to ease the heat of the summer sun. Lapsat was basking in the shade of the old oak tree some distance from the boat. Inside would be intolerably hot from the mid-day sun and would remain so into the evening even with the windows open and the cooling breeze. I contemplated joining Black Persian under the tree but as a few white fluffy cumulus clouds were disrupting the sun's rays I chose to lay on the solar panel, my favourite vantage point and wait to see if the young student girl would pet me on return from school.

Boss-man was also enjoying the sun. He had set out a camp chair in the grass, filled a large glass with dark malt beer and was engrossed in reading a paperback book. A black baseball cap adorned with a gold logo perched on his head, while a pair of brown tinted sunshades rested on his nose. While I watched him for some minutes it became apparent, he was not reading but had nodded off to sleep. There was no movement and the book resting in his lap remained open to the same page.

I was amused to see a mother moorhen gliding over the water with a plump of moorhen chicks bobbing up and down behind her. The chicks were small bundles of black fluff. She was encouraging them to keep together with a 'wupwup' sound.

The tranquillity of the scene was rudely interrupted by, of all animals, Tess the vivacious cockapoo. She had spied a squirrel foraging in the hedge just round the bend of the canal. Like lightning the squirrel bounded towards the oak, Tess in hot pursuit. It was a close match with squirrel only just maintaining a safe distance until it hurtled skywards to the safety of a habitat it was fully accustomed with. Defeated, Tess pulled up short at the trunk and looking up at the mocking squirrel gave a loud bark: "Missed you! Drat! Get you next time."

The bark which destroyed the peaceful ambience, caused Alex to stir from his slumber with a jerk, which in turn caused his drink to spill, and book to fold and land closed upside down on the grass. "Wretched dog. Disturbing the peace. What's wrong with you?" he asked of no one in particular.

"Oh, I'm so sorry." It was Fiona who, seeing the chase, had hastened to catch up with her charge. Being an older woman, she had lagged behind despite her best efforts to subdue the unruly dog. "She just can't help herself. Cats and squirrels. She just has to chase them. I don't like to keep her on a lead all the time." Tess' mistress moved towards him to attach a lead to his harness, but on seeing him laying below the tree panting, and giving her the 'sorry, was there something you wanted?' look, she relented and turned back to Alex.

"Turned out nice today," Alex said.

"Quite pleasant, sun was rather fierce though, until the clouds rolled in. What is the forecast for tomorrow?"

"Oh, Um, not sure." Alex produced his mobile phone, tapped away and then added: "Fine again, with a risk of an occasional shower."

What is it with these humans and the weather. Obsessed. For us felines we sniff the air, if it is going to rain or it is already raining, we stay indoors or find a dry place of refuge. If dry, time to roam. Why worry about tomorrow, we live for the moment.

"How's your mother doing today?" Alex's question was sincere but took me by surprise. Until the previous Tess encounter, I was not aware of 'the old lady' upstairs, but it seems Boss-man was.

"Grumpy! Says she is feeling under the weather today."

There we go, talking about the weather again, I mused.

"Can't you get her out for a walk sometime, she might enjoy the fresh air."

"Great idea, but I would need to get her into the wheelchair and push her along the path. She can't walk very far now, and these paths are not easy to negotiate."

"That's true, but if you could get her here on a fine day, I could produce some tea, and who knows, perhaps a piece of cake."

"She always liked Battenburg, I remember it was her favourite when I was young. Naturally she knows this canal like the back of her hand, she has lived here since she was married at nineteen."

I lifted my right paw and looked at the back of it. No. Don't understand that.

It was right about this time that the incident occurred. Everything happened within an instant, but I can still replay the events clearly in my mind. It began with Tess giving a single warning bark that we all ignored. A young man wearing khaki trousers and riding a green sports bicycle came into view at speed along the path. It seemed clear that he was heading for the main road that crosses the narrow brick bridge. However, instead of following a straight path, at the last moment he veered off course towards Alex and Fiona. I raised my head just in time to see him grab at Fiona's tote bag that was resting on her shoulder, and with a deft and well-practiced move, jerk it over her head. The move would have been perfect if it were not for her auburn hair, which being long, snagged the strap. The cyclist held onto the bag as Fiona turned awkwardly and fell to the ground like a large bag of cat biscuits!

I was not the only observer of the incident. As the man started to pick up speed, carrying his ill-gotten trophy, Tess had seen it all and started off in pursuit from his resting place under the oak. I have already explained how fast this young cockapoo can move, but to chase and bark at the same time! It was a challenge for the energetic dog to catch the bike, but swiftly she gained ground until she was snapping at the heels of the man. Unnerved by the ferocity of Tess attack the bike wobbled and the man fell clumsily to the ground. I doubt I have ever heard such intense barking, that is until the man kicked out in anger with his left foot and size ten boot accompanied by vitriolic swearing. Tess was in just the wrong place; she rolled over backwards and gave such a heart-rendering yelp it genuinely upset me. The dog groaned and then became silent and still.

Was it the yelp of Tess or Fiona clutching her ankle and groaning or not, but something inside drove me to action. Now my head was telling me to do the sensible thing and scram, look for a safe place, and wait for the chaos to subside. However, an inner subconscious propelled me in the direction of the youth in khaki and his stricken bycycle. I leaped from the roof of the boat to the grass in one swift movement, and propelling myself forward with powerful hind legs I covered the distance in record time. Why I should want to be in the centre of the action I really did not understand, perhaps my subconscious wanted me to swipe him with a claw extended paw, but having seen what had happened to Tess who was much bigger than myself I doubt it. Rather, I stood my ground and gave the man the 'evil eye' as he struggled to extricate himself from the machinery that made up his conveyance. In the mayhem the cream leather tote bag had fallen a few feet away from the bike. He moved as if to retrieve it, but I was in his direct line, that's when I hissed my fiercest taunt, and to my surprise he straddled the bike and rode off without the bag.

    I could not move. In the briefest of moments, we had faced each other, and eye contact had been made. The face aroused in me a terrifying memory, this was the man, the khaki young man, who had punched 'Pinky' causing his fall and death. It was the face of Cracker!

#

A whimpering sound aroused me from my stupor. It was Tess. I turned to see her trying to roll onto her belly.

Suddenly I had a growing admiration for this loyal companion to Fiona. There had been no hesitation in providing protection to her mistress despite the obvious danger to herself.

"You okay?" I lamely inquired.

Tess groaned again, "just bruised, I think."

There was little I could do myself to help her, but I moved forward and rubbed my nose gently against hers. "You did good. Come on you will be just fine," I said without conviction.

I glanced over to where the bag lay undamaged except for some grass stains.

"You did well to save the bag, can we get it back to my mistress?"

"Can you stand?" I asked her.

Gingerly Tess raised herself onto four paws, a few whimpers accompanying the move. Hobbling she reached the bag and took hold of the loop handle near the leather handbag and made her way back to where Fiona had been attacked. I followed at a discreet distance.

The scene in front of us was not so good. Alex was helping Fiona to her feet, and it was clear to me that she was having problems putting her left foot to the ground. Tess stopped just short of the couple and stood, bag in mouth watching the proceedings. Despite her predicament Fiona caught sight of Tess and joyfully exclaimed: "Tess, you got my bag. oh Alex, look, how wonderful. Thank you, Tess, thank you so much."

I had a momentary pang of jealousy; it was me after all that had prevented Cracker making off with the item. Nevertheless, I am not a jealous cat, and I was delighted she was so happy to have it restored to her. Boss-man reached out and took the bag from Tess who rather warily relinquished it to him rather than her.

"I've got the bag," Alex proclaimed unnecessarily, "now you hold on and we will get you inside the boat."

It was a distressing ordeal as Fiona limped forward grabbing on to any suitable support available. As she descended the wooden steps her hands grasped the steel hatch and took the weight from the damaged ankle. Once inside she manoeuvred her way through the galley to the saloon where Alex rushed to make the master arm-chair available with a stool to rest her feet. Tess followed protectively behind and lay in a watchful pose at her side. Lapsat had already acquired the window bed having slipped in unnoticed while we were all outside. I came in last and curled myself into a small ball beside the unlit fire, just to give the impression I was not concerned with the present antics.

Being the kindly man he is, Boss-man went back to the galley, and I heard the familiar sound of the stainless-steel kettle being filled and the gas burner ignition being fired. Before the tea was made, he returned with a balloon glass containing a small quantity of rich orange liquid, the sweet woody aroma permeated the boat.

"Get this down you, it will help with the shock."

"Thanks, but I'm okay really."

"That's what people always think at first, but the aftereffects of any sudden shock can mess up the bodies equilibrium, I've seen it happen before."

"I'm not sure exactly what happened?"

"It was the guy on the bike, he snatched your bag, but it caused you to fall, I guess you have twisted your ankle or something. Can I take a look?"

"It's very painful, do you think its broken?"

Alex carefully removed both shoes, which conveniently were not laced and came off easily. Even to me it was clear to see that the left ankle was swollen compared to the right. Alex knelt at the woman's feet and gently felt the area, even manipulating it slightly in a circular motion much to Fiona's protestations. Tess raised a concerned head at the sound of her mistress in pain.

"Not broken," he announced, "twisted, swollen and will be very bruised by tomorrow. Wait here a minute!"

"I can't very well do anything else," Fiona said with a smirk on her face.

Alex returned to the kitchen just in time to turn the gas off under the singing kettle. He returned with a pack of peas he had been storing in the freezer.

"Right then, we will start with the ice pack."

"And then we'll eat them for dinner." This woman had a sense of humour then.

Ignoring the jibe Alex continued: "Then later I will put arnica cream on the ankle and wrap it in a bandage. I'll take you back to your cottage in the car."

"Oh, you're too kind, but really it is only just through the bridge, I can walk slowly."

"No you don't, you will have to rest the ankle for some days and that means not walking on it more than you absolutely must. I can come by twice a day and take Tess for a walk, after all she got your bag back from the scoundrel."

Really the audacity of it, our Boss-man taking another person's dog for a walk, and a mischievous dog like Tess, well, I must talk with Lapsat about this later. It seems Tess is fast becoming the hero of the hour, but what about ME, I know who did it!

"Hey, Lapsat, you awake?"

"Wasson," Black Persian mumbled.

"Your cat is making noises," said Fiona, "is she okay?"

"Oh yes, 'talkative' one that one, always meowing."

"Guess who tried to steal the bag?" I continued, "it was that Cracker, you know, remember him, the one I told you pushed Pinkerton into the canal when he died. It was him I tell you, same guy. Nasty piece of work that."

"Ee pulling my leg?" Lapsat was engaged with me now: "Really, same bey."

"No kidding. I wish I could explain that to the humans."

Alex had taken a seat on the small wooden folding chair he used with the writing table after he had made them both a hot tea 'with lots of sugar' to help the shock. He seemed obsessed by the effects of shock. Silence descended on the little gathering for a short while, then both humans spoke at once:

"Ops sorry, after you," Alex volunteered.

"Just wondering how easy it will be to get up and down stairs to help my mother."

"Is she confined to her room?"

"Well not really, but she is quite poorly now and since I moved in about a year ago, after the fall when she broke her hip, she says she prefers to stay upstairs. It is quite self-contained, with bedroom and ensuite bathroom with a walk-in shower that we had installed."

"Does she get many visitors?"

"Not really, but she is somewhat reserved, always has been, not bothered with parties and gatherings. My brother who lives in Scotland visits occasionally and when he does, perhaps two or three days at a time, he sleeps downstairs on the couch. Otherwise, a few in the village call around from time to time."

"You said she has lived in the same house for many years, she must know people in the village."

"Nineteen, a child bride. Huh, they married young in those days. I guess today young couples just move in together, but mother was from a strong Christian family and was expected to maintain a good moral standard. Many of the locals she knew as a young woman have moved on or died now. There are a few in the village who ask after her when I go shopping, and I dare say one or two might come and help out for a few days if I asked. I'll give Rosie a call. She is the village post mistress, and her daughter Melissa, a teenager, is so kind and helpful, she might call and take dinner upstairs."

"How about the landlord of 'The Lock Inn' he might prepare some meals which I could bring round for you and your mother, save you standing in the kitchen?"

"Do you think he would do that?"

"I know him quite well; I like a pint or two some evenings. I'll pay him of course. They have a simple menu, but the food is good I understand."

"That is so kind. How will I repay you?"

"Don't mention it. Happy to help. I'm sure you would do the same for me."

Alex stood up, and removing the peas, started to rub arnica into the suffering ankle which he then wrapped tightly in a bandage. As he did so, my roving eyes came to rest on the magazine rack in the far corner. At the front was the local paper from two days after the death of 'Pinky'. I made my way over to the paper and looking at the photograph of the two ruffians who were caught on CCTV I wondered if the humans would understand who had attacked Fiona. I pulled the paper from the rack with difficulty and dragged it across the wooden floor. "What are you doing Kippy?" Alex asked me without expecting a reply.

I pushed the paper toward the adults and with my paw I patted the photograph of Cracker. "Curious cat you have there Alex," stated Fiona, "is she trying to tell us something?"

"Doubt it, just being a nuisance, aren't you cat. Just a pest, love you really. Oh, and you too Lapsat." He said as he transferred his gaze to Black Persian on the hammock.

"They are good company for you, just like Tess is for me. I wouldn't be without her now." Tess upon hearing her name, looked up longingly. "Well, better get you home then, oh, and see if mother is alright."

"Absolutely." Said Boss-man as he gathered up the paper from the floor and cast it aside. Ah well, I tried.

## 8 — LOCKSIDE COTTAGE

Black Persian had been gone for much of the morning. I wandered around most of her usual haunts in search, but she was nowhere to be found. Boss-man was also missing, but I knew where he was. Since Cracker had worked his evil, over the last couple of days our provider would take Tess for a walk in the morning and in the evening collect food from the pub which he would deliver to Lockside Cottage for Fiona, and her mother.

I had taken ownership of the window hammock, at least for the present, and was occupied licking my genitalia clean while my left leg stretched skywards. Pardon? Well, how am I supposed to keep clean? Us felines are very proud animals when it comes down to personal hygiene. You humans might use soap and water in your man-made waterfall, but we have a rough tongue and lots of saliva to do the job. I must say that we do a pretty good job too, it keeps the old fur in excellent condition. It is only as we get older and it becomes harder to groom ourselves that our coat can become matted, then we must rely on you humans to help us.

It was while carrying out this daily ritual that I heard the cat door at the bow of the boat click open and closed. Lapsat sauntered in casually and jumped up onto Boss-man's favourite chair, made three circles and lay down.

"So, where have you been?" I demanded before she became too settled. There was quite a long silence during which time I began to think she would not answer.

"The cottage."

"Wayside Cottage. But I looked for you there."

"No silly. Lockside Cottage. Ee know, where cockapoo lives, what's 'er name?"

"Tess."

"Tess, yes 'nd mistress, 'nd mistress' mother."

I was shocked. "But, but, that's beyond the bridge."

"Right on."

"You went beyond the bridge?" I stated again incongruously, "why?"

"Don't ee want to know where Boss-man goes each day?"

"I know he is helping Fiona since she broke, er, I mean twisted, her ankle. Have you seen her? Is she improving? Can she walk now?"

"Doing just fine. Proper job. Ee should go take a look. Nice place, isn't it?"

"Is it safe? I mean, beyond the bridge?"

"Sure, go check it out," she said as she buried her head deep between her paws and wrapped the tip of her tail over her eyes. I guess that was the end of the conversation.

It would be the following day when, trembling inside, I ventured beyond the bridge.

I have described the old brick bridge before, but what I may not have mentioned is that the towpath runs under the road in a small, low headroom, tunnel. This was used by the bargee to lead their shire horse or more likely pony or mule under the road while the boat was being lowered in the lock. Leather harnesses and straps fitting comfortably on the animal had a stout length of rope attached that would stretch back to an anchor point on the boat a few feet from the bow.

It had rained slightly the previous night, and a small muddy puddle had formed on the towpath under the bridge. As I gingerly straddled the puddle, I stood on the edge of a new world experience. New of course to me. Naturally the canal continued ahead of me, with the path hugging the water's edge. Far in the distance I could distinguish a number of trees fully laden with summer leaves. To the left an embankment rose up to meet the road above the bridge. But what really caught my eye was the brick cottage with enclosed garden and a small pathway leading back to the road that was now behind me. In the drive was a smart three-door Mini Cooper in British Racing Green. Was this Lockside Cottage? Is this where Fiona and her mother lived? Was this her car? If so, she had good taste in my opinion.

As if to answer my question, the gate opened and from behind the tall hedge Alex appeared with Tess on a lead. I had a moment of panic, should I return to a safe location and take cover? I did not need to fear as both human and canine set off away from me down the canal path.

From the bridge to the cottage the path was well worn but firm and dry. Much of the cottage was surrounded by a tall green privet hedge obstructing the view. However, once I had reached the gate, a simple wooden design with upright slats, I could peer into the front garden with ease. Knowing that Tess was not at home, I slipped easily through a gap in the gate and feasted my eyes on the neatly trimmed lawn surrounded by a fine array of flowers, and shrubs, many of which were in bloom. The garden was so delightful and the flowerbeds so soft and inviting, I could not resist digging a little hole, no doubt the smell would drive Tess mad when she came home!

The two-story cottage was brick built with two elegant chimney stacks pushing their way through the slate roof. On one chimney was a weathervane taking the form of the grim reaper with his sickle. As there was a gentle breeze blowing today it pointed south-west, the direction of the prevailing wind. There was no wisteria as we previously had on the walls of the Devon Cottage; oh, how a distant memory tried to overwhelm me. In its place were rosebushes that extended red, yellow and purple blooms to the height of the Georgian timber windows that had been lovingly painted in a brilliant white gloss.

Central to the property and evenly spaced between the two ground floor windows was the Georgian style front door with a beautiful brass door knocker in the form of a lion's head. I doubted it was the original door, nevertheless it was lovingly painted with a high gloss finish in dark green.

The garden was split into two areas, either side of the gravel path and small lawn. On one side were daisies, foxgloves and hollyhocks of varying colour, while on the left was a kitchen garden. I delighted in the rich smells from mint, thyme and other herbs which grew alongside lettuce, carrots and radishes.

Naturally the front door was closed so I worked my way around the corner of the cottage to the rear. Here above the coal bunker was a small window that had been left open. Cautiously I jumped onto the bunker and peeped in through the window. Well, you can't accuse me of being a 'peeping tom' because I am a lady cat!

Inside a cabinet was pushed up against the window in just the right position to make a good point of entry. So, I did. It was the downstairs toilet. The convenience door was ajar, thus, as is my usual custom when exploring a new environment, I poked a head cautiously around the door jamb. The downstairs corridor leading to the front door lacked light and ventilation. There was a musty dampness in the air and the once vibrant coloured Axminster carpet was threadbare and worn. I was about to explore further when I heard voices. Fiona's, I recognised at once, the other must be her mother.

"I don't know why you moved into my home; I can cope you know."

"Yes mother," came the exasperated reply, "you have been saying that for nearly a year now. Alex will be back soon; I'll ask him to fix your television. I expect it needs re-tuning."

"Who? Who's Alex."

"Mum, remember, Alex is the nice man who helped me when I twisted my ankle."

"Twisted ankle, I haven't twisted my ankle."

"Not you, me! I told you before, I twisted my ankle when the young man on the bicycle grabbed my handbag, and Alex helped me home."

"Who's got a bicycle?"

"It doesn't matter mother."

"I don't know why you moved into my house. I don't need your help you know."

The banter was interrupted with a bark. I knew that bark. Time for a quick escape. Back to the water closet, onto the cabinet, through the window, down onto the bunker and round to the front of the cottage. Horror! Tess was sniffing at the freshly dug earth in the flowerbed. I backed up and returned to the rear of the property. I was relieved to find another exit point over a low wall, which led to the car in the drive. I ducked under the car and waited to make sure all was safe, then I quickly made my way back to our home on the boat.

#

The following morning Tess came to us. Alex went as usual to collect her for the daily walk but instead he brought her back to the boat and tied her lead to the totem post at the front of the boat. I did not wish to be unsociable, so I pushed my way through the cat flap and sitting on the front of the boat watched Tess as she ate some of the longer strands of grass. The men had not cut the grass for a few weeks and as Alex had been busy, he had not done so either.

She didn't look too well to me. After a while she burped, then she arched her back and started to heave. No problem, this is something both Lapsat and I do when we get a hairball.

"That's better," Tess said after bringing up some bile and green grass.

"You okay, Tess?"

"Been a bit yuck since I got kicked, think it bruised my stomach." She was uncharacteristically quite for a few moments, then: "So, you been sniffing around our place, have you?"

What should I say? Had she seen me? Was it my digging in the garden flower bed? Was she cross? I did not reply.

"No matter. 'Curiosity killed the cat' so they say. Or is it 'Tess who killed the cat?'" she spat out with venom, and then seeing my startled reaction she laughed: "Joking, just a bit of fun. Used to be a wharf you know."

"Wharf, what was a wharf?" I puzzled.

"The cottage was built thirty to forty years after the canal, so I have been told. The site used to have a wharf, a wooden jetty. It was eighty feet long I understand. The cargo boats, mostly carrying coal would come down the canal from Wolverhampton, and the occasional carpet would come up by boat from Kidderminster and be unloaded at the wharf to be taken into the village. The wharf fell into disrepair a long time ago and was abandoned. The cottage was built with the same type of brick as many of the bridges and locks in the vicinity, and a wharf manager lived on site."

"How do you know all this?" I demanded.

"Chalky, pub cat. You know Chalky?"

"Oh yes, I know Chalky!"

"He knows everything about the canal round here!"

Tess stood up and stretched then sat back on her hind-legs and continued: "The old lady has lived there since she was nineteen, they say. Married a carpenter's son from the village and his parents rented the cottage for them. Then Fiona and her brother were born and grew up in the cottage. Husband died some years ago it seems then last year the old lady fell when visiting the village post office and broke a hip. That's when Fiona and I moved into the cottage to help out, but she doesn't like the arrangement much. Going a bit silly I suppose. Repeats herself. Stays upstairs most of the time. Could come downstairs but doesn't unless it's for doctor or hospital or something special. Grumbles a lot. Recently she has been calling out in the night."

"Walkies!" the voice of Alex drew my attention from Tess ramblings, "come on Tess, walkies!"

Boss-man untied Tess lead from the totem-post and led the excitable canine up the towpath towards Wayside Cottage. Tess was jumping up and down, doing circles and generally being a nuisance. Unlike us, dogs can be so boisterous and demanding. Just before they walked out of sight, about the location of the narrowboat 'At Last', Tess made three or four circles, crouched down and emptied her bowels. Boss-man using a green bag picked it up and tied a knot in the top. Oh, how disgusting! Dogs don't even try to cover over their filth, but quite happily leave it for humans to collect and carry. It has been noted by both Lapsat and I that some humans fail to pick up after their dog, usually if they think no one else is watching. However we see it, and we do not approve, especially if it is near our home. Most inconsiderate.

After Tess and Boss-man departed I made my way onto the boat roof to take up my usual and preferred vantage point. From here I observed a flock of ducks that made their way from below Kinver lock and settled themselves on the grass verge no doubt in the hope of a quiet few minutes. Most of the birds were mottled brown females but there were two drakes both with iridescent green in their heads and a rich variety of browns adorning their bodies.

Much to my surprise I caught site of a pair of slightly smaller ducks that stayed apart from the main flock. The male had a rainbow of colours, orange plumes on his cheek, with mauve, brown and blue blended on his torso. A striking crimson and white beak finished the regal effect. His mate was dull by comparison, with a grey head and brown back. It is rare to see Mandarin ducks but a delight, nonetheless.

Unfortunately for the ducks, Tess was on the warpath. Rather unwisely in my view, Boss-man had allowed the mischievous cockapoo free reign, and upon their return she spotted the flock on the side of the canal and went 'hell for leather' directly at them. They were too quick for her naturally. Thus ended the peaceful sojourn at Kinver lock for the party of ducks who escaped just in time onto the safety of the water.

"Great sport, what," barked Tess in my general direction. I ignored her. "Nothing like chasing the wildlife."

"What would you do if you caught one?" I demanded.

"Well, I would, um, I would, catch them, and then I would, grrr, worry them, and snap at them and …"

"Sounds to me like you don't know what you would do."

Tess let out a loud aggressive bark just to let me know how fierce she really is. What Tess did next was not good and made me ashamed to admit knowing her.

A young mum was pushing a toddler in his stroller. The small lad had a rather nice-looking hedgehog plush toy in his little hand. Tess, no doubt frustrated with my reaction to her upsetting the ducks, strode over and snapped the toy from the little boy. I was horrified and said so. Tess ignored me. She stepped back from the buggy and violently, shaking her head, shook the toy back and forth with venomous fury. This lasted for about ten seconds, when perhaps coming to the understanding of what she had done, she stopped, and meekly pushed the plush back into the face of the child.

At first when Tess snatched the toy, the little lad looked as if he would burst into tears, but watching Tess antics he burst out laughing, and squealed with delight at the show put on, it seemed, just for him. When Tess returned the hedgehog, she allowed the boy to pat her head and make a fuss of her, then, rolling on her back she invited the young mother to rub her belly. Really, how embarrassing! Nevertheless, all parties ended up entertained.

Alex, who had missed most of the action due to being inside the boat, appeared and putting Tess back on her lead, about time too I might add, walked her back to Fiona's cottage.

Not many minutes later, Chalky sprang from the pub, rushed across the lock and up the oak tree to a vantage point on the first branch. "Pub's on fire!" he exclaimed between breaths.

"What?" I said as I turned my head 180 degrees. A steady trail of greyish black smoke was ascending from the back of the pub near the car park. "What happened?" I queried of the ginger tom.

"Don't rightlay know. Kitchen, Oy think. Oy didn't hang around to find out."

A small gathering of apprehensive patrons spilled out into the carpark, including a very concerned looking publican and two bar staff. It was several anxious minutes until we heard the first wail of a siren, it turned out to be a blue and white marked car, like the one that turned up with the policeman to speak with Boss-man about the chip shop receipt. A full two-tone siren announced the approach of the fire truck. Comings and goings continued into the evening, long after Boss-man had returned, observed the activity, and walked round himself to speak with the landlord.

I learned later as Alex spoke with the Sausage dog walker; it had been a kitchen fire. Not too serious, and the pub itself remained undamaged, but the kitchen was to be out of action for the foreseeable future. That evening Alex bought fish and chips from the village and delivered them to a grateful Fiona and her mum, who was less grateful.

As it turned out, that would be the last time Alex took a meal for Fiona as apparently, she was 'making a good recovery and thank you for your attention, but she would be able to cook for her mother and herself now.' I learned all this from Black Persian who had stealthily slipped into the cottage before Alex returned with the fish supper. Being the wily old fox she is, well cat I mean, she was able to purloin a small piece of fish. That evening while we both went roaming outside together, she informed me of her exploits and her suspicion that with the pub kitchen fire, Boss-man might well get cooked fish from the store. Why am I not as cunning as Lapsat?

When I ventured out that night the waning gibbous moon had risen high in the night sky and cast harsh shadows across the landscape. The remnants of a torn photograph and withered flower stems hung depressingly from the totem post. The sky was cloudless, and I could hear tawny hooting in the distance. Along with the noticeable chill in the air there was the faint, almost imperceptible smell of smoke from the pub blaze. Emboldened after my previous exploration I wandered back to the bridge and through the archway. On sight of the two luminescent eyes glowing in the dark I froze. The vixen turned and trotted away towards the cottage, two cubs following closely behind their mother.

Somewhere faraway was the sound of a motorbike disappearing into the distance. All that remained was the sound of cascading water from the lock gate, which itself amplified the silence of the night. A disturbance in the long grass caught my attention. Light from the moon illuminated a small area a few feet in front of me and exposed a small water vole that was busy chewing grass. With his petite brown body with bushy tail, blunt nose and little ears he was going about his business oblivious to my proximity. I choose to leave him to his activity undisturbed as I was in a reflective mood and not hungry!

I lay for some time gazing upon Lockside cottage. Since Brenda had departed, our protector had been alone, alone that is except for us felines. I understood that a human, while enjoying our company needed interaction with others of his genus. There had been no humour or jollity such as we had enjoyed in Wisteria Cottage. On many occasions Alex had spoken with passers-by, but with no substance. The weather, the news, directions to the village and so forth. He had helped Fiona when she was in need and just once he had responded with a smile to a humorous comment she had made. More than the time of day had passed their lips. Could it be possible that she might be the catalyst for a recovery? Only time would provide an answer.

## 9 — ALEX DEWHURST

"We are going away."

I was laying on my back on the boat roof. Against a bright blue sky with puffy white patches, a sparrowhawk was circling, rising higher and higher, searching for signs of a tasty meal in the field below. My reverie was interrupted as the voice barked again: "Did you hear me? We are going away!"

Promptly I rolled over and sat up in one smooth movement. Tess was standing on the grass below calling for my attention. She got it!

"Yes, I heard. What do you mean, 'going away'?"

"Last night I heard my mistress telling the old lady we are all going to see whales."

"Don't you mean Wales, as in Welsh Wales, across the border?" I guess this dog is lacking in brain cells! Dumb mutt.

"Perhaps? Some place sounds like clan-drid-nod-wellies. Well apparently, there is a nice little park home with two bedrooms and everything we need."

"When?"

"When what?"

"When do you go, stupid?"

"Oh, I don't know, soon, perhaps soon."

I know about boundaries. My boundaries are set close to the boat, outside them are other felines who do not like me snooping about. But borders? Well, I remember Lapsat telling me about other countries and borders you must cross. For some borders humans need a little book thing that may or may not be stamped by a person in a smart uniform. I wondered if Fiona and her mother would need a little book to cross into Wales? I glanced across at Fiona who was chatting to Boss-man. Was it my imagination or was he looking a little downcast?

"See you!" Tess said quite casually as she trotted off to be at Fiona's side.

I rolled onto my back again. The sparrowhawk had gone, but a wedge of noisy geese were crossing the blue expanse in a vee formation. So that was it then. Four simple words: 'we are going away,' and the path of life takes a turn. Why did I suddenly feel hollow, it was not as if I was fond of Tess, but I have to admit she and her mistress had added a new dimension to our lives.

#

As each day past with no Fiona walking Tess, it became apparent, that they had gone away. Gone away to Wales? Perhaps, how should I know. My curiosity forever goading me to investigate danger and peril was now spurring me to visit Lockside Cottage and see for myself. The first indication something had changed was the absence of a car parked in the driveway. Naturally this was inconclusive evidence as Fiona frequently took the car out for shopping and other activities. I pushed my way through the wooden gate. The small lawn, usually in pristine condition was growing dandelions. Glancing at the cottage windows I observed they were all closed, and the curtains in each were partly drawn. Purposefully I walked around to the rear and jumped onto the coal bunker. I was about to jump up to the small lavatory window when I realised, that it too was closed. Never had I seen this window closed before, something was definitely amiss. I made my way back to the front and looking up at the Georgian sash window I could make out the corner of a picture still hanging on the wall inside where I had seen it before. The lampshade in the centre of the ceiling was still the same. Perhaps a removal van would come to collect the contents of the cottage, just as it had done last spring at Wisteria Cottage before we left.

Feeling rather dejected I made my way back to our home on the boat. Lapsat was waiting for me.

"Wasson."

"What's going on? What do you mean?" I quizzed grumpily.

"Boss-Man, 'e be ma-dde as a bar-bed wire baddger. Grumpy like."

"Oh, that's because she's gone."

"Who be gone?"

"The woman with the cockapoo. I checked out the cottage. Empty."

Lapsat did her usual silent thinking bit while licking a front paw. "That explains it. Now ee mention it, they not be round these parts lately."

Inside, Alex was busy in the kitchen. I heard a glass shatter on the floor followed by an expletive, which for him was very unusual. As for me I was none too bothered not to be looking over my shoulder all the time just in case Tess should be in the vicinity and feeling roguish.

#

The first signs of autumn were making themselves felt in the trees and hedgerows. Small red hawthorn berries, oval rich dark sloe berries of the blackthorn and the bright orange elongated rosehip were prominent in the hedge along the lane. Multi-coloured spent leaves from the oak, beech and ash started to form a carpet of reds, orange and deep yellows. A few leaves that fell on to the water were carried down the canal, drifting inevitably towards Kinver lock. They were starting to form a multi-coloured leaf soup, which would get caught up in the propellers of passing boats, much to the annoyance of the novice boater who wondered why the engine was struggling to produce the usual forward momentum. However, on the other hand, the experienced boater periodically gave the prop a quick burst of reverse thrust to clear the clogged mechanism.

Days were regular and routine now. Cats like myself appreciate an orderly routine. Set times of day for food, grooming, exploring, sleeping and of course lots of times for naps which do not need set times. We also have favourite places to go. During daylight hours I favour the solar panel on the boat roof, for where I can watch the world go by without fear of attack by predatory canines.

Humans apparently like routine also. Each morning, weather permitting, an elderly gentleman from the village walks from the bridge to the wooden seat opposite our boat. The bench has a small brass plaque that Chalky says dedicates the bench to 'Audrey Brighton, loving wife, mother and local schoolteacher. She loved life, family and canals.'

I watched the old man make his way slowly up the path, leaning heavily on his malacca cane. In his left hand a small grey leather bag which he placed on the seat next to him. From it he produced a thermos flask which contained strong black coffee and a small sandwich or sometimes a piece of cake. For about an hour he would sit and watch the world go by while sipping his coffee. Boaters who knew him would wave or shout a cheery greeting. Dog walkers, joggers, pram pushing young mothers and others would smile, some would pass a comment about the weather, occasionally another lonely soul would stop and join him on the memorial bench to share reminiscences of life and days gone by.

From a distance I heard Alex call over to the gentleman. "You okay?"

"Guess so!"

"Can I join you?" Alex sauntered up to the old man. They both knew each other as acquaintances, because most days Alex waved or passed a comment which was reciprocated by the old man. Perhaps, due to reluctance in making new friendships or a reclusive attitude it was apparent to me that Boss-man had avoided in-depth conversation with others. Today proved different.

"Be my guest. I only have one sandwich!" he commented with a small grin.

Alex joined him on the bench and said: "Chill in the air, guess autumn is on the way."

"Right there. I put the central heating on last night."

Boring! Here they go, talking about the weather again. What is this obsession humans have? I turned my head away and decided a short nap was the order of the moment.

"Nice boat. You live here on your own?"

"Right. I have the two cats of course."

"Seen them about, the white fluffy thing on your roof, and is the other the Black Persian I see sometimes."

"Yes, they are great company for me, since the wife died you know."

"No, I didn't know."

"Just a year ago now. Brenda. Got the cancer. Less than six months and it was all over."

"Wow, so sorry for you. My wife died nearly fifty years ago, it was car accident. Drunk driver crossed the carriageway up on the bypass, and we had only been married fifteen years."

"Did you never re-marry?"

"No, I had a lady friend or two, but I guess I was always comparing them to Tara. She was perfect in every way. Well, that's how I like to remember her.

"Children?"

"One son. He was only fourteen when his mother died. Messed him up good and proper. I tried of course, but I was never going to be a mother figure. Perhaps I was too hard on him, but he chose to go and live with his aunty in Middlesex, then when old enough he went to Australia, one of the last of the 'ten-pound poms'. I don't hear much from him now, and he never visits me."

Alex didn't reply for some time, but my interest had been piqued, so I jumped down from the roof and slipped under the bench to listen more clearly.

"Sad story. You still remember her fondly; how did you meet her?"

"Oh, yes, that takes me right back, right back you know, to my first job."

"Where was that?"

"I left school at fifteen and my father got me a job at Tooley's boat yard on the River Severn. They took in all kinds of craft for maintenance and repairs. Naturally, being a young skinny runt, they got me making tea, sweeping the yard, cleaning the toilet in the outhouse and so on, you know the way it is.

"It didn't put me off, I was dead keen, and loved boats. They had previously employed other 'boys' who did not last long, so they didn't expect me to continue. But I did. I worked hard, and the foreman soon noticed I was serious about my work. He took me under his wing, so to speak, and got me working with the welder. I made progress and in a couple of years, when the site welder took sick, I carried on his work. Soon I was known as 'Steel Mike', as I could repair most steel hulled boats. The modern fiberglass was a different story altogether. I didn't want to know them."

"Tara?" Boss-man chipped in.

"Ah-ha. Yes, stunning she was. Just a hint of Asian background, raven black hair, short, eyes slightly squinting and a small flattish nose. Ops, sorry. Running ahead of myself.

"I had been at Tooley's for seven years. There had been girls, naturally. Took them to the Picture Palace, Bert's Big Diner and walks around the park. For one reason or another they were not for me, or perhaps I was not for them. I still clearly remember the day I saw Tara.

"I was twenty-two at the time and had been given a job to repair damage to an old barge used for dredging. I went to the office to order some spares for the welding kit when I saw her tapping away at the old Remington. I will admit, I was stunned, talk of 'love at first-sight'. 'Ethel not here today?' I heard myself stammer. Ethel had been the yard's previous secretary. She was ancient and dull, had ginger hair and always wore the same forest green cotton blouse and straight skirt. The site manager simply said: 'Tara is the new secretary.' Tara was so different!

"I remember I was so shocked I just turned and walked out, quietly closing the door behind me. Later that morning, during tea break I asked 'Sparks' the electrician if he had seen the new girl, 'Oh, yes, that's the owner's daughter. Giving her work experience. Quite a good typist by all accounts,' he must have seen something in my eyes, as he added: 'now don't you go messing with her if you value your job!'

"I did value my job very much but ... temptation was also too much, you know."

"I am getting the picture. Quite a girl was she?"

"Her black hair was pixie cut just like Audrey Hepburn and she wore cat eye multicoloured reading glasses. Turned out she had Chinese blood from her mother's grandmother. She wore a white blouse under a modern turquoise blue jacket and matching skirt. Stylish! I desperately wanted to go back to the office after lunch but could not pluck up the courage to do so, thus, imagine my delight when she came out of the office looking for me! 'Did I need parts for the welder?' How did she know? Who cared. I looked up, right into her sea-blue eyes, and I saw the fire burning within.

"I invited her to the 'Picture Palace' for Friday night. 'Great,' she said eagerly, and from that moment we didn't look back. We were married just four months later. One year later our son was born. She doted on him, and so did I. Life was rich, and our little family was so happy until that day the world ended."

The old gentleman went quiet for some time. I knew Alex wanted him to say more but refrained from speaking. After a while he continued in a melancholy voice: "Strange the things you remember. I remember the police man and woman who called on the house to tell me there had been an accident. They didn't say she was dead at first, but when they did, I was looking passed them in a stupor. Looking out into the garden at the rosebush by the gate. A branch had snapped, and a very beautiful red rose hung down looking pitiful. To this day I can clearly picture the rose dangling, bereft of support."

Abruptly the old man stood up. "Must be going, things to do, people to see, places to visit. Good to reminisce with you. Bye now." And with that he walked off, leaning very heavily on his cane. Alex did not speak a word. I slipped out from under the bench. Boss-man was staring straight ahead at nothing. Had the old man's story stirred in him his own memories and loss. No doubt it had.

#

When did I last have a nap? I can't say I remember, but a few 'winks' would not be inappropriate. A suitable place would be the old shed in the field below the towpath. I made my way warily to the hideaway, checking carefully there were no other inhabitants of the sanctuary. I curled up and was soon enjoying the bliss of sleep.

How long before I became semi-conscious, I am not altogether sure. I became aware of a change in temperature, the autumnal day was cooling as evening approached. There was also a haziness in the daylight, a dull grey film of stillness. Looking carefully through the dusk I could see the lock, Kinver lock, and two figures approaching. A human, tall, a woman, medium long full auburn hair with whisps of grey and soft curls. At her side a dog, a cockapoo, thick apricot woollen coat. I sat erect watching them slowly, very slowly walking towards me. I looked back at the woman, Fiona! Fiona and Tess, they were back, not gone away at all. I wanted to rush forward to greet them, but something was holding me back. Then I looked again at Tess, no not Tess, this was a huge black Alsatian with open mouth drooling and baring its teeth. The woman was straining to hold the dog at the end of a chain. The woman, no not Fiona! I could see clearly now, she was tall, with raven black hair. It was Brenda! It was my Brenda; she was still alive! She was putting her arms out to me, calling me to her. I wanted to rush toward her, but the dog! Suddenly the woman let go of the lead and the dog leapt into the air and charged towards me. Run! Run! But I was transfixed like a deer in the headlight of a car.

I felt a jolt, a pushing, a shaking of my shoulder. Suddenly I was fully conscious. My heart was racing and

Lapsat stood over me, pawing my right shoulder. "Ee okay? Ee don't look good to me."

The nightmare was over.

#

It was three days before the elderly gentleman returned to the bench with his vittles. Boss-man joined him, and curious to learn more stories of yesteryear I sauntered over, rubbed my head against both Alex and the old man's legs and then took up a relaxed position under the seat. There followed the usual small talk: 'notable change in the weather to come, flooding in China and forest fires in Australia.' 'China and Australia' I pondered, perhaps locations beyond my boundary, or were they across the border? Then they started on the more interesting conversation.

"So, I told you my story, how did you meet, what was her name, Barbera?" the old boy began.

"Brenda."

"Oh yes, Brenda. Was it 'love at first sight also?'

Alex made a snorting sound, which I found disconcerting. "More like 'hate at first sight'," He expostulated.

"Ah ha, sound interesting, tell me more."

"I was in the British army based at Aldershot Queen Elizabeth Barracks. I started training at Sandhurst Royal Military Academy and slowly over several years worked my way up through the officer ranks to Captain."

"An army fellow, that's a good career to have," the old man confirmed.

"For most of that time I had little interest in women, I guess you could say I was 'married' to the army. That was my focus, and I did not want to be distracted by the fairer sex the way I had observed so many of my compadres had been. There were a few brief flirtations, but they never amounted to much."

"What happened to change your mind?"

"It started with a letter. It was from the vicar of St. Saviour's Church, Eastbourne. It turns out I had a long-forgotten great-aunt or did have. She had recently deceased, and the funeral was in a few days' time at the local cemetery. Being no other known relatives alive it was suggested I might like to attend the service, and following the burial, the vicar would be pleased to receive me at the vicarage.

"I took compassionate leave and travelled to Eastbourne, staying at the Grand Hotel for the duration. At the church I made the acquaintance of the vicar, and he invited me to visit him the following day in the morning. The old aunt had ended her days in a care home, and all the arrangements and disposal of her few remaining artifacts had been organised by the home. In sorting the papers, they had found a 'Last Will and Testament' and reference to myself. The document it seems had listed me as executor.

"Back in Aldershot I puzzled how to handle the probate and requests of the Will, this was not something I was familiar with. When I happened in passing to speak with the Medical Officer who grew up in the local town, he suggested I go to a solicitor and let them handle the matter. He assured me that any costs would come from aunt's estate. I asked him if he had any suggestions, and without hesitation he suggested 'Messrs Clifford and Sons', 'You'll find them in the High Street,' he added.

"Off I go to find the offices with my leather document case containing various papers and the Will of course, under my arm. I had phoned ahead and arranged an appointment with the secretary, who assured me that a suitable legal representative would accommodate me at eleven o'clock on the Friday. Now this is where it all started to go wrong! The name on the plaque beside the door had a subtle but important change, it read, 'Messrs Clifford and Associates'.

"The secretary invited me into the waiting room, and five minutes later led me to a corridor with rooms behind closed doors. She stopped at the first door and knocked. On the door was a brass plaque. 'Ms. Brenda Cornell, Paralegal'. I remember thinking something was not up to my expectation but failed to register the problem in my mind. The door opened and there she was! Ms. Cornell had a stern countenance accentuated by the tortoise shell glasses resting low on her nose. Her auburn hair was parted down the middle and swept back. She had broad shoulders, and she wore an unfashionable grey trouser suit. She proffered an outstretched hand, which I ignored."

"Oh, no, surely you didn't?" the old man commented.

"I never considered myself a misogynist, but my reaction belied my claim. 'Excuse me, but I came to speak with a solicitor,' I announced inflexibly. 'Yes Mr. Dewhurst,' she said: 'you have come to the right office. I am a paralegal solicitor; you want to see someone about handling a relatives' last wishes I understand? I would be the someone you need to speak with.' Then I really upset the applecart: 'No, you don't understand, I need to see a Mr. Clifford, a gentleman of this establishment!' I declared inconsiderately!"

At this point of the narrative, the old boy was rocking in mirth on the bench and said: "You really know how to charm a girl!"

"Exactly! Well as you can imagine this did not get us off to a good start. She assured me that she had trained as a Chartered Legal Executive for five years and was fully qualified to handle my aunt's affairs. However, if I was unhappy with her services, I was free to take my custom elsewhere! Somewhat wrong-footed I meekly explained what was required, left the documents in her 'capable hands' and made a quick exit.

"Two weeks later I was summoned back to the office to be updated on her progress. I must admit she had done a fine job and made such great progress in such a short space of time. There was still a tension between us. When I entered her office, she did not stand, did not extend a welcoming hand, and did not smile! Back in the barracks I considered sending a suitable card with my apology, expressing profound regret at my insensibility, and thanking her for her work thus far, but I could not bring myself to do so!

"Six months later, it was all sorted and it turns out I received a sizable inheritance, which was unexpected but most welcome. I visited the office one last time and this time we parted with a handshake, although it was half-hearted and weak from both of us. I assumed, incorrectly as it turned out, that our paths would not cross again."

"So how did the romance develop?" the older gentleman asked.

"Well, I thought no more of the woman until I was in the precinct searching a particularly favourite bookshop. I purchased a 'Shakespeare Compendium of Three Plays' and decided because I had some free time to visit the 'China Tea Pot' for light refreshment. Inside the cosy establishment I choose a two-seater table in the window. It was adorned with a white linen tablecloth and a miniature glass vase with a small posy of primroses. The anorexic young waitress took my order for 'tea and cake' and retreated behind the counter. When she returned, she carried on a small tray a white teapot, sugar bowl with tongs, milk jug and beryl green teacup and saucer with spoon, all of which she placed on the table. Finally, the cake, also on a beryl-green plate, which she set down on the table beside the teapot. It was a light and airy pastry, oozing with fresh cream and topped with strawberry jam!"

"I think you are getting carried away now!" said the old man.

"Ops, sorry! I admit to a sweet tooth. Well as she left, I heard the brass bell above the door tinkle and another customer entered. I glanced up, and there she was, the lawyer, Brenda! Our gaze met and without a word, recognition was established. She chose to sit at a small table against the wall. Out of the corner of my eye I could just see her, and I was quite certain she was glancing very casually in my direction. I glanced back. Then horror of horrors, our eyes met. I looked away immediately, but the damage was done. A connection had been made.

Was it my imagination but did she look different. Her auburn hair was trimmed and stylised like Farrah Fawcett. The grey trouser suit replaced with white blouse beneath a white jacket with light brown trim which matched the pleated skirt. Trendy! Her face sported a minimal amount of makeup which emphasised the fine lines and high cheekbones, however, darkened eyebrows and eyeliner gave her a slight gypsy roughness. I detected a carefree nature, so different from her office persona.

"I was watching a small boy holding his mother's hand outside the window when she approached me as she was leaving the tea shop. 'Shakespeare!' she said looking at the book resting on the table, 'Shakespeare. Good choice?' I replied with a monosyllabic 'Yes.' Pointing to the second of three titles on the cover, which was Othello, she continued, 'Lago, he was a misogynist. His attitude is contagious and picked up by Othello himself, who refers to both Emilia and Desdemona as 'whores'. A fundamental mistrust of women. Shocking attitude. Perhaps reading Othello will help you adjust your views of the fairer sex.' 'Miss Cornell, I am most terribly sorry for my attitude toward you. Please pardon my indiscretion.' I said passionately.

"She was very magnanimous about it. 'Remember, any further legal matters you need assistance with, just go around the corner to Windsor Way, they have male lawyers there!' The sarcastic comment was completely neutralised by the wide grin on her face, which transformed her stern countenance into the face of a goddess. The shop bell rang once more, and she was gone."

"So how did you repair the damage?" the curious gentleman wanted to know.

"I knew that the Odeon cinema was showing 'Hamlet'. So next day, just before five o'clock I went to the legal offices in the High Street and sat on a bench waiting for her to finish work. Precisely four minutes past five she appeared at the door.

"'Frailty, thy name is woman!' I called over to her, 'Hamlet was a misogynist as well.' A smile broke out on her usually demure face. 'Mr. Dewhurst I do declare.' 'Hamlet is playing at the Odeon, have you seen it?' she had moved toward me now, 'starring Anthony Hopkin.' 'No, I do not frequent cinemas on my own as an unmarried woman.' 'Perhaps I could escort you.' 'When?' 'Tonight?' 'Not unless you buy me dinner first.' 'Deal!' I said enthusiastically. 'Barnard's Smokehouse, or a Wimpy burger?' The smile transformed into a full-blown laugh, the sound of a happy angel.

"We courted for many months before we became engaged, and even then, circumstances did not allow us to get married until spring of 1980. She gave up her work as a paralegal and we moved into officers' quarters at Doniford Army Camp near Watchet in Somerset. Ten years later I took early retirement, and with my army pension and the inheritance from my aunt we bought a little cottage in Devon, on Dartmoor. We were happy in our country life until the day Brenda got sick."

It was at this point I caught sight of Chalky ferreting about near the bridge. He was a welcome distraction as the conversation had stirred a distant memory in my sub-conscious. Fiona and Tess, I wondered if Chalky knew where they had gone. Chalky knows everything. Suddenly I had a strong urge to ask him.

## 10 — CRACKER

Something was definitely wrong. More than six months now I had been observing the antics of boaters on the canal near our floating home. It was the latter part of the day when Chalky and I, peering over the lock side, observed a hire boat at a 30-degree angle in the lock below. We had both been attracted to the lock by the commotion of a small group of men who were quite obviously worse for alcohol and noisily blaming each other for their predicament. The men had scrambled out of the boat and were stood on the far side staring at the stricken vessel.

"What happened?" I asked Chalky.

"Got it stuck on cill. See that ledge protruding below top gate, get yow boat too far back in lock, as water goes down, it gets 'ung on edge."

Not being in full command of their senses they had been slow to stop the water flow and now the lock was drained with the nose of the boat dipped in the murky water.

"Just re-float it you morons," one member of the group expostulated at his mates, and promptly ran around closing and opening paddles. The water rushed into the lock, sloshed around the prow, and started to inundate the well-deck.

"Shut it down, shut the paddle you fool!" It was a voice I recognised. Alex running towards us was waving his arms and shouting: "You can't refloat it. You are filling the front with water, and besides you will have damaged the rudder and mounting. We need to call for assistance."

I was proud to see my owner taking charge and initiating the salvage procedure. The four unshaven men of middle age, due to their negligence, had brought their weeks holiday to an untimely end. They stood around helpless as their intoxication quickly dissipated and the reality of their misadventure took over.

Chalky was distracted by a lady cat that passed under the road bridge and set off in pursuit, while I remained to observe the proceedings. To me it seemed a long time elapsed before the first vehicle arrived with a man who would provide assistance. It was a medium sized van with light and dark blue paintwork and a large white circle logo. The Canal and River Trust workman stepped out of the vehicle wearing a dark blue windcheater and storm waterproof black trousers, and wandering meditatively towards the lock he peered down at the stricken boat. Alex joined him and they chatted a while, occasionally calling over to the men on the opposite side, who by now were looking very contrite.

Soon after the arrival of the CRT inspector, a black Mercedes screeched to a halt next to the van and a well-built middle-aged gentleman in designer clothes added his presence to the small crowd. He was an angry middle-aged man, and justifiably so. It was obvious he was the owner of the hire-fleet of which this brightly coloured specimen was a part. A few choice words were exchanged with the penitent group of would-be revellers. Pulling out his mobile phone, he started to make several calls. The CRT man also set about communicating with head office, after which he availed himself with yellow and black warning tape from the van and started to wrap it around various iron work fixtures on the lock.

Alex was called into action as a liveaboard couple pulled up at the lock landing in their relatively small narrowboat 'Agape', and were disappointed to learn that they would be unable to use the lock any time in the foreseeable future. The CRT man, having finished with his yellow warning tape, assured the couple they could moor on the lock 'mushrooms' until the canal was reopened to passage. Alex for his part, made observations about the village, general amenities and 'if you need anything let me know.'

A petrol blue Skoda taxi drew up alongside the CRT van and the boat owner parcelled up the four men and sent them on their way, telling them as he closed the taxi door, that any personal effects recovered from the boat would be forwarded to them later along with insurance claim forms.

The whole area was fast becoming a novelty attraction as passers-by, those with and some without dogs, stopped to take in the sorry scene. The CRT man was chatting to Alex again, and I casually approached, curiosity ensuring I would hear what the recovery procedure would involve.

"No danger of fuel leakage into the canal," he stated.

"Of course. Diesel tanks are at the stern which is well out of the water," Alex replied, "what about electrics and gas?"

"I will get on board now and isolate the electrics with the battery master switch and shut the gas off at the cylinders."

"Is it secure?"

"Safe enough until the recovery team arrives tomorrow morning. I just need to padlock the sluice mechanism, so no one tampers with it, then I'm off home."

The inspector gathered padlock and chains from the van and spent a few minutes ensuring all was secure. After climbing into the boat very carefully, due to the slanted angle of the decking, and shutting the utilities down, he returned to the van and drove off. Night-time drew in quickly now we were into autumn, and Alex had already returned to the boat for the evening. I wandered about for a while before considering the small pit feeling in my stomach.

Lapsat had already eaten her 'diced lamb in jelly' and had bagged the window bed for a few hours snooze. A small dish of choice meats consumed; I looked around for a resting place for my excitable head. As Boss-man had just risen from his armchair the vacant space, a comfy warm cushion, was most tempting. Now as a rule, I do not attempt to take Boss-man's seat as just as his bed, I know it annoys him. However, on this occasion temptation prevailed. I jumped up, did two full circles, and settled down in the warm dip, to dream of salmon swimming against the current.

"Come on you, off!"

"But please ..." I started to voice as a firm hand pushed me from behind.

"You know not to sit on my chair, now scram you little tyke." Against my better judgment I resisted. Well, it was just so comfortable, and I was just so tired, and well ...

The push became a shove. I opened an eye to see Alex carrying a small tray with tea and biscuits and a face saying: 'I am not playing games.'

I hissed: "Leave me alone, go away," and flashed my stern look, "I am so very comfortable," I miaowed.

I don't like to consider myself a looser, and generally my developing stubbornness pays off, but on this occasion, I was doomed to failure from the start, and to be honest I knew it all along. I jumped down on to the rug and putting on my face a 'it doesn't bother me' look, I sullenly turned my back. Glancing up I became aware Lapsat was watching and rather amused by the whole episode.

"'e got ee good 'nd proper,' she scoffed.

I chose not to respond, but had my honour restored when after Alex had settled, he allowed me to jump up on his welcoming lap and continue my salmon dream.

#

Next morning a weak daylight glow penetrated the small bathroom porthole. It was accompanied by noises from the direction of Kinver Lock. I did consider it was rather early to rise, but as I was curious to see the events unfold, I skipped breakfast, jumped onto Boss-man's bed, clambered over a recumbent body, and slipped through our very own cat door to welcome the early morning outside.

Men had arrived. Inspections had been made. Work had begun. A large white van with RCR in striking blue letters was parked next to the lock. From it, strewn about were pumps, generator and various inflatable tubes. The two men had donned Hi-Viz yellow jackets and black 'Crewsaver' life-vests. One man had just finished an internal examination of the boat and was calling his mate for the inflatables, when the CRT man arrived in his blue van. The inspector removed all the padlocks and watched the RCR man place tubes around and below the front of the boat and large flexible black pipes were handed up to the man on the lockside. The generator was started, and following an initial heavy thud, it settled into a steady regular purring sound. A couple of pumps attached to hosepipes were lowered into the front well deck and saloon area. With the pumps steadily pushing water out of the boat and into the canal below the lock, one man raised a paddle on the lower gate.

Connections were made, valves turned, and the inflatables started to fill with air. The boat did not move! However, when the water being expelled from the pumps started to reduce in volume, the top sluice gate was partially opened, and the lower gate sluice closed. Now there was a noticeable movement upwards from the nose of the narrowboat. As the water level equalised and no more water was being pumped from the boat, the men allowed the lock to fill, floating the vessel and allowing it, after opening the top gate to be dragged back onto the lock landing 'mushrooms'.

The liveaboard couple were delighted when, mid-afternoon the yellow warning tape was removed, and they were assisted through the lock to continue their sojourn on to Kidderminster. Job done the CRT man drove off just before designer man in his black Mercedes took his parking space. A discussion was had with the RCR men and all three inspected the inside of the boat. The hire-boat owner collected many bags of personal belongings, which he pushed without ceremony into the boot of his vehicle.

Generally, life on the canal is slow and relaxed, which suits us cats just fine. Thus, the stricken vessel remained around five days at the lock landing before a scruffy middle-aged man in dungarees was dropped off by yet another small van, this time with an orange logo, something to do with 'Diamond Marina'. He had a sizeable bag of tools and with them effected a temporary repair to the rudder. It took him some time to do this as he had to push and pull, attach ratchet straps and even at one point wearing waders, lower himself into the canal to make adjustments under the swim, getting the rudder into the cup on the skeg.

I hope you are suitably impressed by my knowledge of all things boaty? Having befriended Chalky, the pub cat, we spent many happy evenings in the saloon bar of 'The Lock Inn' discussing boat life, history and boats in general. I don't pretend to know where all his knowledge came from, but being more of a feral cat, he has been about a lot and spoken with many other animals along with listening to boaters enjoying a pint in the saloon bar of the public house.

After some final checks, our dungaree clad human, started up the engine. It took three attempts for the machine to fire, but when it did a large cloud of black smoke puffed from the exhaust. Lowering the throttle, the engine settled into a happy and regular puttering noise. Satisfied all was running acceptably, he grabbed a windlass key and set the first lock of his journey. Lock gate open, he returned to the narrowboat and proceeded to embark on his voyage to the nearest dry dock, which Chalky had informed me was at Stourport. Once in the dry dock, resting on wooden blocks, the underside of the hull could be carefully examined, and repair work completed safely. Only then would the vessel be returned to the hire company for future holiday use.

#

It had become clear to me that there are good days and bad days. No, not for me personally. After all, to me every day is a good day. Lapsat and I have food provided by Bossman, along with a cosy home where we can spend time grooming or resting. Outside there are many places to satisfy our curiosity or snooze. Generally speaking, I enjoy a catnap, the occasional rest or even a full-on sleep for around 16 hours a day, this seems quite reasonable to me.

Let me explain, good and bad days relate more to events that happen on certain days. Thus, the incident with the stricken boat in the lock was a bad day. The day Pinkerton died was a bad day, and so was the day Cracker tried to steal Fiona's bag. On the other hand, there are many good days. One such occurred when I saw the two women and the toddler. I had been catching up on some well needed rest when, hearing voices, I opened an eye and caught sight of a mother holding the hand of a little girl. With them was another older woman who I took to be the grandmother of the toddler.

Happy chortling sounds emanated from the beaming chubby face as she tested out her immature legs. She took one step forward with the right leg, then half dragged the left in its small white plastic shoe and lacy white sock, to join its companion. Having progressed a few feet, she stopped looked around at her mother who stood behind her, caught sight of a squirrel, turned quickly, pointed towards the rodent, and lost her balance. She sat down with a small thump on her padded bottom, and I watched her homely round face turn from a confident picture of joy to a distraught representation of anguish. Her mouth opened, her little eyes squinted, and her soft round cheeks reddened.

This was too much for me. Quickly I leapt from the boat roof and rushed to the little girl's side. Deliberately I brushed my soft furry torso against the chubby legs. The effect was instantaneous. The wail and tears were stifled, and her little face relaxed into one of intrigue with eyes wide open. Tentatively she raised a hand, finger outstretched and poked my neck. Under normal circumstances I would have complained, hissed and moved away, but I understood her desire to touch me, even though she had yet to learn how to do so gently. A female voice from above expressed her enthusiasm at my presence and the toddler looked up to her mother, her blue eyes questioning if it was alright for her to touch me.

Naturally I was pleased with my intervention and the effect it had produced, so I moved to rub my head against the long shapely legs of the mother, who rewarded my attention by stroking my head and saying: 'nice pussy,' which to be perfectly honest I found condescending.

I sat in the middle of the path licking my right fore-leg for some time after the little group of women had moved away. It had been a pleasant encounter and would ensure that this was a good day, or that is what I thought. Unfortunately, some good days are overshadowed by troublesome events. This was to be one of those days.

#

The silence of the night was only punctuated by the sound of our resident tawny owl marking its territory and communicating with its mate. As you must know by now, I do like a nocturnal meander, just checking the surroundings for possible prey, although I am not really nocturnal, but instinct dictates I should check my surroundings both dawn and dusk. I like to think I am checking for predators who may have evil designs on our Boss-man. This particular night my watchman duties would pay off big time.

I waited until Alex had turned in for the night and when he was settled, and as Lapsat was already outside, I slipped quietly through the cat door and sniffed the cool clear air. For an hour or two I made my usual rounds. Down towards the dark shadows of the lock and the main road still with an occasional vehicle crossing. Round by the horse's field, Black Beauty and Dobbin were sleeping in a standing position, how do they do that? A quick check on my favourite shed. Then, along the towpath to Wayside Cottage where all the lights were extinguished, and peace had descended.

As I considered returning to the boat following my patrol, I noted a dark figure standing near Alex's Yaris. Immediately I sensed danger and made a detour via the shadow of the hedgerow. The figure was up to no good, that was clearly obvious. Working my way along the hedge I was able to slip under the rear of the car and move closer to the suspicious character. All I could see from my restricted viewpoint were a pair of legs. Dark khaki covered legs! No, it could not be, could it? At that moment the man dropped a solid chrome spanner of some considerable size, causing a distinct clatter which he followed promptly with an expletive that I have no intention of repeating.

Convinced trouble was in the making, I made a dash from under the car to the front of the boat, onto the gunnels, into the well-deck and through the cat door, in one smooth movement. As I disappeared from view another obscenity hit the air, obviously aimed in my direction, but too late, I was safe inside my fortress.

Safe, yes, but was Alex's car safe? No! What to do? I could not tackle the villain alone. The dark khaki cargo trousers kept coming back to my mind. Was this Cracker? If so, he could kill without a second thought! I needed to arouse Boss-man from his slumber. Jumping on the bed I purposefully pawed his face, claws retracted. It seemed an age of time before he reacted. When the reaction came it was not what I expected. Rather than be grateful for my concern, he pushed me forcefully away from him, causing me to lose balance, roll over, and almost fall off the bed. I extended my claws in order to grip the duvet and save myself from an undignified fall.

Undeterred I returned to my task and placed a paw on his closed eyelid. Irritated, Alex semi-woke and tried to shoo me away again. That's when we both heard it. A single crash and tinkling. Alex wide awake in an instant sat bolt upright, and in doing so caused me to roll over a second time in just a few seconds.

It is without doubt that Boss-man is a highly organised man, well prepared for many kinds of situations. No doubt in my mind this is because of his army training.

Exiting the bed at whirlwind speed he grabbed a rechargeable torch that was located near the front doors. Flinging the doors at the bow of the boat open, he stepped into the well-deck with me keen to see what transpires, close on his heels. A strong beam of white light from the powerful torch lit a small area around the front of the car, I noted a bird had left a message just above the righthand headlamp, annoying! Alex quickly moved the beam to the left and caught the unmistakable colour of dark khaki trousers, which as the light rose came to identify the familiar features of Cracker. He was standing next to the broken window with the spanner in his hand but in the glare of the spotlight he looked weak and cowardly. The spanner fell to the ground with a clatter and the face vanished from view as he made a rapid escape from recognition. It was too late. Alex shouted after the departing figure: "Cracker! You scoundrel! You Troublemaker! Your days are numbered!"

While Alex slipped back into the boat, I stepped onto the path, safe in the knowledge that our would-be assailant was not returning anytime soon. Boss-man returned to the scene of the crime dressed in a black dressing gown with a cream stripe across the pocket, and with a word in white lettering and a golden harp embroidered below. I wonder what that means? Torch in hand, he made a careful examination of the broken window, established Cracker had not had enough time to take anything from the little Toyota and with a pocket handkerchief, picked up the spanner. After returning the tool to the boat he returned with a large piece of card and gaffer tape to make a temporary repair to the window.

There followed a restless night, where neither of us slept well. I could hear Alex tossing, turning and mumbling. Now, I know he does not like me on the bed with him, but I had to see if he was alright. Laying on his back he was fully awake staring at nothing in particular. I jumped up, climbed onto his belly, pawed his chest a few times and then lay flat, my stomach on his, staring expressionlessly into his face. This non-verbal communication worked well as when he began stroking my soft head he started to relax.

#

Next morning brought a small flurry of activity. Following breakfast as usual on the galley floor, and having enlightened Lapsat of the previous night's events, as she had been out on a rodent search and missed the fun, Bossman started making phone calls. The first visitor arrived mid-morning. DCI Blackwood looked tired and stressed, stepping out of the brightly coloured Volvo, which he parked next to Alex's Toyota, he stretched and briefly examined his black shoes.

"DCI Blackwood, how nice to see you again."

"Three cars stollen in the village last night!" He declared. "Superintendent called me into the office at six this morning. Wanted a full investigation. Been a real problem around these parts over the past month."

"Is it an organised gang?" Alex asked curiously.

"You bet. They move around the area targeting different locations on different nights. Last night they were in Kinver. They spend time in daylight scouting potential vehicles to steal, then under cover of darkness they return, taking three or four in one area during the night."

"Are the residents not warned when the alarms go off?"

"Seems they have a device, electronic device, pull the cover off under the wheel arch, unclip the lights wiring loom and plug in the electronics. The device overrides the car electronic system, disabling the alarms and unlocking doors and activating the Start button. One of the rogues jumps in, starts the car, and away. Simple."

"Where do they take them then?"

"Ah, this is the clever bit. They drive them to housing estates some miles away in Wolverhampton and abandon them. As there are numerous vehicles on the estate, no one questions an unusual car when seen the next day. Then after a day or two, if the owner has not tracked the car and recovered it, which I must say is a very rare occurrence, they return and remove it."

"And the purpose in all this?"

"They hire lockup garages or old warehouses. Put the car inside, out of sight. Then they get the angle grinder and start hacking the car to pieces. They are pulling out valuable spare parts which are shipped abroad to unscrupulous characters who sell them to unsuspecting individuals as spare parts for their car. Just occasionally a whole car, if it is valuable enough, will be loaded into a shipping container and sent all the way to the middle east to be sold in its entirety."

"Oh, this can't be good. You catch any of the crooks?"

"Nope! No sooner than we track a gang down and find the warehouse than they have long gone and started up somewhere else. So be it. Now, this incident last night, you say you know who it was that tried to break in and that he is a wanted man?"

"Absolutely!"

I can't say I relished listening to all the details, so I took up a restful position under the old oak where, out of earshot I could still watch the proceedings. Blackwood seemed most interested in Alex description of events, and upon handing over the chrome spanner, he was positively ecstatic. Carefully he lowered it into his specimen bag, sealed it and placed it into the police car. I must have nodded off for a while because the next thing I noticed was the multi-coloured police car joining the main road at the bridge and disappearing from view.

Later in the afternoon a grey transit van in need of a wash arrived. A portly man in a dark boiler suit set about gathering up the broken glass, and fitting a new pane in the driver's door, all the while whistling a merry tune. I had rather lost interest in events at this point, and as the mechanics music making was distinctly out of tune, I considered it was time for another nap, so I went in search of my favourite haunt in the old shed next to the horses.

I must have slept late as when I awoke darkness of the night had descended. Steadily I made the short journey back to our floating home. Inside Alex was watching the moving image screen and Lapsat was busy on her window bed grooming her long black fur. I sniffed out the food bowls in the galley. Lapsat's was empty of course. Mine contained rather unappetising pile of meat in some sort of gravy. I looked at it, sniffed it, but didn't eat it. Rather, I complained to Boss-man: "Um, excuse me, what's for dinner?" I miaowed plaintively.

"Kippy, what's wrong, your dinner is in the kitchen."

"Yes but, it's, well not very nice," I grumbled.

Boss-man went through to the galley, took one look at the bowl, picked up a small spoon and mixed up the meat in the dish, and pushing it forward with his foot he said: "Look, duck in gravy, yum yum."

I looked at it, I sniffed it again, and I ate it! Wow, this was more like it, very tasty!

After dinner my feline companion said: "Ee missed television news. Didn't ee?"

"Yes. So?"

"Them showed picture of that military looking kid."

"Who? You mean Cracker?"

"Seems they got fingerprints now. 'e's a wanted man. The nice inspector said if anyone sees 'im them should phone police immediately."

"And just how am I to do that when I don't have a phone?"

## 11 — FIONA FULLERTON

Now I've seen some boats in my months on the canal, but none quite like the one that drifted noiselessly passed one cool autumnal day. Despite the chill in the air, it was not raining, and I do like some fresh air, thus I had taken up a relaxed position on the roof's solar panel, from where the usual mixture of passers-by and occasional boat could be monitored. Not so many boats now the main boating season had ended. Mostly liveaboards and die-hard souls who cruise at any time of year and in any type of weather.

This boat was a sight to behold. The first object I observed was a very worn and sorry looking front fender, if you can call it that. It most certainly had seen better days, but now was hanging by just one chain at a lopsided angle across the prow and was well covered in moss. As more of the boat drifted into my line of vision, I considered the paintwork. Green? Well yes and no. It was certainly green, but it was clearly mould, algae and mixed plant detritus. I suspect the underlying colour was off-white, but I could be wrong. On the front well-deck was an assortment of objects, mostly rusty or just plain broken. An old bicycle which rested atop the pile seemed to be in working order however, nonetheless a good clean up would not go amiss.

As the boat moved further into my path of vision, I noted on the roof a solid collection of old tins, rope, firewood of various shapes and sizes, a lifebuoy, ladder (broken) and a hose reel. The windows were covered in grime with some grey material haphazardly hung inside for privacy. By now, my curiosity was well and truly aroused, and I sat up, intrigued to see who might be at the helm of this sorry excuse for a boat. No one!

I shook my head, closed my eyes, opened them again and took another look. No helmsman! The boat was moving through the water at a very slow pace making hardly any ripples on the surface. I strained to see what was happening at the stern of the boat, how could there be no helmsman? At first, all I could see were wooden boards pushed up against the stern rail. As the vessel drifted level with my position, I had a better view and noted a young man in torn jeans and old blue sweater half crouching over the engine bay. He had set up some pully with a handle and webbing strap and was winding the apparatus with enthusiasm with one hand, the other loosely guiding the tiller of the boat to provide some direction.

"You okay down there?" Alex shouted at him from the stern of our boat.

"Hello, old bean. Am I permitted to moor here next to you?"

"Uh, well, this is private, but as the owner of this mooring is having his boat repaired, he will be away for a while. Why not pull in. I'll help you."

"Jolly good show old fellow."

Alex grabbed the rope the young man threw and helped him secure the boat to the mooring rings. A long conversation ensued, of which I have no intention of relating in full. However, the curious situation of the young man is of interest.

It appears, from what I overheard, that he comes from a well-to-do family in a big city called London, wherever that is. He descended from family grace when he fell for a waitress in a coffee bar in the financial district. His family were disgusted to say the least and turned him out of the house. He moved in with his new girlfriend, but after a few months she also turned him out! No home, little money and no prospects, he bought an old narrowboat to live on while he tried hard to restore some order to his life.

He told Alex it was not going well. He had brought the boat up the river from Gloucester docks, but to save on diesel costs, after he left the river, he had rigged up a simple method of propelling the boat by muscle power. The webbing was wrapped around the prop shaft and as he turned the handle the propeller revolved, slowly, but enough to produce forward propulsion.

Despite his appearance he was a personable young man with whom Alex spent the next couple of days in animated conversation. Now, I am not certain, but it seems Alex pulled a few strings with some contacts he had from his army days. When he departed it was under engine power as Alex provided him with a couple of gallons of diesel, warm clothes and a bag of food items. More than that, it was arranged for him to abandon the boat at Ashwood Marina where it could be put up for sale, as if anyone would want to buy it, take the train to Aldershot where he would attend a couple of job interviews. All going well Alex said, this should get him back in the mainstream.

"When you've re-established your life, you can go back to Ashwood and buy a nice boat for your holidays!" Alex shouted with a grin on his face as the warmly dressed young man set off in a northerly direction.

"I can't thank you enough old sport; will keep you updated on my progress," he replied with an accompanying enthusiastic wave. And with that he was gone. I guess that was a good day.

#

The next day turned out to be another good day, well at least it was for Boss-man, perhaps not so much for me!

Boss-man had been out in the Yaris that morning and had returned with some groceries from the supermarket. As there was a noticeable chill in the air again, and I knew the area under the engine would be warm and cosy, I had curled up in a relaxed manner under the little car.

How long I was resting I am unsure, but it was yet another rude awakening. I doubt anyone likes to be woken suddenly by a loud bark, especially if you are a sensitive cat like me.

"Hey Kippy, it's me, I'm back. You glad to see me or what?"

It was Tess, piercing eyes focused on me as she crouched down on her belly with front paws outstretched to look under the car. "Oh no! go away," I instinctively reacted.

"Hey, don't be like that. Aren't you pleased to see me again after all this time?"

How long it had been I was unsure, and to be brutally honest, I had not really expected to see Tess or her mistress again. I crawled out from under the car, as it was too low to stand up, and stepping forward pushed my soft stumpy nose against her cool and wet snout. Without another word she wandered off in the direction of her mistress who was speaking with Alex.

"We went to Llandrindod Wells and stayed in a park home," she was telling Alex.

"Did you have a good time?"

"Oh yes, mother enjoyed it. She stayed in the home much of the time, but I was able to walk Tess around the countryside."

"How is mother doing?"

"Not very mobile, and she does get confused at times, but otherwise alright."

Glancing around I noted Chalky striding across the lock gates. Stopping on the grass he casually examined a front paw, a few licks, and an air of mischief in his eye. Turning my head, I realised Tess had also seen Chalky and was taking a positive interest. Dipping my head from side to side as if watching a game of tennis, I saw Chalky move slowly in the direction of the wooden bench, Tess tensing with each step. The impish feline increased his pace, the cockapoo started to tremble as she took up a sprint position. Without warning Chalky froze, looked innocently around and then briskly trotted towards the old seat. Too much temptation! Tess took off in style, hurtling at full pelt towards the seemingly vulnerable animal. Sensing imminent danger, Chalky leaped onto the bench, did a right-angle turn, jumped over the back, along the fence, up the oak trunk a few feet then hurled himself forward towards the canal, pulling up short just in time and executing a 180-degree spin he shot back across the path towards a small hole in the hedgerow. Tess followed. Unable to jump the bench she took the long way around the back, was close on Chalky's tail as he used the oak for a springboard, and narrowly missed falling headlong into the canal.

It was obvious to me what Chalky was doing; baiting the dog into a chase. I knew it was not going to end well for Tess and it seems Fiona who was watching realised the same thing at the same time.

"Tess, stop, NO! come back, Teeessss!" she hollered.

Tess took no notice and ran headfirst into the hedge, the gap being big enough for an athletic feline, but not a well-built canine. Brought to a sudden halt, Tess struggled to free herself by wriggling backwards from the entangled branches, bracken and teasles. The result was not good! The cockapoo's fur was a magnet for the spiney teasles which had attached themselves like glue to her face and ears. To make matters worse Tess started pawing at them which caused them to matt her fur to a greater degree.

Fiona rushed over to Tess who was now stressing out. "Help me, help, ouch, oh no, it's stuck, help, help," she whinged. When Fiona tried to calm Tess, rather than being grateful she fought with her, growling: "Leave me, go away, oh no, oh help, don't touch me." It was a sorry sight.

During the commotion Boss-man had grabbed a small towel and rushed over to assist in the subjugation of the distressed animal. Grabbing Tess in the towel he picked her up and took her inside our boat. Fiona followed him; I followed them.

"In the pot by the table," Alex was saying to Fiona: "cat comb, yes that one there."

What! My comb! How dare they use my comb on a dog, and Tess of all dogs! I could do nothing but watch. I jumped up onto the window-bed as Lapsat was not at home and watched the proceedings with some sense of vindictive pleasure. Tess was not enjoying the humiliating experience. Despite her best efforts to bite, scratch and escape from Alex, Boss-man held her muzzle while her owner slowly worked away at each teasle one at a time.

After about thirty minutes the job was done and a very weak and contrite dog was allowed to go free, which she did, laying flat on the floor, front paws extended either side of a sad and ashamed face with soulful eyes. I couldn't help but smile, but as I am a cat, my smile is not recognised by the humans.

"I reckon we deserve a drink after that kerfuffle. Brandy?" Alex asked Fiona.

"Very kind," she replied.

Boss-man returned from the galley with two round-bottomed glasses with a rich orange liquid. A sweet fruity aroma permeated the air.

Fiona had been looking at the double silver photo frame. "Picture of you and your boat," she stated as he returned. "Who is the woman?"

"My wife," he replied in a matter-of-fact manner.

"Oh!" An awkward silence broke the conversation. "I'm sorry, didn't know you were married. Perhaps I should leave."

"She passed away just over a year ago," Alex stated with a melancholy tone that Fiona detected. Another awkward silence followed.

"I'm so sorry. I didn't realise. Never thought to ask. I don't know what to say." It was obvious to me that Tess' mistress was feeling very uncomfortable at this point. Alex put a hand to his forehead, at that moment I had a terrible foreboding he was going to weep. Perhaps due to his army background, Alex rarely shows emotion however, the moment passed, and in an instant, his downhearted demeanour changed, a warm smile of a distant memory lit up his eyes and he pointed towards the large smiling face.

"Brenda. Look at that smile and her ginger hair, not unlike yours, but you are more auburn."

"Very striking. She looks a glamourous woman. What did she do?"

"She was a paralegal when we met," Alex chortled. "That's quite a story, will tell you one day. And what about you? You been married?"

Fiona had relaxed, the tension of the moment had passed. She pushed herself back into the armchair while Alex sat on his little upright seat at the table which was cluttered with papers surrounding his laptop. I was intrigued by the way she twirled a few strands of her thick hair between the fingers of her left hand while thinking.

"'Caught him in bed with a younger woman'," she said dramatically. "Actually, that's not really true, just a cliché. We were married in '89, summer wedding. Geoff, that was his name, Geoffrey Fullerton, he was a little older than me, but a real dreamboat. Big muscular man with a rugged outdoor physique. He was keen on rugby and played for a local team in Wolverhampton.

"My brother and I were brought up in the cottage, Lockside Cottage. When Geoff and I married we moved to a two-bed semi-detached in Wightwick, on the edge of Wolverhampton. He worked in Staffordshire District Council in the planning department. For some years we were very happy together. Each day he would go to the council offices, and I would go to work three times a week at The Manor Hotel just walking distance from home. In the mornings I cleaned rooms, in the early evening I waited on tables in the restaurant."

"Any children?"

"No, there should have been at least one, but things went wrong. Some 'abnormal chromosomes' the gynaecologist said. Well, after that we just didn't really try. We were happy enough just the two of us, or at least that is what I thought."

"So how did you find out he was having an affair?"

"It was over a long period of time and naturally when I found out the truth, I was so distraught that the man I trusted had deceived me. Honestly, I think he had been deceiving himself also.

"The first warning sign I missed completely and only recognised it later when other events came to light. I had been speaking with Aunt Maud who lived near Geoff's office, she was spring cleaning her kitchen and couldn't get behind the large freezer. As I didn't like to disturb Geoff at work, I waited for his lunch break. Every day he took a packed lunch which he ate in the canteen, that's when I called him on his Nokia cell phone. Would he 'call in at Aunt Maud's to help her before coming home.' 'Sure thing,' he said. He was a very kindly man, and although he had some poor habits, he would do anything to help you. I didn't think any more about the call until later in the afternoon. I remember thinking, 'there was background music, country music, Dolly Parton, playing in the background. Strange, I did not think they allowed music playing in the offices or canteen.'

"On his return home that evening, and after he assured me Aunt Maud had cleaned behind the freezer with his help, I queried the country music. 'Music?' he said after a pause, 'You must have imagined it.' But I didn't. I know now he was not in the canteen for his lunch break, but I did not understand that at the time.

"Geoff was always punctual leaving work so when he came home late it was unexpected. Naturally, it started a little at a time. First it was thirty minutes or so, 'traffic delays,' 'running an errand for the boss,' 'a puncture.' You know the sort of thing. The puncture was a key event. 'Flat tyre in office car park, fitted spare wheel, took old one for repair at Nobby Barrow's garage,' he said in a matter-of-fact manner. Now it just so happened that the evening of the puncture was bin night, so I went outside to put the rubbish out for collection and as I was doing so, I noted the tyres on the car. I checked each one casually at first, then disturbed I went round again. Dirty! All four were dusty, no sign a wheel had been removed, no markings of a tyre being repaired and restored. I expected some evidence of manhandling. Nothing!

"I didn't say anything at the time, but when the bank statement arrived two weeks later, I looked for an entry from Nobby Barrow's. Nothing!

"Suzie, Geoff's secretary at the office invited a few over for Christmas dinner that year. It was a relaxed and friendly party, not over the top and the food was good. Geoff's boss and his wife were there along with two of Suzie's girl friends from the glass club in Stourbridge. It seems they spent time learning glassmaking techniques. Suzie's home was a small one bed apartment, so we were rather cramped for space, but I did admire the assortment of pictures on the walls, faces of family and some country music legends.

"Geoff liked rugby and followed Wolverhampton rugby in the rugby league. He also like to play amateur matches with 'the boys' usually at the weekends. It was about this time when I realised, he was going to more matches than he used to. Sometimes with little advanced warning, which I did find odd as the league table was set out months in advance.

"Then my mother got sick, and I came to spend the day with her one Saturday at the cottage. When I got home, Geoff was setting out the table. A wonderful smell announced his culinary efforts with lasagne, which was still in the oven. I disappeared upstairs to the bedroom to put my earrings on the dresser and realised I had forgotten to straighten the bottom bed sheet from the previous night. I am fastidious when it comes to making the bed. I pulled back the duvet, and to my surprise the sheet was smooth and tight. He might be a good cook, but one thing Geoff never could do was tidy up or make a bed. I puzzled over this all evening.

"The following week I went to mother's again and stayed the night. On the Monday I gathered up the dirty clothes from the bedroom floor and wash basket as usual. I told you he was untidy; he would just discard used clothes on the floor beside the bed. Into the machine, turned on, left it to do its thing. Later, I caught sight of something small and pink going round and round! When I pulled the wet clothes from the machine, guess what I found?"

"I don't know, but I can guess!" said Alex who was hanging on to every word.

"A pair of lady's intimates! Not mine!"

"How were you so sure?"

"I don't wear pink. I always wear black!"

"Whoa! Too much information!" Alex hurriedly expostulated.

"'Skimpy black lace frillies' to be precise," Fiona said with a big chuckle.

Now I have no idea what they were talking about, but Boss-man went red and burst out laughing, so much so I thought he would injure himself. While Fiona obviously enjoying the moment started rocking with mirth in the armchair. This apparently was too much for Alex, who disappeared into the galley and when he returned was dabbing his eyes with a kitchen towel. It was some time before order was restored and the anecdotal story continued.

"As I stared at the pink undergarments it all fitted into place. The phone call, the puncture, the rugby, the bed. When Geoff returned, he found the offending briefs on his dinner plate at the table. 'What's this?' he said. 'Well, you should know!' I retorted.

"The next day he moved out of our house in Wrightwick and into his country music loving secretaries' house in Tettenhall. She was 32 and he was seventeen years her senior."

"You must have been devastated."

"Stunned, distraught, bitter, angry, oh and lonely. I blamed myself at one point, silly really. I could have tried to get him to stay, but ..."

"No, you could never trust a man who had been so deceitful. You did the right thing. But how did you get over it?"

"I took a few days holiday from work and went to live with mother for a week after he left. However, I knew I had to get back to routine and face my new circumstances. The girls at work were very supportive and a couple of them invited me on a cruise around the Mediterranean they had been planning. Over the past seven years I have become more stable in my emotions. I have friends of course, male friends, and ladies at the bridge club, but no close friends. 'Once bitten twice shy', they say.

"When, three years later, Aunt Maud died and left me a sizeable legacy I gave up working at the Hotel. That, and the divorce settlement ensured I was comfortably off. The following year, lacking a purpose and still somewhat lonely I got Tess as a puppy. Eighteen months ago, I sold the house in Wrightwick and moved in with mother as she was not doing so well on her own."

"You have certainly had your fair share of challenges in recent years."

"You still haven't told me about your wife, Brenda, was it?" she said as she took another look at the photograph frame.

"Yes, Brenda."

"Oh, look at the time, I must get back to mother. Perhaps you could come over for dinner one evening. Mother could do with some interaction to stimulate her mind, and I could try out my Thai red curry recipe. Ah, do you like Thai curry?"

"Definitely, that sounds good to me."

"Shall we say Sunday about five?"

"Thank you very much, looking forward to it already."

"Then you can tell me about Brenda. Tess, let's go."

Tess jumped up eagerly and rushed for the stern doors. I on the other hand rolled over and started to wash my face using the back of my paw as a flannel. To this day I still wonder what 'skimpy black lace frillies' are.

## 12 — COLONEL PARKER

Peering through the old gate which had seen better days, with its peeling paint and rotten wood, I could see a light on in the downstairs living room window. Darkness descended earlier in the afternoon now, and all over Kinver, village inhabitants were drawing curtains and switching on artificial light to compensate. Lockside Cottage was surrounded in darkness being just set back from the canal and main road. I squeezed my way through the gate and made my usual pathway to the rear of the cottage. Usual? Well for some time I had not visited the property as I knew no one was in residence except the spiders and woodlice.

I found the small toilet window open and so into the cottage I scrambled. I was confident that the only occupant would be the old lady, and as the only light in the cottage was on downstairs, I assumed she was in the front room. Previously, I had waited patiently for Tess to take her mistress for their usual walk along the towpath before risking a stealthy reconnaissance. My relationship with

Tess was complicated. Complicated by her I should clarify. I would tolerate her most of the time, and even found some conversations to be informative, but she was unpredictable. One minute she was happy to see you and sat around chatting, the next, without warning, she was chasing you with determined aggression. I am not really sure what she would do if she caught Lapsat or myself, I don't think she has thought that far ahead, however, being more agile and light-footed than the dog we get away to safety quickly enough. Both of us know how important it is to be aware of our surroundings, checking escape routes and knowing where to find safe places in case of predatory attack. I understand she has met her match in Chalky, who unless he deliberately goads her into a chase, will stand his ground, hissing and snarling, which causes Tess to back off in a sheepish manner.

The sound of roars and growls along with someone with a deep booming voice could be heard from the living room. I crept forward guardedly. As the door was slightly open, I poked a curious head cautiously around the opening only to discover that the large wall mounted television was showing pictures of big cats in vast plains of savanna. As the human voice was speaking over the pictures, I figured it was a documentary about my distant relatives. What exciting lives they must live. Sometimes I dream of prowling the wide-open spaces, making friends with big cats, and tearing into fresh wildebeest for dinner. Then the scene changed to a big white man holding a rifle and looking triumphant as he stood over a prostrate and very dead lioness. Perhaps life in the African National Parks is not such a great place. I guess I feel safer here with Bossman and Lapsat.

A foot extending beyond a recliner chair moved slightly and caught my attention, more of a fidget movement than anything with purpose. The foot, which jiggled up and down in an irritating manner, was attached to a heavily bandaged leg, of which my sensitive nose detected the slight odour of decay. My guess, later proven correct, was a leg ulcer which the district nurse, who I also discovered visited three times a week, was doing her best to treat. I moved forward into the room and into the old lady's line of sight.

"Colonel Parker!" Her words causing me some measure of alarm. I crouched down instinctively and quickly looked around the room. Who in the room was she speaking to? Where was Colonel Parker?

Apart from the two of us I was unaware of anyone else present in the room. "Come here Colonel Parker," she said obviously addressing her words in my direction. Unnerved but curious, I approached the side of her chair. An arm extended and she started to stroke my head. Friend not foe, I decided as I purred and brushed against her leg. Reclining in the big chair, Fiona's mother looked relaxed and comfortable. Standing on my hind legs and placing my front paws on the edge of the extended leg rest I gazed up at the lady, contemplating if I should jump up onto her lap or not.

I considered the woman to be ancient! This deduction I made from the lines on her face, the heavy sunken eyes and the mousey grey hair which while full-bodied was cut short. I clambered up into her lap and she immediately caressed me starting with my head and then my back, which I arched in approval. Her hands were gnarled and misshapen and lacked the strength and firmness of Boss-man. I didn't mind, she approved of me and that was what mattered. I expressed my appreciation by purring loudly, "Nice to meet you. Are you quite well? What do you think of Tess? Will they be home soon do you think?"

The old lady seemed rather distracted and didn't answer me but appeared to be mumbling something while watching the pride of lions on the television. Nevertheless, I deemed it appropriate to avail myself of a short rest on a cosy lap while it was vacant.

All was going very nicely until I heard the front door open. Tess bounded into the room full of energetic enthusiasm. In an instant I was fully alert, and in the same instant, the vivacious cockapoo seeing me on the old lady's lap, gave a violent bark: "Kipepeo, you scoundrel! How dare you come in this home. This is where I live, and you are not welcome here." Following the pronouncement, she hurled herself at me, crashing into the elderly woman's bandaged leg and causing her to issue a sharp rebuke. I was also subconsciously aware of Fiona, who by now had entered the room, shouting at Tess to 'stop,' and 'come here now.' She didn't!

As for myself, I leapt from the old lady's lap onto the carpeted floor, around the armchair, across the coffee table, almost knocking over a vase of flowers, and up onto a high bookshelf, on which there was just enough space for me to stand and snarl back at Tess: "That was unnecessary. I cause you no harm. Stop bothering me." Along with other such platitudes.

Despite her best effort and vocal exclamations, I was out of reach of the mutt. In time she calmed down and while Fiona grabbed her collar, I made a hasty exit from the lounge and out through the still open front door.

I ambled slowly back to the boat where Lapsat was blissfully ignorant of Tess' designs. I enlightened her on the troublesome nature of the animal and warned her of entering the cottage if the disagreeable canine were to be at home. She on the other hand seemed unconcerned but thanked me for the advice.

"Oh, er Lapsat."

"Wasson?"

"Who is Colonel Parker?"

"Colonel who?"

"Parker."

She meditated for some time before replying: "Well, I think 'e were manager to some famous singer years ago like in a faraway land. Wye?"

"Oh, it doesn't matter. Thanks."

Now, why would the old lady think I was a manager to a performer? Didn't make any sense.

#

Next day, sometime in the mid-morning, Tess and her mistress came passed the boat on their regular walk.

"Morning Fi. How you doing?" Alex called out as she passed.

"Doing good Alex, doing good. Did you get to adjust the alternator belt yesterday?"

Alternator belt? Perhaps this is what Boss-man was doing while I was making the acquaintance of the old lady. It seems to me he often has his head inside the engine bay, poking about at something, or grumbling about something else. I did take a peek inside one time when he had the cover raised. A huge machine covered in oil, grease and dirt. Not the place for a clean white Persian to be seen, and oh for the smell of diesel, not my scene at all.

Tess had a red and yellow ball in her mouth. I had noticed that on many occasions when she passed us, taking her mistress for a walk, she carried a ball.

"You still mad at me for being in your house yesterday?" I asked innocently.

"Mm a uu, mm nn be mm ysss day."

"Drop that ball you stupid dog, I can't understand a word you are saying."

The ball released from the canine grip, fell onto the path, and rolled a few feet stopping on the grass verge.

"Mad at you, I don't remember being mad yesterday. Why should I be mad at you?"

"You don't remember?"

"Remember what?"

"Oh nothing, it doesn't matter." A dog of few brain cells as I have said before.

Fiona picked up the ball and threw it with all her might down the path. It bounced two or three times before Tess with lightning speed caught up with it, gripped it in her mouth and returned. She trotted up to her mistress and dropped the ball at her feet. A second time she hurled the ball into the air. This time it went high but not so far, and Tess caught it before it bounced.

"Make a good fielder in a cricket match," said Alex.

Fiona laughed. "Not always so impressive." The ball went up again, high, and long. This time Tess was in place as it descended, but a failed attempt to catch it saw the ball bounce off her nose towards the canal. With great dexterity she spun round and made a second attempt to rest the ball's travel, but again it slipped away, back towards the hedge where it lodged itself in among the nettles. Tess stood erect staring at it for a few seconds, then gingerly put a snout into the vegetation and retrieved the colourful ball very carefully.

"Butter-snout," I joshed.

"Can't win them all," was the reply as she continued her morning walk with Fiona along the towpath.

#

Alex had gone missing again, and so had Lapsat. There was a cold north wind blowing and the stars that I had seen just half an hour ago had vanished. I suspected rain was in the air, so I retreated inside the boat and as Lapsat was out, I got to snuggle up on the hammock besides the window.

The sound of rain pounding on the steel roof of the narrowboat was comforting and sleep inducing. Somewhere out there in the cold precipitation were Alex and Lapsat. I wondered where they were, but as I could do nothing about it, I curled up in a ball and fell into a deep trouble-free sleep.

I vaguely recall the sound of the cat door as Lapsat made a hasty entrance, followed by the very disconcerting noise of the rear hatch being opened and Alex entering and grumbling about the weather. It turns out they had both been to Fiona's home; Alex for dinner, and Lapsat to snoop around and satisfy her curiosity. Later that night, as the weather was bad and neither of us felines were inclined to prowl outside, Lapsat gave me a running commentary on the evening and events in Tess' home.

On arrival Lapsat had been greeted with the most interesting smell of Asian curry, however she felt it was too strong and thus it would not be good for her delicate stomach, which is just as well as she was not offered any. Alex and Fiona, it seems enjoyed it very much. Neither human nor canine seemed bothered that Lapsat was among them, perhaps taking pity on her for the poor weather. In fact, Lapsat told me she felt so much at home she jumped over the stair gate and went upstairs in search of the old lady.

The bedroom that Fiona's mother occupied was well laid out. Spacious with two windows, one facing the canal and one at the rear of the cottage facing the brick wall of a small business premises. A steady rain was battering the canal side window behind the drawn velvet curtain. Beside the bed was a comfortable upright but well-padded orthopaedic chair in which the woman was sat. Across her lap was a table on wheels which when Lapsat arrived held dinner, mutton stew Lapsat thought it was, peaches in custard and a hot drink which my loyal friend thought was probably a malt beverage of some kind.

What was really interesting was what happened later, when Fiona came upstairs to collect the dinner plates. Lapsat repeated the dialogue:

"Colonel Parker was here yesterday when you took Tess for a walk," the old woman had remarked.

"That's what she called me when I was there," I repeated to my companion.

"Yes, she remembered ee, but called ee Colonel Parker." Then Fiona said: "Sorry, mum, that wasn't Colonel Parker, that was Alex's cat Kipepeo."

"No, it was Colonel Parker!" Apparently, the old lady repeated in some state of irritation.

"But remember, poor Colonel Parker died over five years ago of liver disease. You are confusing Kippy with your old cat."

"Don't argue with me young lady, I am your mother, and I know my cat when I see it."

It seems, according to Lapsat, that Fiona just let the matter end there and took the dishes back downstairs.

"So, there ee are, they old lady thinks ee are 'er previous cat. Ee must look alike, I guess. Per'aps 'er memory is not good."

Now I understood why she had called me Colonel Parker. But why was the old lady so confused?

#

Everything was wet and damp. I had remained in bed for most of the morning, partly as it was so miserable outside and partly because I had the hammock which was more than comfortable, and I knew when I left it Lapsat would take over. However, nature called so finally and reluctantly I rose, stretched and jumped down from my warm sanctuary. A quick breakfast taken, I slipped outside and what do you think was the first sight to greet me? Tess! Bounding along, full of the joys of spring even though it was early winter. The downpour from the previous night had left its mark. Not only was the ground and surrounding vegetation wet, but the soil was mud and there were numerous muddy puddles scattered around.

Tess likes puddles. At first, she tiptoed through a small one near the boat. This pleased her greatly, so she bounded through a larger one that had formed near the old oak tree.

"No Tess! Come here now!" Fiona called.

I feel sure that this cockapoo has a hearing defect. I have noticed that there are many times she just does not hear her mistress calling, while on other occasions her hearing is so acute, she can hear the rustle of a 'treat bag' at fifty paces.

Splosh, splash, splish-splash. Tess had moved away from the oak and found a very muddy large puddle which had formed near to the canal edge. She was now prancing up and down through it.

"Tess. Get here now!"

Alex had poked a head out of the stern hatchway and was laughing at the show.

"It's not funny!" Fiona reprimanded Alex while trying unsuccessfully to supress a huge grin.

Tess was in full naughty mode now. Rushing headlong into and out of the water, kicking up the mud, even laying on her belly in the mire. Finally, obviously having run out of mischief, she came back to Fiona dripping wet and looking bedraggled.

"Oh Tess, now you need a shower when we get home." As if in agreement she stood beside her mistress and shook herself violently from side to side. The result was hilarious I must admit. Fiona covered in spots of muddy water, let out a screech of dismay. Boss-man on the other hand was having hysterics, which only seemed to annoy Fiona even more. "Don't you encourage her. Now I must try to wash her down in the back yard. She won't like that."

"You must admit Tess enjoyed herself. Don't go too hard on her. Oh, by the way, do you want me to look at that garden gate this afternoon."

"Alex, you're a good man."

"Oh, I know!"

"Cheeky so-and-so. Yes, it needs attention. I'll go to the bakers and get a date and walnut cake to go with our coffee. See you later."

"Sure thing. Have fun washing Tess."

With that the show ended, Fiona and Tess set off home, Boss-man disappeared inside the boat, and I went off looking for a patch of soil that was not too muddy to scrape a hole.

#

The weather turned out nice in the afternoon. Boss-man picked up a large bag of tools and set off in the direction of Lockside Cottage to attend to the rotten gate. I chose a few more minutes nap, which I should inform you, turned into a couple of hours. However, finally when I did follow Boss-man, I arrived to find him clearing up and admiring his handy work. Sawdust had gathered in little piles where the wind had carried it, and there were off cuts of wood that needed removing.

At the back of the cottage was a wooden hut which I was aware of, but had never explored, as it was of solid construction and always locked when I visited. Today it was open. A single naked bulb burned bright as it hung from the roof on a white cable, its light illuminating the contents of the shed. A small grass mower, some gardening tools including shears, rake and garden fork. There was also a small workbench which had an assortment of woodworking tools, tape measure, rules and a metal square. I was curious as to why Fiona and her mother, the only occupants of the cottage, apart from Tess, of course, would have such instruments for maintenance work. In the far corner was a goodly selection of timber pieces, of which obviously Boss-man had been making good use of to repair the gate.

There was a strong smell of coffee coming from the open kitchen window, which, while Alex set about coating the gate in protective wood stain, drew me inside by way of the front door which had been left open. I do like the smell of coffee, but not the taste. There was one occasion when Boss-man, much to his consternation, spilled a mug of coffee in the galley, and before he was able to clean up the brown mess, I took a large lick. Disgusting. Not my 'cup of tea'. I was very jittery for the rest of that day.

I took a quick look in the living room, but the old lady was not there. A simple leap over the gate at the foot of the stairs, which stopped Tess ascending, but did not stop me, and I was on my way upstairs to visit Fiona's mother. The first room I came to was the bathroom. A simple layout with a walk-in shower, toilet and sink. Nothing unusual here, except the colour. It was coral-pink in Edwardian style. What bad taste some people have. Perhaps it was the in-colour years ago when it was fitted, but it certainly could do with a makeover today.

On the far side was the first bedroom I examined. A large bed dominated the room, dresser, wardrobe and a small bookshelf. No occupant. I crossed the landing to the second bedroom. This was about the same size as the first but appeared smaller due to the amount of furniture and clutter. True, the bed was a single, but it had a large metal frame and some sort of controller with buttons dangling from the side. There was another television, smaller than the one downstairs, resting on a glass topped unit, which also supported an assortment of pictures, ornaments and miscellaneous junk.

Beside the bed and facing the television was a leather covered easy chair, which like the bed, sported a button controller. Reclining in the chair was the old lady. Her eyes were closed, but I felt strongly she was not sleeping so I miaowed: "Hello granny, it is me, Colonel Parker!"

Eyes opened and the corners of her mouth rose slightly as she smiled. "Hello, pussy. Where have you been? Have you been chasing the birdies in the garden again? You naughty boy."

What, wait, I remonstrated with her: "Hey, I never chase birds, and I am not a boy you know, I'm a girl cat." I guess she didn't understand my reply, but I understood.

Her old cat the Colonel obviously was a naughty male feline who caused trouble among the bird population.

Taking up a comfortable position on her lap I allowed her to stroke my head. Despite the room being decidedly warm, being heated by a radiator under the rear window, her hands were cold. While she pampered me, I looked around the room. Two photographs hung on the wall. Both were in black and white and must have been taken many years ago. Not only that but taken in a foreign country no less.

The first photograph was of three dark skinned boys, African young men perhaps. They were sat on a rocky outcrop looking away from the camera towards a distant snow-capped mountain. The simple monochrome scene was sublime in its simplicity. Deep shadows from the rocks were harsh against the pure white of snow on the distant mountain.

The second photograph was of a white Land Rover with a large Maltese cross painted in the centre of the driver's door. An African woman wearing a simple patterned dress, which I knew had it been in colour would have been vibrant and exotic, was holding a small child on her hip, and on her back, peeping out from behind her right shoulder was the beaming face of a small baby. Beside the mother was another native woman dressed in a smart white uniform, the same uniform design that the third woman wore. The third woman was not a native. She was a white woman in her mid-twenties. The more I gazed at the western features of this woman the more I saw a resemblance in the old woman whose bedroom I was now visiting.

Could it be the same person? Was this Fiona's mother in younger days? Some investigation on my part would be called upon. But not now. That could wait for another time. Now it was time for a quick nap.

## 13 — A FOXY TALE

It was cold. I poked my nose out of the small plastic door at the bow of the boat and breathed in a lungful of icy air. Carefully jumping down, I landed on crispy frosted ground and took tentative steps across the once green but now silvery grass towards the path. As I did so my feet crushed the frosty blades under them, and the sound of crunching shards of ice assailed my ears. The path was no better. Smooth and slippery under foot, I carefully worked my way towards the hedge. I had no longing to extend my travels that evening, so instead of looking for soft ground further up the towpath, I chose a spot tucked behind the hedge nearer to home. The ground too was frozen and refused my best attempts to claw soil over my deposit.

Despite the cold, which I was gradually becoming accustomed to, I had no desire to return promptly to the warmth of the boat. The day had been spent indoors and now was time to absorb the freshness of the still night air. The friendly robin was the only soul I encountered that evening, but even he refrained from singing while nonchalantly watching my wary steps along the hedge. Below in the field Black Beauty and Dobbin were standing huddled close together for warmth.

The old wooden shed was calling me inside. I was unaware at the time that the cold air had dulled my sense of smell, which was an important part of my predator protection alarm system. Nonetheless, I felt no concern as I slipped through the rotting gap in the wooden side of the shelter. Inside, all was still and calm. My usual sacking was heaped up in a corner and thus after a couple of circles I settled down for a well-earned snooze. As my eyelids became heavy and drooped, I became aware of the darkness, accentuated by a shaft of silvery moonlight penetrating a split plank at the eve of the shelter. I slept.

I cannot tell you for how long I dozed but something was niggling my mind as I became conscious. I opened my eyes without moving my body, and I listened intently. A second sense was alerting me to a danger unseen. The shaft of moonlight had moved as the lunar satellite was traversing the night sky. Nothing was visible to my nocturnal vision and no sound was audible to my acute hearing. Nonetheless, something was not right. I lay motionless for what seemed like an eternity. Then I heard it! A slight, very slight rustle followed shortly after by an almost imperceptible sigh.

All my senses were on full alert now. My brain was calculating my escape route, distance, angle, exit strategy, it was all computing. Rather that make a hasty escape, which after all might provoke a predator to pursue me, I moved my body slowly into an upright position. The nearly full moon still moving in the night sky cast light that penetrated the shelter and moved almost imperceptibly with it.

I had been staring at the far corner behind the small pile of logs for some time before I saw them. A pair of luminous eyes fixed intently in my direction. It took less than a second to flee through the gap in the wooden wall. Outside I stopped and looked around. No sound of movement from within. No chase. Did that mean no danger? At the top of the mound before the path I paused again and thought carefully. There was something about the eyes, a something that was not as it should have been. What was it? I mused on the problem until I recalled that they were dull, they were close together, they were hardly open at all. My terror turned to curiosity, but rather than return I decided to wait for sunrise and ask Lapsat to investigate with me. After all, there is comfort in having a wise old friend at your side when facing the unknown.

#

Lapsat was at first reluctant to assist. I guess age had caused her to lose some of her curiosity, and she enjoyed the quiet life, curled up in the window bed or in front of the fire. However, only a little persuading was needed and so we set off together mid-morning to investigate the fearsome creature within the wood-shed.

"I be go first, ee follow," words that I had no intention of arguing with.

Pushing her way through the gap in the shed, she led the way, I on the other hand, keen to investigate in a safe manner, followed close behind. Daylight outside, albeit winter gloom, caused us out of necessity to pause and allow our eyes to adjust to the darkness within. Some dull grey light did penetrate the shelter and after a short time Lapsat stepped forward.

"Behind the logs," I whispered.

Stepping to the side of the aforementioned pile, Lapsat stopped and sniffed. At that same moment I caught the smell. Fox! Why had I not detected the odour last night? Drawing alongside my companion we stood together staring at the soft bundle of baby fur that constituted a fox cub.

"Is she dead?" I murmured.

Lapsat stepped closer and after a long silence announced: "No. Not dead, but very nearly. They be one very sick 'nd very cold fox cub."

"Oh Lapsat, what can we do?"

"Not much I rec'on. We just 'ave to let nature take its course."

"No, no, we can't," I gesticulated, "there must be something we can do."

"Nothin' we animals can do, but I guess 'umans could. We would 'ave to get Boss-man down 'ere."

But how? We stood wasting time, contemplating the sad bundle and the insurmountable problem of drawing attention to the little creature.

As we were mulling over the situation, we both heard a loud bark from the pathway above.

"Tess!" I cried. "Get Tess to help us."

"Uh, yeh right on," Lapsat replied with credulity.

I wasted no further time and sprinted up the bank to find Fiona and Alex in deep conversation and Tess barking to gain attention, complaining that she wanted to chase a ball.

"Tess, Tess, you got'ta help us!"

"Your grammar is not so good this morning."

"Oh, shut up idiot."

"Help you, with your grammar and you calling me an idiot. Huh, I don't think so."

It didn't take long for me with Lapsat's help to appeal to the canine's sense of adventure and enlist assistance in gaining the attention of the humans.

"Help, we need help," barked Tess in an authoritarian manner.

Boss-man and Fiona ignored the attempted interruption and continued their chat. Tess seemed unsure of the next move and started to turn away. I on the other hand was not to be dismissed easily and started to paw at Fiona's left leg while pleading: "Hey you guys, we need help here, fox cub, sick, very weak, how about it?" Fiona was very nice in her attempt to brush me aside, but I was not deterred. With ever increasing intensity I wrapped myself around her legs while Lapsat set about Boss-man in a similar manner. Tess, seeing the determined nature of us felines joined in with renewed zeal, barking and running up and down.

Phase one of the campaign was successful as we now had full attention of the humans. Phase two would be more difficult. A brief appraisal of the circumstances and location of the stricken cub enlightened Tess to the need to enlist human help. Tess rose to the challenge and started running up and down between the fence and the humans while barking anxiously.

"What is the matter with that demented dog of yours?" Alex said to Fiona.

Then to assist the campaign, Lapsat and I trotted off towards the fence, stopped, turned, walked back, and repeated the action again. The combined effect had success as Fiona concluded: "It seems they want us to follow them."

We kept up the deliberate actions passing under the wooden fencing and down the slope to the shed. There was a brief moment when the humans stopped at the fence and seemed disinclined to follow. However, more barks and a few well-placed miaows found both Boss-man and Fiona climb the fence and join us outside the shed.

Phase three would be troublesome. How to get them inside? The small gap in the wooden planking was too small even for Tess to pass through let alone a human. Our canine friend knew just what to do as he stretched his body at full length up against the door of the structure and pawed the woodwork.

"She always does that when she wants me to open a door," Fiona said.

Much to my amazement Boss-man simply lifted a wooden bar that pinned the door closed and pulled the creaky and weak structure open.

Light penetrated the darkness and Fiona was the first to sight the cub.

"Alex, look! A fox cub curled up behind the log pile. Oh, but is it asleep, or …"

The sentence was unfinished as she backed away with a grim look on her face. Alex stepped passed her, and kneeling felt the little bundle for signs of life. "Still breathing but looks very sick to me. Quick, keep watch, stay here, I'll get a blanket." We stood silent and motionless in the doorway as Alex hurried back to the boat for a blanket. I wondered just what they could do to help the poor creature.

We didn't have to wait long to find out, as when Alex returned, they both bundled the fox cub in the grey woollen blanket and Fiona gingerly carried it up the embankment and back to the path. Opening the rear door of the car, she placed the bundle on the back seat.

The situation that I found myself in next was rather disturbing! Alex ushered both us cats back onto the boat with Tess. "You animals stay here and don't get into any trouble." The boat was locked, and we heard the little car drive away. So that was the thanks we got for initiating the rescue; locked up inside the boat, our boat, with Tess, not even our dog!

#

"Nice place you have here," said Tess as she stretched herself out on the saloon floor. I couldn't help noticing her muddy paws. I guess mine were just as muddy from the embankment, but then I had a right to bring mud into our boat, as a visitor she should have wiped her feet on entry.

Of course, we were not locked inside the boat. Lapsat and I could leave anytime we liked by the cat door, but the dog was most certainly a prisoner, although she did not seem to be bothered by this situation. Quite casually she rose and started sniffing around. First, she found a small piece of wood that was destined for the fire and started tossing it in the air, then chomping on it causing small splinters of wood to be scattered on the floor. Bored with the wood, she pulled a cushion from Alex armchair and began vigorously smashing it from side to side on the floor. Discarding the cushion, she went sniffing around the galley, checking out our food bowls, which were empty, and drinking water from the water bowl. All this was irritating me intensely until Lapsat said: "Wonder where them 'ave taken cub?"

Lapsat's comment refocused my mind. Even Tess stopped her inquisitive wanderings and taking up a thoughtful pose beside the fire, contemplated the question. We waited some considerable time before the little car returned. Naturally it was Tess who heard the approaching vehicle first, and promptly rushed up and down the boat, unsure at which end her mistress would appear. The moment the rear doors opened Tess was gone and peace returned to our floating home. Boss-man entered with a melancholy countenance but said nothing. Does he not realise we understand human speech and wanted to know what had happened to the cub. Left in the dark, metaphorically speaking, we had no answer. Was the cub dead? Had it survived? If so, where was it now? How would we get answers to our questions?

#

Day turns to night, night becomes day. Time drifts by and life continues. Little changed in our routine over the next few days. Alex came and went, leaving us for long periods of time. For the first few days he would drive off in the Yaris, but lately just walking in the direction of Fiona's cottage. I asked my feline companion if she knew anything of the fox cub, but she lacked interest in the story. She did suggest I visit Lockside Cottage, where she thought, perhaps, just perhaps, I might discover some information on the subject. That suggestion appeared good to me and besides I had not seen the old lady for a while.

Ambling down the towpath it took me only a few minutes to make the journey to the wooden gate. Alex handy work had made it impossible for me to just squeeze through the wooden slats, thus I pushed hard on my hind legs and skimming the top of the gate cleared it easily in one movement. I landed gracefully with all four paws upon the path, pushing myself into a standing position, and promptly initiating a security sweep of the immediate surroundings. At the same moment as the smell registered, I spotted the hastily erected wooden hutch pushed into the corner of the garden where the path led around the back of the cottage.

The cutest little face with bright sparkling round eyes surrounded by soft reddish-brown fur with white patches and a solid black nose caught my gaze.

"Hello, have I seen you before?" the cub quizzed.

"Yes, I think so," I replied. "My friend and I found you in the old wooden shed. I'm called Kippy."

"Oh, I don't have a name."

I thought for a moment, then said: "Well, I will call you Foxy."

"I don't remember too well, but your face is familiar. I remember being cold and hungry. I also recall a human lady took me away to a very clinical hostel where a man in a white coat gave me food and water and a warm bed in a metal cage."

"How long were you at the vets?"

"Vets?"

"Yes, vets are people who help sick animals to get better."

"Oh, I don't know, but this lady with another man brought me here two days ago."

"That would be Boss-man and Fiona. Boss-man is our master and looks after us, while Fiona looks after Tess, the cockapoo."

"Oh yes, Tess is so kind."

"Er, what was that you said? Kind?"

"Oh yes, she is like a mother to me and keeps coming out to see me, checking I am getting better."

"Speaking of mother …?"

"I don't think I have a mother now. I don't know much of my early life, but I remember my brother and I following our mother as she foraged for food, when I heard a loud crack sound from a distance and the next thing I knew, my mother was laying on her side making pitiful yelping sounds. A second later another bang and my brother also collapsed. I ran as fast as my little legs would carry me and ended up in a gorse hedge. I wandered for some days I think, hungry and tired, until I found a little gap in the wooden shed and pushed through."

"That's not a good start for a young fox. But you are safe now. Will you stay here with the lady?"

"Oh no. I am a wild thing. I must explore and seek out a new path for my life."

"Right."

"I'll stay a while of course. Then one day, you will find me gone."

"How will I find you if you are gone?" Foxy was not making much sense, but he was a happy little creature, and I touched my nose to his black snout, then rubbed my head along his soft frizzy fur. I had a new friend, at least until he was gone.

Jumping onto the wooden hutch I was able to gain access to the path that led around the cottage to my usual entry point. Deftly negotiating the open toilet window, I soon found myself inside the cottage, which due to the cold outside, had a warm dusty smell of burning ash and oak which created a cosy atmosphere. The front room was empty of humans, only the mischievous cockapoo, asleep near the fireplace. My human companions I discerned, were in the kitchen because of the conversation along with the sounds of pots and pans being moved.

Making my way upstairs I found the old lady sat in the large chair beside the bed watching some game show on the television. She was delighted to see me and called out to me: "Colonel Parker, there you are. Come here and tell me what you have been doing."

I was used to the name now, and ambled over, demonstrating a casual take-it-or-leave-it attitude, to help her realise she needed me more than I needed her. Nevertheless, I jumped on to her lap and chatted away in purring tones.

My early evening siesta on her lap was rudely interrupted by Boss-man who upon entering the old lady's room, pulled the curtains across the window to close out the night and told me to 'jump down' and 'leave the nice lady alone.' I stayed put.

"Who are you? What are you doing in my room? Go, just go!" The old lady was getting rather upset, but I couldn't understand why.

"Hello Enid," Alex said in a slow drawn-out voice.

"How do you know my name? Who are you?"

The distress in her voice was becoming more evident, and Alex seemed unclear how to handle the situation.

"It's okay Enid. I am a friend of your daughter. Remember me? I helped you when Fiona hurt her foot and couldn't cook your meals."

"You're not my friend, you better leave me now."

"No problem Enid, but I will be back with your dinner tray soon. Fi is just preparing it in the kitchen." Then Boss-man turned his attention to me: "Kippy, what are you doing here?"

"That's not Kippy, that is Colonel Parker!" She corrected.

"Sorry Enid, that is my cat you have on your lap."

"Kippy, you will have to go now, Enid's dinner will be ready soon."

Enid. So, the old lady has a name. I didn't much care for being told what to do, so I caused a little fuss to show my displeasure, but reluctantly I jumped down from the warm lap and took up a recumbent position under the television. Alex was contemplating the pictures on the wall with a certain amount of interest.

"That's you, isn't it?" He commented while looking at the photograph of the three women in front of the Land Rover. "Yes, that is definitely you!" in Africa with St. John Ambulance. Am I right?"

"A long time ago, a very long time ago," she concurred.

"You were quite a looker I do declare!"

"You cheeky little minx," Enid replied, although I noted a smile of pleasure adorn her wrinkled face. "I worked for St. John Ambulance in Kenya for three years you know. That was before I married Fiona's father and came to Kinver. I was a midwife, helping the natives with their families. It was a good life, I enjoyed it very much."

"You look as if you are enjoying yourself. What of these three African boys sat looking at the mountain."

"One of mine."

"Your what?"

"My photographs. I liked photography. I had an old Voigtlander German camera and took many black and white pictures. The boys are looking out over Mt. Kilimanjaro."

"What wonderful memories you must have. Do you remember your visit to Llandrindod Wells last month with Fi?"

"Where?"

"Llandrindod Wells, in Wales."

"Never been to Wales in my life. You still here?"

"Apparently." Alex said as he made a tactical withdrawal.

As I did not want to overstay my welcome, I also made a retreat and worked my way back to the boat. This simple action was not without its share of trauma. Descending the stairs was simple enough, but on jumping the stairgate I came face to face with Tess who was fully refreshed following her fire-side rest. Needless to say, I bolted down the corridor, into the toilet, and out through the window in record time. The hapless canine hard on my heals and making a fearsome racket into the bargain.

It was another cold night, even more noticeable after leaving the comfy warmth of the cottage. I hurried along, keen to seek shelter and perhaps a small portion of tuna or turkey in gravy. As I approached 'The Lock Inn', I couldn't fail to notice thousands of multi-coloured lights twinkling around the eves and windows of the old pub. In the carpark, the small silver birch tree had been festooned with white lights that hung from lofty branches. I felt sure the illuminated display had not been there the previous evening. I would have to ask Chalky about it when I saw him next.

On entering the narrowboat, I found Lapsat sat in front of and staring at an empty food bowl on the floor.

"He's at Lockside," I simply explained.

"'e be forgettin' us now 'e got a lady friend."

"I'm sure he will be back soon, then we will get our dinner."

I proceeded to tell Lapsat about my visit and how the old lady remembered events in her past but had forgotten who Boss-man was and where they had been in Wales.

"Sometimes 'umans be like that, forgetful 'nd confused."

"Must be distressing for Fiona. Will she get better?" I asked.

"No!" My friend abruptly replied.

Lapsat was right. However, neither of us realised how challenging the next few weeks that lay ahead would be for Alex and more significantly, Fiona.

## 14 — THE OLD LADY

I don't generally take kindly to being woken abruptly from my slumbers no matter what time of day it is. Someone was banging on the side of the boat and shouting, a woman's voice I recall. I guessed it was midmorning, as a grey winter daylight was illuminated the inside of the boat, and as I had been scouting much of the previous night, I had returned in time for breakfast and then fallen into a deep sleep in the window hammock.

"Coming Fi," I heard Alex shout from the bedroom.

What was Fiona making such a fuss about? Awake and on full alert, I jumped down and rushed outside to see what the commotion inferred. Tess was pacing up and down. "The old lady has gone missing."

"Sorry, the old lady what?"

"Disappeared in the night it seems. Mistress went to take her breakfast this morning and when she found the bed empty and then the front door unlocked, she got into quite a panic. Dragged me out to look for her, up and down the canal, then hauled me up here to get your master."

"Don't you know where she is? Can't you track her down?"

"I would but mistress is dragging me up and down and ignoring my attempts to take her towards the public house."

Following a brief exchange with Fiona, Alex grabbed his coat, put on his grey loafers, and locked the boat. Being less emotionally attached than Fiona, Alex had a clear head and thought the matter through. He took hold of Tess' lead and encouraged her to follow the trail. "Where is she Tess? Can you find her?"

Now free to follow her instincts the cockapoo set off with earnest pulling on her lead and taking the anxious humans towards the bridge. I watched them cross the bridge towards 'The Lock Inn' where I lost sight of them and decided to slip back into bed as all the excitement had made me feel drowsy.

#

"Aye up babbie. Ow do?"

"Hello Chalky."

"Why yow sneaking round here then?"

When I awoke in the afternoon, I remembered the fuss about the old lady, and wondering if she had been found, and as Boss-man had not returned to the boat, I sauntered over to the pub to see if she had been seen there. Chalky, the tomcat, was curled up on the doormat. "Did you see the old lady last night?"

"Sure did babbie."

"And?"

"Oy was just about to catch that peskay little mouse round by wood store, when this old woman in her dressing gown and slippers stumbles upon me. Very confused she was. Sat on some bags of coal and fell asleep."

"Didn't you get any help?"

"How was Oy gona get 'elp? So, Oy sat and watched 'er 'til that 'orrible dog from Lockside came by with two 'umans."

"She is not horrible," I snapped. I can't believe I just said that!

As Chalky had nothing more to add to the story I made my way down the towpath to the cottage to see if I could get an update on the previous night's events. The first thing I noticed was the old wooden gate left open. Strange! Slipping through the open gate into the cottage garden I immediately noted the absence of foxy. The rickety and hastily built den stood empty. I could not even detect the odour of fox cub. Without doubt, fully recovered the little bundle of fur had decided it was time to make his own way in the world and slipped through the gate, which must have been left open deliberately. So, it wasn't just humans that went missing. Well, I wished the little fox all the best in his new life, I hope it would be a happy one.

Getting over my initial sadness upon seeing that foxy had left, I had developed quite an attachment to the little chap, I made my way, by the usual route, into the cottage and up the stairs to the old lady's bedroom. Someone was in the bed, but I couldn't be sure it was Fiona's mother, so using the recliner chair at the bedside I jumped up and now I had a good vantage point where I could see it was the old lady and she was warmly tucked up and fast asleep.

Downstairs in the kitchen Alex and Fiona were having a serious conversation. As they took no notice of me when I entered, I jumped up onto the washboard and sat quietly listening.

"Really worried about mother," Fiona was saying.

"I understand."

"What if we had not found her quickly?"

"I know Fi, try not to worry. We found her with Tess help, and the hospital said it was just mild hypothermia and she will make a full recovery soon."

"Yes, but why did she wander off in the night like that. I mean, she doesn't even like to come downstairs anymore. In her room all the time, confused about your cat, thinking it is her old tom that died years ago. Oh dear, dear oh dear."

"Try not to worry Fi."

"You've just said 'try not to worry' twice. Not worry, not worry, how can I not worry?" Fiona said in an agitated and raised tone of voice.

Alex was sat at the solid oak kitchen table with a mug of coffee, while Fiona was pacing up and down near the sink. Her face a picture of stress with her eyes staring at the floor. A troubled soul.

"I mean ..." she continued, "what if she goes out again tonight? What if she falls in the canal? What if ...?"

"Might I suggest you take the key from the door when you lock it tonight and put it somewhere safe where she will not easily find it. I know this is not ideal but at least you will not have to worry about her going outside while you sleep."

At that moment there was a loud thump as something heavy fell in the bedroom upstairs. Fiona uttered a sound of anguish and disappeared up the stairs.

"Hello Kippy. You come to keep us all sane, good girl." Boss-man got up and came over to me to stroke my head. Perhaps my presence would help calm the fevered brow. He then set about washing, drying, and putting away the coffee mugs. He is so domesticated.

Fiona returned to the kitchen. "Knocked the bedside clock onto the floor. Last night it was the cup of coco, it was a terrible mess, I even had to change the bed sheets. The demands of caring for her day and night is getting too much for me. Can't sleep properly at night in case she needs me, always cleaning up after her."

"Your brother, can he help?"

"No chance. He lives in Edinburgh. Runs a very popular wine bar. Married with two teenage girls. He only visits us occasionally and always says he can't stay long before he hurries home. No, he's no help at all."

"But have you told him about his mother?"

"Well, he knows she is not too well, but I haven't mentioned the confusion and forgetfulness. I don't want to worry him."

"I do think you should keep him informed."

"You know, what I do about mother is my business. Leave me to sort it out my way."

"Have you thought of asking social services what assistance can be provided?"

"Certainly not. I don't want charitable hand outs and other people interfering in my life."

"They don't want to intrude, after all it's only what you deserve."

"I think you are meddling in my personal affairs."

"Sorry Fi, I didn't …"

"No, don't 'sorry Fi' me. I think you should go now," she said in a raised voice while pointing to the door, "and take that cat of yours with you!"

Now that was uncalled for. What had I done to upset her? Needless to say, Alex grabbed hold of me, and we exited the cottage together, both with our tails between our legs.

#

Alex was cleaning ash from the Squirrel stove the next day when I heard Tess complaining to Chip the Sausage dog about the weather. I slipped outside and sat on the front of the boat watching. Tess was off her lead sniffing at patches of ground and the occasional solid object such as the totem post. Fiona was standing some distance away and looking absently towards the village, unwilling perhaps, to be seen by Alex.

"Hey, Tess, what are you sniffing for?" This was a habit I had observed her doing many times previously.

"Oh, just checking."

"Checking what?"

"Checking my wee-mail."

"Pardon?"

"Wee-mail. When I sniff, I can identify other animals, dogs mostly, to see if they have left any messages, like who they are and where they are going. Some I recognise, others are new to me."

Strange dog! As I was watching Tess checking her canine communications I saw Boss-man emerge from the boat with a small bag of rubbish that was destined for the wastebins at the utility point. Alex caught sight of Fiona as she turned away.

"Morning Fiona, how's mum?"

After a long pause Fiona half turned towards us, "I'm sorry Alex."

"What for?"

"I was beastly to you yesterday. I'm just so confused and tired all the time. I have not been sleeping well since she went night-time walk about, and it makes me irritable."

"Hey, I understand, think nothing of it, come inside and warm up for a bit."

Alex dropped the bag of waste beside the path and they both went inside the boat. Tess followed. Really the nerve of that animal! I choose to go back inside just to keep an eye on the pesky rascal in case she decided to chew up more of the firewood.

"It's a difficult time for you," Alex was saying. He was making some hot drink in the kitchen while Fiona had seated herself in the armchair with her eyes closed. Tess was in the corner eyeing the tassels on the scatter cushion. I was keeping an eye on Tess.

"I understand how stressful these situations can be," Alex continued. "When my Brenda was dying of cancer, I said and did some very foolish things."

Brenda? Something nagged at my mind. Did I know a person called Brenda? I rather thought I did, but then my memory is not what it once was.

"She is getting more forgetful you know," Fiona said in a raised voice so Alex could hear her.

"Have you asked her doctor for a diagnosis. You might be able to get some professional assistance."

"The district nurse comes three times a week and said in her opinion she is sure it is dementia. It is a real struggle to get her to the surgery for a doctor appointment, and they don't like to come to the home anymore."

"Perhaps if you can make an appointment for her, I could help get her in the car." Alex said as he brought two steaming mugs of hot chocolate into the saloon. The smell was divine, and even Tess looked up longingly.

"Thanks," she said as Alex handed her the mug along with a chocolate covered biscuit that Tess sat begging for at her feet. What a cheeky dog she is, you wouldn't catch me begging for treats, well not chocolate biscuits!

"No Tess, not for you, chocolate is not good for doggies."

"I have a plain digestive, can she have that?" Following an affirmative answer and despite my remonstrations, Alex gave the persistent cockapoo a plain biscuit.

"You know," continued Fiona, "I do think Tess keeps me sane. She senses my mood and provides me comfort, especially when my mother upsets me by things she says and does."

"I know it's hard but try not to say or do anything in your mother's presence you might later regret. Remember that she has a real illness, just because it is not physical doesn't mean it is less traumatic for her or you.

Also, there will be a time when she is not with us, and you don't want to ever think back and say, 'Why did I say that?' or 'I regret doing this'."

Fiona put her mug down on the small side table and said: "Thanks, Alex, I do appreciate your support. I must be going back now, as the nurse is due soon."

#

Days came and went. Weeks followed. I knew spring was on the way as fresh green shoots emerged in the grass, buds appeared in the hedgerows and bird song became more prevalent in the mornings.

I made it my mission to visit the old lady as much as possible to keep her company and calm her anxiety. I waited patiently when the district nurse came to dress the leg ulcer, even though the smell was repulsive to me. I was there when Boss-man and Fiona made a supreme effort to get her down the stairs and into the car for a GP appointment in the village surgery. I was there the day the radiator went cold in her room and Boss-man came to fix it.

"Who are you?"

"Hello Enid, you know me."

"No, I don't. What are you doing in my room?"

"Is quite okay. I'm Alex, remember."

"No, I don't remember, and I have a good memory for faces, but I don't know you."

"Right, well I'm Alex, your daughter's friend."

"What daughter?"

"Come now Enid, you know Fiona."

"Oh, that stupid woman. She is no daughter to me. Doesn't do anything for me that one. Now my son Brian, he is a good boy, I like Brian, he puts all his toys away after he has played with them, and he likes to build railways."

"Your Brian is married with two daughters of his own now."

"Don't talk gibberish, he is in the garden playing with Colonel Parker."

"Yes, well there you go then. I'm just going to look at this radiator."

"I wish you would go; you annoy me."

The old lady was getting very confused and rather argumentative at the same time. Boss-man bleed the radiator with a special key, catching surplus water in a large rag and then he left without uttering another word.

#

I wasn't there the day the old lady fell down the stairs. That is a day I will always remember and will always regret.

It is sad to say but things went from bad to worse. Enid was no longer just confused but with the confusion she became argumentative and stubborn. As a general rule she stayed all day in her bedroom occasionally using the bathroom next door. On rare occasions she still came down the stairs and if she could negotiate the stairgate which stopped Tess getting up the steps, she would wander into the kitchen or living room.

Frequently on such occasions Fiona would shepherd her gently towards the sofa in the living room and turn on the television. Lately however, I had notice that she would get up from the sofa, her bed or her reclining chair and absentmindedly pace the room. When Fiona found her like this, she would shepherd her back to her seat or bed, but on most occasions she would resist. Neither did she like to be touched. While coaxing her, if Fiona put a hand on her arm or shoulder she would pull away at the same time as grumbling: 'Don't touch me, I'm not a child.'

It became more and more apparent to me that Fiona was finding it hard to handle the situation. Without doubt the lack of sleep, constantly being on call and being the butt of antagonistic and caustic comments did not go down well. Alex came by frequently to offer moral support and on a number of occasions to bring a meal he had cooked himself or fish and chips he had purchased from 'The Frying Plaice'. Tess, however, seemed oblivious to the tension within the home.

I asked him about it one day, but all he said was he did not understand the old lady at all and felt it was better to keep out of the way where and whenever possible. I on the other hand wanted to provide as much support as I could even though I was only a cat. I think I did a good job, that is until the day she turned on me!

I had been enjoying the spring scents of the well-established cottage garden when I heard the old lady raise her voice in what was obviously an animated conversation with Fiona in the bedroom. I took my usual route around the cottage and up the steps to the landing. The dialogue that followed went something like this:

Fiona: "Sorry mum but you can't go to see Brian he lives in Scotland."

Enid: "Wrong, he lives above the barber's shop in the village."

"That was over forty years ago mum."

"Don't you argue with me young girl."

"Mum you are upsetting me. Now, what do you want for dinner? Cottage pie?"

"Huh, I'll have to put the oven on first."

"No, mother, I will cook it as usual, you just stay here."

"Send Brian up will you."

"Brian is not here, I told you he is in Edinburgh."

"Go into the village and get him to bring a cottage pie, he lives above the barber's shop."

"Yes, alright mum, I'll ask him to bring the pie. I will be back with dinner soon."

When Fiona had left the room, Enid's attention turned to me. "Arg, a rat, a rat," she shouted at the top of her voice.

I legged it out of the room to the strains of: "Get that thing out of here." Trotting back to the peace of our little boat I decided not to visit the old lady again for a while. That is why I wasn't there the day the old lady fell down the stairs.

#

Lapsat was out again when I pushed my way through the cat door. I don't see so much of her these days, we pass in the night, we pass in the day. I have noticed she has become slower in her movements, not jumping off the prow of the boat as easily as she used to. I guess age is catching up on her. She was born some five years before me which means she is really ancient now.

I was in a melancholy mood that day. I had not been to visit Lockside for at least a week and to make things worse I had inadvertently trodden on some snowdrops while making a toilet stop at Wayside Cottage garden. I do love snowdrops, crocuses and daffodils, don't you? Perhaps it is because they herald the spring and warmer weather, perhaps it is because my sensitive nostrils detect in them the gentle fragrance of new life dawning after the wintery night. Whatever the case I had turned suddenly upon hearing a 'woof' from a passing canine and trod on two or three. I stepped back and looked at the delicate petals crushed into the dark damp soil. Humans just don't understand how sensitive us felines can be.

Alex owned a small flat device which I understand is called a mobile phone, which at that moment started vibrating rhythmically on the desk. I don't know why it does this, but every time it does, which is not so often really, Boss-man picks it up and speaks into it. This strange behaviour is something I just can't seem to understand or get used to.

"Hi Fiona." Alex said to the device. He listened intently for a few moments then said: "I'm on my way." Phone stuffed into his pocket he put on his loafers, grabbed a coat, and left home.

On his way to Lockside Cottage in a hurry, that much was self-evident. Something was a foot and I needed to know what. I didn't stop to put on shoes or coat, I don't have any and don't need them. As I hurried along the towpath towards the tunnel under the road, I caught sight of a vehicle approaching, it had blue lights flashing. The lights were similar to the ones on the police car I saw on the day they found Pinky in the lock, but this vehicle was bigger and squarer. As I emerged from the short tunnel the ambulance was backing into the little driveway where Fiona's car was parked.

From the gate I observed some commotion around the front door and the bottom of the stairs. Tess was sat upright inside the gate ever watchful but keeping a discreet distance.

"What happened?" I asked her.

"Fell down the stairs! Silly old woman was coming down the stairs and slipped, hit the stairgate which stops me getting up the stairs and got her leg stuck at a funny angle. Daft old biddy."

"Tess, how dare you be so rude."

"Well, how careless can you get?"

"She didn't do it on purpose you fool. She is elderly and these things happen when you are old."

"Huh, not me, I'm not going to be a silly daft old mutt who slips downstairs every five minutes."

I didn't much like the tone of this dialogue, and as the doorway was full of people, I made my way to the ambulance, the lights of which were still flashing and the rear door of which was wide open.

I jumped up onto the running board at the back, then cautiously, spurred on by curiosity, I sniffed around the clinical environment. There was a strong smell of antiseptic. Metal both chrome and painted white glistened and gleamed in this sterile world.

Looking at the black leather bed on the trolly with wheels I was contemplating a few moments curled up as I could not remember the last time I had snoozed, when I found myself, quite literally, being dragged off the vehicle by a woman in a sharply pressed uniform. Dumped unceremoniously on the path I watched the woman deftly pull the trolly from the ambulance and wheel it around to the front of the house.

When both paramedics returned with the trolly I was distressed to see a dressing gown clad figure laying on the leather. It was the old lady. As they effortlessly loaded the trolly and human content onto the vehicle I noted Fiona in a state of anguish looking on. Alex was with her; he had an arm around her shoulder.

Tess, looking somewhat penitent was now standing beside me, and the four of us watched the ambulance as it turned on its wailing siren and pulled out unhindered onto the main road. No sooner had the blue lights turned the corner by the pub than Fiona locked Tess in the cottage and both humans climbed into the Mini Cooper and followed. Unlike the previous vehicle however, their departure was hindered by other cars on the busy main road.

I looked at Tess and she looked at me, but we said nothing.

## 15 — BENEATH THE SYCAMORE

"No supper in my bowl again," Lapsat grumbled.

I was busy trying to remove a particularly thorny twig from my furry tail but took the time to explain to my long-suffering companion what had happened earlier that day at Lockside Cottage.

"Boss-man went off with Fiona following the ambulance and hasn't returned yet," I added unnecessarily. Dark clouds had been gathering as the sun went down that day, and I could now hear the patter of rain drops on the boat roof. Along with the rain came a steady howl of wind which was increasing into what would become a full gale, a prelude to a violent downpour which would last well into the night. Boss-man didn't return until the early hours and when he did, he looked tired and drawn. Both of us cats kept out of his way as much as possible initially, but it was Lapsat who first caved in and miaowed, wrapping herself around his legs. Despite his forlorn appearance he quickly realised we were hungry and filled the food bowls and placed fresh milk in the water dish. We ate voraciously.

Alex slept on late the next morning, and when he did finally wake, he started a long conversation on his hand-held device. The conversation was muted and subdued, but I assumed he was speaking with Fiona about her mother. His mood changed little during the day and when the evening came, he fed us as usual and went out again in his car.

I strode down to Lockside after dinner, but it was all quiet and closed, a solitary light burning in the front room. I rightly presumed that Alex had taken Fiona to the hospital, and I also assumed Tess was inside on her own, but as I was in no mood to make small chitchat with her that evening I left as quietly as I had arrived. I longed to have more information as to what was happening to the old lady, but Boss-man said nothing to us on his return home and when he was speaking on the phone to Fiona, I could only catch snatches of the conversation.

I did receive a valuable update however two days later, when a gentle tapping on the galley window heralded a visitor. Boss-man went to open the stern doors and in rushed Tess, who upon seeing me darted directly in my direction. I stood my ground and hissed back at her: "Pack it in you fool, you know this is our boat, that is no way to behave as a visitor." Tess seemed somewhat put out over my reaction. Perhaps she had expected me to run away, and then she would have given chase, but as I mature in age and understanding of the cockapoo's behaviour, I realise I must stand my ground, especially when on my home territory.

Suitably chastened, Tess made a couple of circles in front of the fire and laydown.

"She has come round from the operation, so the nurse informed me when I called earlier," Fiona was saying as she passed Alex in the galley and took up the favoured seat in the saloon.

"Good, good, so how is she?" Alex inquired.

"Well, I don't know yet. All the nurse was willing to tell me was that mother was comfortable and the hip replacement was successful."

"Shall I drive you into the hospital again this evening to visit?"

"Oh, no, not tonight. I was told in no uncertain terms that she would not have recovered enough from the operation for visitors yet. It must be quite an ordeal for her."

"Her dementia was really affecting her badly yesterday wasn't it."

"Afraid so. I think she is already in a poor state, but the pain killers and no doubt the shock of falling down the stairs and breaking the hip has made matters worse."

"Can we visit tomorrow?"

"I was planning on going in the afternoon tomorrow, but you don't need to come."

"Are you sure, I mean, really I don't mind."

"You have a dentist appointment in Wolverhampton, don't you?"

"Well remembered. I had almost forgotten myself, but yes, I do. I could change it."

"No need. I don't expect any meaningful conversation with her. I do want to talk to the doctor and try to arrange a social worker to assess her needs. I need to make provision for when she comes home."

"Fi. Um, you know, I was thinking, do you think she really can come home. I mean I don't want to doubt you, but can you cope with her, now she is less mobile, and her memory problems are much worse. Also, how will she cope with the stairs."

"Stair lift. I have been making enquiries."

"Right, sounds possible, but …," Alex paused then continued: "getting into and out of bed, using the toilet, washing, you know."

I had been watching Fiona carefully, and I saw her head droop, she hesitated to reply, and Alex swiftly passed her a small pack of tissues. A pang of pain stabbed my usually carefree heart.

"Oh, Alex, what am I going to do?" she blurted out between sniffles.

"Hey, don't worry. All problems can be worked out. We just need to think carefully and plan ahead. I suggest the first thing for you, is to speak with the doctor, and then organise a social worker who will have many ideas, after all they have handled these situations many times in the past."

There was a lull in the conversation at this point. Both parties obviously thinking of scenarios that might manifest themselves in the days ahead. I suspected Fiona's scenarios were negative rather than positive.

"Alex, I don't want her in a care home. I couldn't live with myself if that happened."

"Okay, I understand, but don't think too far ahead. Let us handle one stage at a time. Also remember not all care homes are bad places. Belmont Care Home in the village is very modern and well run."

I had heard enough to satisfy my curiosity by this point, and as nature called, I slipped outside for a meander along the towpath. So, the poor old lady had broken her hip when she slipped on the stairs, and in hospital they had given her a new one. That would restore some physical movement, but what about the mental agility? If she did go to Belmont, I might never see her again because the care home is far outside my territorial boundary.

I was feeling quite sorry for myself, with the old lady and foxy gone at the same time, when my feathered friend, the small male robin flitted onto his stump in the canal and started to sing of spring and regeneration. Nature has its own way of providing a healing balm to the troubled soul.

#

Days and nights slipped past. I can't say how many, each day was similar. Most afternoons Alex went out, no doubt with Fiona, to visit her mother in the hospital. Sometimes he took the silver Yaris, other times they must have used her little green car. The routine was much the same, leaving early afternoon and returning just before our feeding time. I saw little of Tess during that period of time, but when I did, she made a point of telling me how she was shut indoors most afternoons on her own.

"Very inconsiderate of my mistress, shutting me up all afternoon, and me, well I would like to go and see the old biddy, but no one thinks about me, it's all 'poor mother' and 'is mother going to be alright?' and 'will mother be home soon?'"

We were both laying on the grass beside 'Rumah Saya', Tess in her usual 'sphinx' posture, me rolling on my back with all four legs in the air. There was some warmth again in the spring sunshine and we were happy to bask in it after the cold damp days of winter.

"I mean, it's not as if the whole world revolves around one woman. I ask you, when will we get back to proper walks, and chasing the ball? Mistress is just so busy, coming and going. When she is not out visiting her mother, she's on the phone or filling in forms or talking to your Bossy-man."

"Boss-man! Its Boss-man." I replied somewhat irritated by the selfish attitude of the hound. "You really can be quite annoying young Tess."

"Me, annoying? Huh, it's you that is annoying, laying there with your legs in the air as if you own the place!"

I could see this conversation was not going well and was pleased when a distraction came along in the form of a young girl with her mother.

The girl must have been about four years old, and her mother had dressed her in a lovely bright salmon pink coat complete with a fur-lined hood. Tess who takes exception to hats of any description, stood up and barked loudly at the little girl: "Keep away, keep away," she barked aggressively.

I was about to remonstrate with Tess over her attitude when the girl who had taken a step backwards toward her mother simply said: "Hello little doggie." The sweet little voice had an immediate calming influence on Tess, who I happen to know has a great affection for small children. First, she crouched down on her belly, all the while watching to ensure the full attention of the young person. Springing up, she ran swiftly along the towpath a few dozen feet suddenly stopping, crouching and running back again. She continued this springing and sprinting action for some time in different directions, all the while keeping eye contact with the girl. Obviously enjoying herself and detecting a broad grin on the girls face Tess dashed behind Boss-man's car and squatted down. The girl stepped forward to look for Tess, who promptly jumped up and ran around the car, squatting down again and waiting for the girl to come back in the opposite direction looking for her. By now the girl was laughing and chuckling so much she couldn't speak. Her mother, watching approvingly as the game of hide-and-seek played out, also had a broad beam on her face.

Our canine companion puzzles me deeply. On the one hand she may chase Lapsat, me or even a squirrel and can be insensitive, even rude. While on the other hand she is full of mischievous fun, sensitive and respectful. The problem is how do you know what mood she is in at any given time?

#

Enid was making good progress in the hospital, or so I gathered from the conversations Fiona and Boss-man had when on the boat in my presence. Amazingly, Fiona had come around to the idea of her mother going to stay in Belmont Care Home 'for a temporary rest' as Alex put it. I gathered from a discussion they had over a Chinese takeaway meal that they were eating on the narrowboat one evening, that all the arrangements were in order, and she could be moved by private ambulance, early next week.

Boss-man had recently obtained another comfy chair with soft green fabric, a little smaller than his existing armchair, which he had squeezed into the saloon, and which enabled them to sit alongside each other rather than him turning his formal desk chair around to face Fiona. Both had lap trays on which to place their plates with steaming Chinese rice and noodles. The atmosphere that evening on the boat was relaxed and contented, so much so that they both fed Lapsat and I little pieces of chicken from the chow mein as we sat beside them. Wisely they had given Tess some boiled chicken pieces in a dish in the kitchen, and having scoffed the lot before anyone else had sat down, she had sprawled herself all over the galley floor, eyes staring at the empty bowl.

"Mrs. Brocklesby, the manager of Belmont Care Home told me the room is ready."

"Well, that is good news Fi. Will mother transfer soon?"

"I have arranged the ambulance for ten o'clock on Monday morning. This weekend I am going to put a few pictures and personal items in the room ready for her. Perhaps the personal touch will help her memory and make her more settled."

"Does she have a television?" Alex asked.

"No, I need to take the one from her bedroom."

"Shall I come and help you on Saturday to set it up."

"Great, let's say midday, shall we?"

The Squirrel stove was glowing with hot coals and casting warm amber light that danced on the ceiling. A joyous and harmonious domestic scene that proclaimed, 'all is right with the world'. But it wasn't! None of us present within that cosy scene knew anything of the grief that was about to upset our simple lives.

#

It must have been a couple of days later, when sat quietly under the oak tree minding my own business, I observed Tess stride up to the boat with a purposeful gait.

"Kipepeo, Oh Kippy," she was calling out. At first, I ignored her, but after a while I realised, she was being very persistent, and I had just comprehended she was on her own, no mistress, and no lead.

Sneaking up behind her I simply said: "Yes, what do you want?" She turned abruptly.

"Oh, there you are then."

"Yes, here I am then." There was a pause in the conversation if you could call it that. I was beginning to wonder if Tess had forgotten what she wanted to see me about. Then she blurted out: "She's dead!"

"Whose dead?" I quizzed.

"The old lady."

"What old lady?" I foolishly questioned.

"The old lady. You know, Enid."

"Don't be silly Tess, she is not dead, she is going to a care home."

"Dead. The old lady is deceased." She was sounding irritated now, and I was becoming uncomfortable.

"Do you mean Fiona's mother?"

"Yes, silly cat, Fiona's mother is departed."

My simple brain was having a problem registering this information. I said: "But I understood that she was doing well in hospital and going to the care home on Monday."

"Nope. I just heard my mistress telling your bossy-man: 'Enid died this morning.'"

"Hey Tess, why are you here on your own?"

"Oh, they were talking, and the gate was left open, and so I just wandered up here to tell you."

"You must go straight home; Fiona will be worried about you."

"I doubt that, she is too upset to notice me."

So that explained why Alex following a phone call earlier this morning, had rushed out of the boat. The old lady had died.

"Now Tess, you listen to me. You must go straight home; your mistress needs you. Oh, and thank you for telling me."

"You're welcome," she replied with an air of superiority on her face. Obviously pleased to be the bearer of information that I had been unaware of.

I learned later, from eavesdropping on human conversation, that she had caught a virus of some kind while recovering from the operation and being in a weakened state she had developed breathing problems and slipped away in the night.

Over the next few days Boss-man came and went. I didn't see Fiona, but guessed she was in the cottage. I wandered down there one afternoon, only to find Fiona sat in the front room in silence, Alex was nowhere to be seen and Tess laying on the floor next to her mistress looked at me with the whites of her sorrowful eyes, as if to say: 'you are wise not to disturb our mourning.' I left. A dark cloud had formed over that little cottage. Now why did that feel familiar to me?

#

I experienced quite a shock when Boss-man emerged from the bedroom. It was a very pleasant warm spring day with few clouds in the sky, but his attire did not complement the weather. He was wearing a black suit, black tie and black shoes with a black look on his face to match. Familiar? Something nagged at my memory. Without a word he left the narrowboat with Lapsat and myself contentedly ensconced within.

"Funeral. Gone to funeral." Lapsat stated.

"Oh." I said: "The old lady's?"

"Guess so."

I spent the next few hours with my head on my front paws reflecting on the twist and turns of life and the special friend I had experienced in Enid for such a short time. I wondered what Tess was doing, I doubted she had been taken to the funeral, so she would be at home alone, reflecting on life, or perhaps just dreaming of chasing a squirrel.

I spent some time considering whether I should go to see her, and finally decided I should make the effort, so I slipped quietly down the path until I reached the cottage. All appeared quiet and I was contemplating just going home again when I spotted a dark shadowy figure around the back where my toilet window entrance was. The passage behind the cottage was narrow and dank being surrounded on one side by the cottage itself and on the other an old stone wall, the boundary of the housing estate beyond.

In all my many visits to Lockside I had never encountered a person in the passage. There had of course been the occasional rat, and even on one occasion, another cat who I did not recognise and had wisely fled the instant it saw me. This figure was undoubtedly human, a little stumpy and shabbily dressed. I did not see a face as the shadow was moving away from me and shimmying over the end wall towards the main road. I did however catch a glimpse of his dark brownish-yellow trousers!

I will admit, that following that gloomy day, the mood of our master, Tess, and her mistress all improved greatly. Actually, I was quietly confident that some normality had been established when something very strange happened involving, us felines, the cockapoo, Alex, Fiona and a plain cardboard box.

#

Both Lapsat and I knew it was to be a different type of day to our usual routine when Boss-man put our harnesses on us. This had not happened for many months, in fact since last year. Our floating home was on the move again. After fussing about the engine, making final checks, and attaching ropes, lifting side fenders and other such necessary activity, the boat came to life as Alex turned the key. I had jumped up onto the roof solar panel as is my usual vantage point, while Lapsat unwilling to miss the excitement had taken up a comfortable position on the cushioned seat at the rear of the boat. We both had leads attached to the harnesses to stop us wandering off the boat and getting lost.

As the narrowboat 'Rumah Saya' was facing south it was obvious Alex would have to set Kinver lock before we could proceed. Grabbing a suitable windlass key, he marched off with a determined air of person on a mission. It had been a long time since we had descended in a narrow lock and at first a feeling of claustrophobia started to overwhelm me as the water drained through the bottom sluices. However, I soon adjusted to the sensation, reminding myself of the long trip we enjoyed together while cruising north on the Staffordshire and Worcestershire Canal.

In the course of time, the bottom gates opened, and the boat drifted slowly out of the lock. A stout rope attached to a centre cleat was being pulled from above, no doubt by the master himself. As the boat cleared the gate and slipped under the road bridge, the angle of the rope under tension changed, causing the boat to slow to a stop just below the lock. Both of us received a sudden shock as a coil of rope fell heavily onto the steel roof of the boat. After the lock gates had been shut, Alex returned to the boat, took the helm and throttled up, and we slipped quietly below the bridge towards Lockside Cottage.

Stood on the bank of the canal in front of the cottage was Fiona and Tess, Fiona was holding a medium sized plain grey box. Alex brought the boat alongside and kissed the bank with the stern as both living creatures stepped aboard.

"Good timing," Alex proclaimed.

"Heard you working the lock," was Fiona's simple answer.

"About ten minutes or so and we will be there."

Fiona didn't reply but Tess on the other hand grunted: "Right fuss and bother, don't know what's going on, do you?"

"No idea," I admitted.

"So, your barge not only floats but has an engine!"

"It's not a barge. A barge is usually a working boat, mainly used in the past for carrying goods. This is our home; our home is a narrowboat."

"Like I say, your barge actually moves, wow!"

Some days you just couldn't get a decent conversation with this canine mutt.

We were drifting steadily passed a kaleidoscope of moored boats. Visitor moorings for the village were laid out below the bridge and several holiday makers had taken advantage of the location along with three 'live-aboard' boats and just the one restored working boat which carried coal and gas bottles to boaters and homes along the length of the canal.

Alex was right in that we only travelled a few minutes until we pulled up alongside a picturesque length of towpath with a steel edge. Boss-man busily set hooks into the Armco bank and tied the boat securely. A reverential silence had fallen upon the two humans. From my vantage point on the roof, I watched as Tess' lead was attached to the back of the boat to stop her wandering off, and the humans stepped on to terra-firma. Fiona carried the box. They climbed up the small embankment to a flat grassy patch where a magnificent sycamore tree provided year-round shelter. What they were doing I could not establish as they were mostly hidden from view, however after a few minutes they both sat down on a wooden bench which overlooked the canal. No words were exchanged but Alex was holding Fiona's right hand.

"Hey, Lapsat, what just happened?" I queried.

"No idea," Tess interrupted.

"Not talking to you dog."

"I don't know either," Lapsat answered, "but the box is empty, look!"

I looked. It was laying on its side at Fiona's feet devoid of content. Puzzling.

#

The nose of the long narrowboat almost hit the middle of the vee shaped canal side.

"Ha, just missed the middle, turned a fraction too soon." Alex and Fiona were chatting away at the stern of the boat while Tess was standing on the open deck at the rear. She was very close to the edge, with her front paws just touching the edge of the steel. I thought she might fall in if she was not careful or if she was pushed!

I had seen this manoeuvre before, Alex was 'winding' the boat so we could return to our base. After the planned stop at the sycamore tree, we had continued for about a mile to a winding hole where Alex pushed the nose into the far bank while explaining to Fiona why it was called a winding hole.

"Winding, as in wind, gale, you know. So, the boaters of years gone by used horses as you know, no engines. Thus, when turning a boat, they would have to haul on ropes from the towpath or use barge poles to get the boat to turn. However, if there was some wind, they would make use of this to help them swing the vessel around. You will find that even a narrowboat or barge of many tons in weight is easy to manage when floating on the water."

I had heard all this before from other passing boaters, and I was in no doubt Fiona knew it all as well.

After all she had lived a number of years both as a child and an adult beside the canal. But it pleased Alex to pass on his knowledge and she gracefully listened.

Once facing north again we slipped through the water like a sharp knife through butter. We passed the sycamore and the visitor moorings and then drew up alongside the cottage. It seems Fiona was not keen to help with the lock today. "It has been rather emotional, and I need to lie down in a darkened room," she announced.

"I quite understand." There was a silence while both were thinking of something to say in parting. "Fiona."

"Yes Alex."

"Well, I don't know, but I …, well I just wondered if you would like a few days on the boat, perhaps we could go down to Stourport stopping at Kidderminster on the way."

"That's a nice idea. I guess I'll have to think about it." She thought about it! "Oh, no, Alex I can't."

"Oh why, I mean I have separate sleeping areas, it would be all above board."

"Absolutely, I know, I do trust you, but who would look after mother?"

There was a deafening silence in which only the sound of lapping water on the steel hull reminded us that our auditory systems were still working. The sound of water was replaced by the sound of sobs as the impact of Fiona's mistake hit her hard. Alex wrapped her in a comforting embrace and held her until she had regained her composure.

Between sniffles she apologised to Alex for being so foolish, and Boss-man, our sensitive hero, calmly explained how she would have many times like this and say crazy things. "It will get better, honestly, and a few days away might be just what the doctor ordered."

As Fiona turned away, Tess impatiently standing at the garden gate, she looked back and said: "Yes please, I would love to have a canal trip, can we bring Tess."

Alex laughed: "You try to stop her."

## 16 — A VOICE FROM THE PAST

The sound of tuneless whistling was coming from the galley at the rear of the boat. Since Fiona had agreed to a cruise on the narrowboat a couple of days ago, Alex had been in a cheerful mood. I curled myself up into a tight ball on his favourite chair and pressed my right leg over my ear. It didn't help. I could still hear his discordant melody. The previous day he had been out shopping for supplies as usual but had returned with numerous victuals in rather ornate wrappings. I had a notion they were fancy chocolates, cheesy nibbles, and sundry snacks. I also had the impression a party atmosphere was to prevail on our cruise down the canal to Stourport-on-Severn.

"Can't take any more of this racket," Lapsat proclaimed suddenly, "I'm going out." And with that she headed off through the bedroom towards the little cat door. A few moments later she was back. "Locked!"

"Pardon?"

"Locked. Our door be locked."

I did know that our personal door could be locked shut from early days spent in the Devon cottage, but I had never known it to be so on the narrowboat. I felt sure Lapsat had made a mistake, perhaps due to her advanced years, not having enough strength or losing the knack to opening it. I made my way to inspect the problem for myself through the bedroom, jumping across Alex bed, and pushing gently on the little door. Stuck. I tried again a little harder, then I tried from a side angle and nearly overbalanced on the step. Locked! My constant companion was right, the door had been closed to keep us inside, but why?

We did not have long to wait for a simple answer. The boat engine started up and in due course we drifted out into the middle of the channel. I took up residence at the window by means of the little hammock which Lapsat was not using. From this vantage point I could watch the progress we were making in moving north on the canal. Boss-man was moving the boat slowly, very slowly. When passing other moored boats, he would slow down to snail pace so as not to cause a rocking motion for anyone on board. He really is so considerate.

As we progressed, we passed the two modern brick houses whose lawn and manicured gardens stretched their gentle arms down to the water's edge. The private mooring was empty as the resident boat was out on a journey somewhere on the vast network of interconnected waterways. Beyond the carefully maintained properties were areas of wild abandon. Somewhere atop the embankment, homes hidden by overgrowth, whose owners no longer valued the waterfront vistas, were hidden from view. A solitary old grey wooden rocking chair, a rubber tractor tyre and attached to an overhanging branch, a rope with wooden seat hung precariously over the water. A reminder of years past when the happy laughter of playful children filled the air as they swung, oblivious of the danger, over the murky canal waters.

At Hyde, our master performed the now very familiar routine to negotiate the lock. From my vantage point I could just see him scurrying around preparing the lock before the boat slipped gracefully into the narrow chamber. Up we rose as water swirled under us and propelled us skyward, inch by inch the water covered the moss that masked the 250-year-old brick work.

Our mini cruise lasted about two hours. Alex took the boat up to Stourton junction where the Stourbridge canal starts its arduous journey towards Birmingham with four inviting locks. After winding the boat, he drew up alongside a waterpoint and refilled the potable water tank while he had easy access to do so. Then back through Stewponey lock, Dunsley tunnel and Hyde lock, before drifting gently towards our regular mooring. Sat waiting for us on the old wooden bench was a sullen looking Fiona, with Tess laying at her feet watching our return.

After Alex had finished securing the boat to the mooring rings, he unlocked the cat flap and allowed us to roam free.

"You okay Fi?"

"Not really. The strangest thing happened to me this afternoon. It has quite upset me."

"Why don't you come inside and talk about it, that is if you want to?"

I followed them both back into the boat as I was curious to know what had so upset the lady. Tess also followed us, the brazen cheek of that dog!

"I went into the village as usual to get some items from the corner shop and bumped into Megan Cornish who lives above the barbers shop."

"Oh, yes I know her, she runs the 'Good Will' charity shop."

"Well, the little flat above the barbers is where Brian, my brother lived for some time when he left home and before he married and moved to Scotland."

"With you so far."

"The strangest thing. She said when mother was still alive, she used to get phone calls from her, anytime of day, but usually in the evening. Many of the messages were left on Megan's answering machine."

"I do remember your mother had a gold-coloured phone on her dressing table. But why was she phoning Megan?"

"That's the thing, she wasn't!"

Do these humans always speak in riddles, I was losing track of the conversation at this point.

"She must have remembered Brian's phone number and dialled it absentmindedly."

"What did the messages say?"

"Well, Megan invited me up to her sitting room and played me some of the recordings on her machine."

"Oh my, that must have been upsetting, to hear her voice like that."

"Yes, but there's more, you know what she was saying?"

"No."

"She thought she was speaking to her mother, my grandmother! She kept saying things like: 'When will dinner be ready?' 'Fiona is playing in the yard,' and 'Tell dad to fix the oil lamp in the hallway, the wick needs trimming.'

There was silence for a while as both wrestled with their own thoughts.

"I'm so sorry about all this Fi, what a shock, not just hearing her speak but hearing the confusion in her voice."

They sat quietly reflecting on the past while I distracted myself by cleaning my front paw. I guess these humans suffer a lot from past emotional reminiscences. Not something we felines bother about. The past is gone, just move forward that's what I believe.

#

To be quite honest with you, I don't really know what is happening with the cockapoo. I have been spending much of my time between our boat home and Fiona's cottage. Following my usual entrance through the rear window, I had checked out the living room where Tess was crouched down on the carpet with a scowl on her face. Fiona was standing in the doorway remonstrating with the animal, apparently to little effect.

There was something in Tess' mouth. At first, I feared it was a mouse or similar small creature, but no, not a mouse. Turns out it was a sock, one of Fiona's black ankle socks. I gathered that Tess had 'stollen' it from the wash basket on the kitchen floor, in front of the washing machine. Just the one sock mind you.

"Tess, come on now, give me the sock."

"No! get away, don't come near, this is mine," she growled in a challenging manner.

"But that is my sock, I need to wash it for tomorrow. Oh really."

It was about this point in the conversation that I heard a small snigger from behind me. Alex from a safe vantage point in the kitchen was obviously enjoying the encounter.

"It's not funny Alex, really, she can be so possessive, it could be ages before I get it back.

"What if I distract her."

"Oh, yes, right, how are you proposing to do that?" she said as taking a step closer to Tess, the wild dog snapped a warning.

"Step away, get back, I've warned you," Tess protested with a louder growl.

"Hey Tess, chewy stick," Alex called from behind the kitchen door. Fiona slipped back into the passage at the foot of the stairs. Tess raised her head and tilted it slightly in a listening pose.

"Try again," Fiona encouraged.

"Tess, Tess, treat, lovely treat. You like treats."

It wasn't working. Tess had learnt the distraction trick and was not giving up her prize that easily, especially as it had a strong smell of her mistress which I knew was all about bonding. The stubborn creature, stood up, took a couple of steps backwards into the room and lay down again.

Boss-man stepped forward, and offered the dental stick around the door, waving it up and down in a provocative manner. He didn't say anything, but the movement had caught Tess' attention. The hound stood and cautiously moved toward the treat as if drawn by an invisible thread. The sock forgotten, she dropped it at her feet and reached for the stick which Alex adroitly drew back into the hallway and then again into the kitchen. Tess' eyes were glued to the new prize and followed obediently. As Alex finally offered the treat to the drooling dog, Fiona struck like a viper, grabbing the sock, and secreting it in her fist so the animal could not see it. She need not have worried; the stupid mutt had forgotten all about the sock and was happily chomping on the dental stick which she had taken back with her to the front room.

As I have said before: 'a dog lacking in brain cells.'

#

The aroma from the kitchen in Fiona's cottage was most appealing. Leaving Tess to her savoury treat, I slipped in through the open door to investigate. I sniffed around, slipping under the table and passed the fridge discovering the pleasant smell came from the oven where no doubt Fiona was cooking a roast dinner for herself and Alex. I sat by the cooker looking up at her as she busied herself with the duties of a cook. A long arm reached down and caressed my head in a loving manner, and then moving the palm of her hand under my chin she gently stroked my jowls, finally massaging behind my ears. I purred my appreciation of her ministrations and curled up on one of the chairs that was tucked under the table. Who knows, perhaps a tasty morsel would come my way later if I waited patiently.

Alex was stomping around on the floor above, and periodically carrying objects down the stairs and outside. His actions provoked a curiosity in me that was hard to suppress.

"Television, radio and alarm clock all boxed and in the outside shed Fi. Oh, and also that rather nice carriage clock, must be worth something?" Alex declared as he poked his head around the kitchen door.

"Oh, great, thanks. So good of you to help clear mother's old room out. Dinner will be ready in five minutes."

"It smells great, I feel famished."

"Is that famished like the poor African children?" Fiona said with an accusative look on her face.

"You're right. We should not say such things while there are so many going to bed hungry, if they have a bed that is. Oh, and by the way that reminds me, what are you doing with the pictures, you know, the three African boys and the one of your mother in the nurse's uniform?"

"I promised Brian, he could have them. I will wrap them securely and then send them to Edinburgh. He wants to hang them in his wine bar, both as a remembrance of mother and a talking point for the patrons."

"I forgot to ask you Fi, did they all get back home safely after the funeral?"

"Yes, the four of them got a taxi back to Birmingham where they stayed in a hotel for two nights so they could look around the canal and surrounding wine bars. On the Tuesday they took the train from Birmingham New Street to Edinburgh Waverley station. Amazing, direct train with no stops. I think the girls enjoyed shopping in the Bull Ring, and Brian and his wife liked the swanky atmosphere around Gas Street Basin."

"Gas Street. Oh my, how that has changed in recent years. That was the first street in Birmingham to be fitted out with gas lighting around 1817. Installed by Birmingham Gas Light and Coke Company. The area around the canal basin with the old working boats and surrounding cut was always run down and salubrious. Now it is a vibrant, clean and safe environment with upmarket hostelries and restaurants."

"Have you cruised the canals through Birmingham?"

"Yes, you can moor right opposite The Mailbox and take advantage of the leisure, shopping and dining on offer. Brenda and I stopped twice in Gas Street when we cruised together."

The conversation between Alex and Fiona stopped abruptly. I couldn't be sure, but it seemed to me that the memory of Brenda was still raw in Alex mind.

"I'll just put the pictures in the shed for you," Alex said by way of a distraction.

As Alex left, Tess marched into the kitchen with an air of superiority as if he owned the establishment, which I guess to an extent he did. I don't think he was too pleased to see me on the chair under the table, but he was quickly distracted as Fiona was grating a large slab of cheddar cheese to use in the baked potatoes.

"Anything for me?" she demanded in her most plaintive tone.

"Hello Tess, have you been a good girl?"

There was no response from Tess.

"You were a little bit naughty earlier, weren't you! pinching my sock like that. You little scamp." I watched as Tess obviously a little embarrassed tilted her head slightly to the side and opened her big brown eyes in a pitiful pose. "Oh okay, I'll get you some cheese, just wait while I finish grating ours."

Fiona was just cutting a small piece of the dairy product when Alex returned.

"Does she like cheese then?"

"Certainly, it's called the cheese tax."

"Excuse me?"

"The cheese tax, when you get cheese out of the fridge and if your dog is present, you must give it small piece. It's called the cheese tax." Tess reached up and gently removed the piece of cheddar from between her mistress' fingers.

Alex, memories of Brenda consigned to the past again, was back to his jolly self, laughing at the concept of being charged to access the cheese, along with Tess pleading expression.

"Okay, all set for tomorrow and our expedition to the deepest darkest reaches of the River Severn? I have some supplies on the boat, and we can go shopping at Kidderminster on the way passed. I thought we could go to the Indian restaurant in Stourport, that is if you don't mind leaving Tess locked up in the boat with the cats for a couple of hours."

Fiona replied: "It sounds good to me."

I thought: "It doesn't sound good to me, but then who bothers what I think?"

I considered it was only right to let them enjoy their dinner together, and besides, Tess looked in a mean mood, so while she graciously accepted the final piece of cheese, I slipped off the chair and legged it down the passage and through my usual exit.

#

I heard a small rumbling sound from inside, and decided my stomach was calling for some sustenance. Homeward bound then, where no doubt, at least hopefully, Boss-man would have laid out some food for us before he came down to the cottage. As I passed the garden shed, I noticed the door was open, and not wanting to pass up an opportunity to investigate a previously restricted area I poked a keen nose around the door.

Someone had been cleaning and generally tidying. Garden implements such as fork, rake and spade were hanging from hooks on the wall, while boxes and other paraphernalia were stacked along the far side. Smaller tools had been rearranged in a neat pile and the workbench under the window had been cleaned and covered in a soft, clean towel. On top of the covering was a collection of boxes of various shapes and sizes. This would be the contents of the old lady's room, neatly packaged and left in storage until they could be sent to a new home. I knew Alex had been carrying some of her personal possessions down to the shed on Fiona's behalf, so I jumped up on the bench to inspect.

Among the boxes were the two pictures waiting to be sent on to Fiona's brother. I looked meditatively at the three Kenya boys gazing upon the snow-capped mountain they had called Kilimanjaro. Memories of a distant past, happier days perhaps, who knows. The second picture with the old lady when she was young as a midwife was a poignant reminder that human and animal alike all travel in one direction on the path of life, there is no turning back, there is no undoing the past. A stumble or lost direction can be recovered or corrected but not undone. I wanted so much to believe she had enjoyed a happy life despite the anxieties and challenges of the last few months. Beside the photographs, television, radio alarm clock and bedside lamp was a stunning carriage clock. This was a thing of great beauty. Panels of champlevé enamel in rich yellow, green and blue adorned the timepiece, while a solid brass case with delicate handle and clear glass inlay protected the interior workings. I sat for a while, mesmerised by the rhythmic ticking, and watching the mechanism slowly revolving back and forth in a circular motion.

The whole atmosphere put me into a trance like state and it was while I soberly reflected on the meaning of life that I heard the door of the old shed close. A bolt was shot, and a metallic clunk announced the locking of the padlocks shackle. Jumping down from the bench I walked casually to the door and pushed. Nothing. Tricky! Methodically I wandered around the base of the shed looking for an opening, something large enough to push my way through as I was convinced there would be a gap wide enough somewhere. All I needed to do was push my head into the space and allow my whiskers to indicate if the gap was large enough for my body to follow.

There was no gap wide enough, and the light outside was fading. Slowly it dawned on me that in my stupidity I had become locked in the shed and there would be no one to rescue me. Would anyone notice I was missing, and even if they did, would they know where I was. What if the humans, Tess and Lapsat all went on their ridiculous travels and I was left here, all alone, and with no food, no water, no toilet?

My stomach grumbled again. Well, I would have to make the best of the situation until help came, and being a practical cat, I decided the first requirement was a full examination of the shed and its contents. This I proudly proclaim was a good move as I soon discovered in a corner of the shed raised on an old, upturned bucket was a small bag of sunflower seeds and peanuts. My assumption was that Fiona had the nuts and seeds for feeding the birds in her garden in the spring. I was attracted to the little collection of food by the smell as there was a small hole in the bag and some of the items had spilled out onto the bucket. Carefully I nibbled at the bag making the hole bigger and spilling more of the contents.

Peanuts are not a good food for us cats as they can get stuck and become a choking hazard, but the sunflower seeds on the other hand are excellent nourishment and most enticing. Separating seed from nut, I devoured enough sunflower seed to settle the pangs of distress in my stomach. There was no daylight left, so I found a small area on the bench with packing material that formed a cosy bed, curled up fell asleep to the rhythmic sound of the carriage clock ticking my life away.

#

I awoke to the sound of a solitary song thrush, hardly a dawn chorus I thought, but perhaps the other birds locally were waiting to be fed the sunflower seeds I had been nibbling on. My mind returned to the problem in hand, namely, how to escape from my enforced confinement. This need was becoming more urgent, not just because I knew today was the day we were all cruising south, but I had a growing realisation that I needed a comfort break.

It was about this point in my deliberations that I noticed Tess taking a morning stroll in the garden of the cottage. Slowly and methodically, she sniffed her way around the garden gate and the adjoining flower beds. As she came closer, I realised my best chance of rescue would be to attract her attention. But how? My eye lighted on a small bicycle bell. If I could ring it, just perhaps, Tess with her keen hearing might notice. Try as I might I could not hold the bell with one paw and press the metal lever with the other. Each attempt caused it to slip out of my grasp and slide across the bench. In desperation I tried again with renewed vigour, but my final attempt caused the bell to fall to the floor making a mute metallic sound.

Tess was close now, just under the shed window. I pushed myself against the glass and pawed at it calling all the time: "Hey Tess, Tess, you hear me? I'm trapped here. Can you help me?" but the stupid mutt was far too busy examining a corner near the shed for the scent of vagrant creatures that might have passed in the night. In my anxiety to be heard I slipped backwards and bumped into a tin can. The can wobbled unsteadily and to my horror it slipped off the bench onto the floor. The contents, old nails and screws, crashed to the ground making a fearful racket which upset me no end, until I realised Tess having heard the sound was looking up at me.

"Hey, Tess, I'm stuck, can you help me?"

"What are you doing in there? You shouldn't be in our shed," she protested in a soft growl. Then, as if suddenly recognising the awkward situation I was in, she let out a loud bark. "Mistress, hey mistress, Kippy in the shed, I say cat in the shed, need you to come now," she barked with fervour. I will give her credit where credit is due, when she barks, she barks! The riotous noise continued unabated until Fiona appeared. This was a woman who was not pleased to have been disturbed, that much was obvious. Her auburn hair was dishevelled, and she had not had time to put on makeup or even dress as she was still wearing a fleecy bath robe.

"Tess, what is all the fuss about? Oh, Kipepeo, are you stuck in the shed? how did that happen?" Promptly she disappeared back into the cottage, which I considered unhelpful, until she re-emerged with the key to the padlock. As the door swung open, I jumped down from the bench and slipped nonchalantly out of the shed, wrapping myself around Fiona's legs with my tail held high.

"You poor cat, have you been there all night?" she plaintively voiced in an almost purring manner.

"Dumb cat, stupid animal, how dare you get trapped in our shed, and look at the mess you have made," Tess gruffly reprimanded me, as if it were my fault.

"Now Tess, be quiet, stop bothering Alex's cat."

Grateful for the reprieve and even more conscious of my full bladder, I disappeared up the garden path in the general direction of the 'Rumah Saya'. Upon arriving back home I did not receive the welcome I had expected. Lapsat was not bothered where I was or what I had been up to, and Alex just castigated me for being out all night when he was trying to get ready 'for the off', as he put it.

As our master fussed about fitting our harnesses, black one for me, grey for Lapsat, he joyfully proclaimed: "Well girls, are we ready for the adventure? Stourport with Fiona and Tess, what fun we will have together."

To be quite honest it didn't sound like much fun to me, not with Tess on board!

## 17 — CRUISING THE CUT

Honk, honk, honk. My peace was shattered yet again. I looked skywards to observe a skein of four streamlined Canada geese in flight framed by wispy white clouds below the rich blue sky. Each bird as they flew in formation, sported a basalt black head and neck with a vivid white patch on the throat.

"Pesky vermin!" Alex expostulated in Fiona's general direction.

Preparations for the wild adventure cruise down the 'Staffs and Worcs' canal to Stourport had been made and Fiona with Tess had walked up from the cottage to join us on the boat. With my comfortable harness fitted, I had taken up my usual residence on the solar panel, from where I observed Boss-man's vehement declaration of disgust.

"Canada Geese! Look!" he said as he extended his right arm in the direction of the path above the boat. Two geese were standing proudly on the towpath staring at the water's edge. "They make such a mess, pooping everywhere."

"You're not much of a fan of the birds then?"

"Well, they are okay I guess, but when they gather in large groups, they leave considerable excrement, it is horrible stuff, I tread in it and carry it into the boat, and the damage it does to the paintwork is nobody's business."

At this point, as if to assist in bird management, Tess who had been eyeing up the offending birds took off at speed in their general direction. The birds, upon seeing the attack unfold, slipped easily into the water, while Tess thwarted in her assault pulled up sharply and barked: "Next time! Just you wait birds, I'll get you."

"Porter Dewhurst at your service ma'am," said Alex as he scooped up the black leather holdall and grey rucksack which Fiona having carried from the cottage had dropped on the side of the canal next to the boat.

"You are so kind, good sir!" she mockingly replied, "do you expect a tip?"

"Happy to be of service," he said as he disappeared below with her baggage.

"Don't talk to strange women!" she called after him.

"Is that the tip? I talk to you and you're strange!" I heard him reply from within the boat.

Tess was sniffing around the edge of the canal, no doubt investigating which other canines had passed by recently. "Don't you go causing us trouble on this trip," I said as she stepped aboard, jumped up onto the rear seating area where Lapsat was already comfortably ensconced and growled: "Move over cat." Poor Lapsat leaped down to safety while protesting vehemently.

"No peace round 'ere. I say what is this creature doing on our boat, no respect from younger generation, that be the problem." With that protestation hanging in the air, she disappeared inside the boat just as Boss-man was returning to collect the remaining luggage.

"What's this big bag here contain?"

"Dog food, biscuits, tins, treats, chews, you know the sort of thing."

Seriously, the way some people fawn over their dogs is just obscene. A little tuna and an occasional cat-nip treat are all Lapsat, and I desire. Well, most of the time."

In short order Alex and Fiona, windlass keys in hand, wandered in the direction of the first lock of the journey. Tess who had been sitting up, looking all high and mighty, now started to whine: "Hey where are you going? Don't go without me. I'm here, left all alone on this boat."

"Stop whining," I demanded. She stopped for a moment, then raising herself up, she put her front paws on the boat roof and stretching full length endeavouring to watch her mistress from a far. The whining started again.

Although Fiona had spent many years in Lockside Cottage, it appears she had never operated a lock herself before today. Together, with Alex taking the lead they set the lock for the descent. Alex returned, cast off, and the slender narrowboat slid gently into the lock.

It was about this time that the proud and haughty Tess turned into a gibbering wreck. As the boat started its descent in the lock chamber the cockapoo started shaking and howling: "Oh my, oh no, no! What is happening? Help, we are sinking, I feel sick, we are going to drown!" She made a complete and utter fool of herself in those few minutes until the lock gates opened and we passed out into open waters again. Naturally, Alex at the helm offered words of comfort and reassurance but to little avail. The panic subsided upon seeing her mistress who single-handedly had opened and closed the lower gates and stepped back aboard. Tess, now the terror of the moment was forgotten, jumped up and hugged Fiona, wagging her tail in excitement.

Alex was full of praise for Fiona's handling of the lock and said: "What great trip this is going to be, all of us together. One big happy crew," but I was less sure. As we drifted slowly passed Fiona's cottage and boats on the Kinver visitor moorings, the humans chatted animatedly together. However, as we approached the sycamore the conversation stopped and a reverential calm descended upon all of us, Tess included.

Next to speak was Fiona: "Look the three houses on the far embankment, they can't be accessed by road."

"Really?" Alex said in surprise.

"There is a footpath naturally, but no roadway. Peter and Leslie live in the middle house, they are good friends of mine."

"How do they get supplies?"

"They carry personal items up the path, but larger items are a problem. Each year the fuel barge calls and drops off wood and coal on the canal side. See the small narrowboat?"

My attention was drawn to a little green boat about twenty feet long, with a small cabin and large flat well-deck. On the side was a name. Being unable to read I wondered what the little boat was called.

"'Mini-Lass', the boat is called 'Mini-Lass'," Alex inadvertently answered my question.

"Yes, Peter had the boat built for them a few years ago. The large open space at the front can be used to carry larger items, like household white goods or furniture. They take the boat up to the road near your narrowboat, load up any item they need to transport, and 'ship' it back down to the house."

By this time, we had drifted passed the houses and continued on passing the winding hole at the corner of the manicured gardens. Standing proud were two more Canada geese, along with several turkeys and a few ducks, all making use of the large well-mown lawn. Alex lined the boat up with the bridge hole and we sailed through with just inches to spare on either side. "Duck!" he shouted as the stern of the boat came close to the bridge and both humans lowered their heads just in time to avoid a nasty headache.

"That's tight," Fiona laughed.

"You got that right. There are others that are even more difficult and can easily knock the chimney into the canal. I know from past experience."

No sooner than we had cleared the little bridge than we arrived at another lock. Alex eased the boat into the side and grabbing the centre line, stepped ashore to bring the boat to a halt, as it was obvious another boat was working up through the lock. Tess took this opportunity to jump from the boat and rush back up the towpath. "Tess, come here," Fiona shouted after her but to no avail. While Alex wrapped the middle rope around a mooring mushroom,

Fiona seeing Tess making circles, trotted up the path in her direction. By the time Alex had secured the boat both human and animal were on their way back. "She's got diarrhoea!" Fiona announced to all of us, while holding up a little green plastic bag with dubious content at arm's length.

"Yuk, is she going to be alright?" Alex queried in a semi-concerned manner.

"Oh yes, look how she is now running up and down the towpath."

Sure enough, I observed the mutt rushing about as if nothing was wrong.

"Poo bin next to the lock by the road," Alex helpfully added and grinned as Fiona made haste to deposit the bag.

"You sick then?" I asked Tess in my most compassionate tone when she returned to the boat.

"Naw, just a bit of explosive diarrhoea. Something I ate yesterday I expect, might have been the bacon rasher I purloined from the kitchen table when mistress was not looking."

"Really, Tess you are so naughty at times."

The loud rattling sound of the top ground paddle being dropped suddenly along with the crash it made when it came to a halt, drew my attention back to Whittington Lock. A rough looking male in his late fifty's was quietly grunting as he pushed on the balance beam with a view to opening the gate and retrieving his shabby looking narrowboat. All of us, except Lapsat who was inside the boat, watched as he accelerated passed.

"You should wind the paddle down mate," Alex commented as he drew alongside us.

"Mind your own business you great stinking cretin," he bellowed in an antagonistic manner while waving a clenched fist in our general direction. The encounter would have been most unpleasant if it weren't for the fact that in his haste to rebuke my master, he lost control of his vessel and nosed it into the opposite embankment. Efforts on his part to extradite himself, seemed only to make matters worse as his boat swung round and wedged the stern into the overgrowth. Generally, I view myself as a hardened animal who is seldom distressed, but the accompanying language and boisterous shouting was most unpleasant. I glanced back to see Fiona holding back a laugh and Boss-man chuckling at the boater's discomfort.

"Making a pig's ear of that," said Tess who had jumped up onto the left-side stern seating to get a better view.

As the uncouth boater finally moved away from us Alex said: "My guess is he bought a boat recently as a live-aboard, having had no previous boating experience, perhaps escaping family problems, and now he is finding out the hard way that boating can be a challenging lifestyle."

We were on the move again. Alex guiding the boat into the lock which had been left open for us. "You will have to close the gate paddle Fi. The uncivilised man left it open. Remember the boater's code: 'wind it up, wind it down'. Dropping a paddle like he did, not winding it down, can damage the mechanism and cause problems for other boaters. Also remember to leave all gates closed and paddles down when exiting the lock."

"Yes captain," was her reply.

"That's a better paygrade than porter I guess."

As the boat entered the lock, Tess jumped off onto the grass. "Gotta go! Must stay with my mistress."

"You're just too scared to stay on the boat in the lock," I happily said, adding to the dog's uneasiness.

"Not me, I'm not a scared-e-cat. I must stay with my mistress to make sure she is safe, and no one harms her."

I didn't bother to reply, why waste my breath.

#

A loud splash from the stern of the boat and an anxious cry of panic from Fiona announced Tess had fallen into the canal. She was not having a good day!

We had left Whittington Lock some time ago and were working our way through pleasant open country towards Cookley, when the incident occurred. The immediate reaction by the human element on the boat was horror, from which Boss-man quickly recovered and threw the gearbox into reverse to slow the boat's forward momentum. This resulted in a sudden and unexpected movement on my part as I slid forward across the length of the solar panel. I was not best pleased.

Alex had the presence of mind not to reverse over the unfortunate animal but hold the boat in a stationary position while Fiona reached out and called to Tess. Lacking brain cells, Tess, rather than doggy paddle towards us, chose to aim for the off-side bank. Even I could see this was a mistake as the canal was too shallow to allow the boat to reverse and the bank was soft clay with no easy means for her to climb out. Alex joined Fiona in calling for Tess to 'come back,' and 'not that way.' Realising the error of her ways, Tess turned and paddled back towards us, finally allowing Fiona to reach down, grab her harness, and haul her back onto the boat.

"Tess!" Fiona screeched as the 'soggy doggy' stood in the stern shaking her whole body and showering the humans with dirty canal water. I, on the other hand, being on the roof of the boat was safe from the onslaught and allowed myself a cheeky grin.

"What happened there then pooch?"

"Don't call me pooch, a little more respect if you please."

"How can I respect a wet dog? How did you manage to fall in?"

"I didn't!"

"Excuse me, you did!"

"No, I didn't. I was pushed!"

"Pushed, you're kidding, right?"

"I was standing at the back by the helm, minding my own business and watching the sheep in the farmers field, when your Bossy-man took a step back and knocked me off the boat." I rather doubt that Boss-man would have done so deliberately, but it did brighten my day to think that Tess had been humiliated, just ever so slightly.

Matters didn't improve for Tess much that day. Following her dunking in the dirty canal, we motored on towards Cookley tunnel. The approach to this short 65-yard tunnel is dramatic because, looking upwards above the sandstone rock are human dwellings, and a main road with various amenities dotted along its length. Not that I have ever visited the area, but my knowledge was expanded as I listened carefully to Alex chatting with Fiona, while I pretended to be asleep all the time.

As we entered the dark and dank tunnel, Boss-man turned on the tunnel lamp and blew the boat's horn. The darkness and the echo from the horn did nothing for Tess' constitution as she revisited her paranoia. We were just about clear of the tunnel when chaos ensued. It appears another boat was approaching the south portal, and as the canal curves sharply, neither boat saw the other until the last moment. Had we been travelling in motorised vehicles, there would have been screeching of tyres and much swerving. As it was, both boats applied full-astern with only the front button fenders of each kissing the other.

As Alex skilfully manoeuvred around the red and black liveried cruiser, pleasantries were exchanged. "Thanks, thanks very much."

"Always on a blind bend!" the passing boater shouted.

"Or at a bridge hole."

"Anyone behind you in the tunnel?"

"No, you're all clear. Good to go."

"Have fun."

"We are."

What nonsense humans speak at times.

#

Debdale was the next lock we encountered, and this had its own particular challenge. As we approached Alex said to Fiona: "Lock ahead! Are you alright doing this one again as it is just around the sharp right-hand bend, and it is easier for me to drop you off and wait mid-stream while you set the lock?"

"Sure thing boss." Ah-ha, so she was picking up my terminology! "Keep Tess on board with you."

Too late! No sooner than the boat stern was close enough for Fiona to disembark than Tess made a dash for it and joined her. As the boat drifted lazily out into the canal Fiona and dog disappeared from view. To the right was an ornate lock keeper's cottage which, having been in a state of disrepair for many years, had recently obtained new owners and a new lease of life. The sandstone walls had been re-pointed, and the windows completely replaced with green tinted aluminium frames and double glazing. The front door, an original in my opinion, being of solid oak, had been completely restored to its former glory and shimmered with a satin stain that emphasised the grain of the old wood.

As 'Rumah Saya' drifted around the corner, the lock in all its glory came into view. Fiona was pushing hard with her back against the top gate balance beam as the water level had equalised. Tess on the other hand was rushing up and down the path and surrounding grass burning off the calories. The boat drifted into the chamber and nudged the lower gates with its front fender. To the left or port side of the vessel I could see a dark opening in the sandy rock. Like myself Tess had also sighted the opening, and running across the now closed gate disappeared inside, much to Fiona's distress. "Tess, Tess come here now." She didn't!

"It's a large cavern cut into the rock. It seems it was used by the navvies when building the canal, and then as stables for the horses that hauled the boats," explained Alex in a loud voice. "The cave, lock and weir are protected as a grade II listed heritage site. There are other caves in this area previously used as factories or for storage, even air raid shelters during World War II."

After Debdale, the canal meandered for half a mile or so narrowing, twisting and turning, constantly hugging the multi-coloured soft sandstone. So soft in one place the whole embankment, roadway above included, had slipped down into the cut. With his usual dexterity, Alex guided the long narrow vessel around the sharp bend and passed the landslip without as much as a scratch to the shining paintwork.

#

"Gongoozlers!" Boss-man announced as we approached Wolverley Lock. Standing proud immediately before the minor road and alongside the 'Rusty Arms' public house the lock demanded our attention. Much to my surprise however, rather than attempting the lock as I expected, Boss-man moored the boat securely to the mooring rings provided and He, Fiona and Tess, now on a lead, disappeared into 'Coffee on the Cut'.

From my roof-top vantage point I could clearly see the small establishment with outdoor seating at the rear. My companions sat at a wobbly wooden table in the garden and proceeded to order and partake of sweet treats from doily covered plates and hot beverages from fancy china cups. Tess was offered a suspicious looking sausage, which predictably she ate without savouring. At the side of the café was a small window or serving hatch, below which a blackboard with chalk lettering announced something to passers-by, of which there were many.

It was the young couple with the toddler in a pushchair that provided enlightenment for me. They stopped, looked carefully at the board, and speaking to the proprietor asked for: 'one scoop choc-chip, and one scoop rum and raisin, in cones, and a vanilla tub for the boy please.' Presently the aforementioned ice-creams appeared at the window, and after parting with money they continued their afternoon stroll.

"A gongoozler is a person who enjoys watching activity on the canals," explained Alex as the three souls returned from their refreshment break. "At the pub there, you see, many people enjoying the day and watching the boats go up and down the lock."

"Okay, here I go then," said Fiona as she grabbed the windlass key, "once more unto the breach dear friend." What is she talking about?

Locking as a solo-boater I realised was very difficult, as I had experienced on our journey northwards on this same canal. An extra pair of hands is very valuable, as one person can remain on the boat as helmsman, while the other runs around preparing, opening and closing the lock gates. Boss-man as helmsman assisted the working of the lock to some degree. After opening the top gate, my master took the boat in, jumped off the stern and pushed the gate closed, then ran to the front of the boat where he vigorously wound the paddle up, ran back and jumped onto the descending boat. Fiona worked the opposite side paddle, then opened and closed paddles and gates as required. This lock was difficult as there was no easy method of crossing the lock chamber when the gates were open. One method was to cross the road bridge, enter the pub property and climb over the fence stile. Alternatively, one could walk the length of the lock and cross at the top gate. Either method was rather arduous.

"Four people is the ideal number for working the locks," remarked Alex as they pulled away from Wolverley, "especially in a flight of locks where they are close together. One helmsman naturally, one lockie on either side, port and starboard, and one to run ahead and set the next lock in the flight."

"You could manage with three."

"Certainly, but that might need a little more running about. On this section of the canal the locks are not close together so three would be fine."

"But we are only two," Fiona stated the obvious.

"Right, so you need to get running more!"

"You cheeky little …" was followed by a playful punch on Boss-man's arm.

#

Wolverley Court lock stands alone in open grassland on the very edge of civilisation. Civilisation being the market town of Kidderminster which grew on the basis of textile, and subsequently carpet manufacturing. Dropping just six feet in the lock prepared us for the final leg of the day's journey to the retail park where Alex planned an overnight sojourn.

No sooner had we arrived and were safely moored under the edifice of St. Mary and All Saints' church, than the two humans locked us animals inside the boat and took their leave. Tess paced up and down the boat for some time. "Gone without me!" she complained. "Yet again, left me behind. How can I protect my mistress when she locks me up in this metal tin can with you felines."

"Quit the fuss, dog. I need some rest," I proclaimed in my most exasperated voice.

The sound of the cockapoo pacing up and down was interrupted briefly by the rich sound of bells. The ring of twelve bells inside the bell tower struck five times announcing the hour in the style of Westminster. We did not have long to wait before Tess with a single loud bark announced: "They're back!"

The sound of happy conversation approaching the boat was a prelude to the unlocking and opening of the stern doors. An all-pervasive smell of hot spit-roast chicken wafted from the supermarket bag that Fiona was carrying in the direction of our olfactory organs. Lapsat who had been feigning sleep for the past hour was first to react. Jumping down from the hammock and wrapping herself shamelessly around Fiona's right leg and quietly purring: "but I am so hungry, you left us all alone with no food, I haven't eaten for days." To be honest it was so embarrassing to watch I considered it my duty to join in the supplication. Both Lapsat and I were totally disgusted when Tess pushed in between us and demanded a piece of the action, or at least a piece of the chicken.

Dinner that night was a fine affair. Cooked chicken for all with the humans partaking of potato salad and coleslaw, followed by some sticky pudding on top of which they poured fresh cream. Lapsat and I received a small amount of cream in our bowls, but as 'Tess is not allowed cream,' she received a dental chew which she nibbled and then guarded with steely determination, not allowing any of us close to it.

Dishes, cutlery and food bowls washed and put away, Alex and Fiona set about entertaining themselves until bedtime. Two chairs were moved, and a small folding table set up in the centre of the saloon.

"Have you played mah-jong before?"

"No never, well not for real. I've seen those silly games you play on your phone."

"Right, well this set is from China. It is a complex game usually played with four persons, but Brenda and I would play using simple rules. Oh, and no gambling! In Hong Kong you can hear the chattering of the tiles behind closed doors. The Chinese take it seriously, so you don't disturb them while they are playing."

Boss-man was opening the ornate miniature case and lifting out trays of white tiles with colourful patterns and bamboo edging. He tipped the tiles onto the table and together they turned them upside down with the 'pictures' face down. Then Alex started to 'shuffle' the tiles by sliding and mixing them using the palms of his hands.

"Mah-jong is locally called Ma-jeuk in Canton, which colloquially means sparrow. When they shuffle the tiles, it sounds like the 'twittering of the birds,' and when they play it's called da-ma-jeuk, or play Mah-jong, literally, 'hit the sparrows!'"

"Okay, what do we do next? It's a wall or something is it?"

"Yes, we build the Great Wall of China." I watched curiously as Alex helped Fiona to build a square wall in the centre of the table, two tiles high. Following a throw of the dice, he started to count around the wall, then count the individual tiles and finally split the wall, passing tiles to Fiona and himself.

The whole game soon became too difficult for my simple mind to absorb. Fiona apparently learned quickly from her instructor and the game became intense, both players silent except for shouts of 'pung', 'kong' and 'mah-jong', the latter shout always producing a yelp of victory or the resigned grunt of defeat. At this point, both humans would laugh and joke, knock the remaining wall down and start 'hitting the birds' again.

It was very dark outside except for the light emanating from the streetlights on the main road which passed the church, when Alex directed Fiona into the bedroom. Tess jumped up, rushed passed them, jumped on the bed, and started to paw at the quilt, moving in a circular motion as she did so. Following this crazy behaviour, she made three full circles and lay down in a tight ball. "Throw back to her ancestors the wolves," Fiona explained to Alex, "when they wanted to make a den, they would clear the ground before settling for the night."

Well, that is all good and fine, but she is not a wolf and should know better. Fancy, jumping on Alex bed and ruffling it up like that. No propriety, that dog.

Once Alex explained how the bathroom doors would provide them both with privacy, he returned to the lounge area where we resided and set about moving furniture. Pushing chairs aside and folding the occasional table, he then unpacked an airbed which, using a small air pump he inflated. A sleeping bag was unrolled. He undressed, turned the lights out and slept. I lay awake for some time reflecting on the exciting day that had passed and how Tess had made a fool of herself on more than one occasion. The church bells chimed eleven times before I too drifted into sleep.

## 18 — AN INLAND PORT

It had been a leisurely start to the day. The warm glow of sunlight from the east pierced gaps in the curtains and struck Boss-man on the face. He awoke and rolled out of bed in one smooth movement. "Morning Lapsat, good morning Kipepeo, another fine day awaits," he announced cheerfully, as he quickly dressed in his casual well-worn boating attire. A loud bark from the bedroom informed us that Tess also was awake and ready for the day. The dividing door parted, and Tess rushed passed us, her mistress, wrapped in a flamingo pink dressing gown, following closely behind.

"Sorry about that guys," she said as she stroked Lapsat's head, "Tess needs to go outside quickly but I need to get dressed first."

"Hey, no problem, I'm up and dressed, I'll take her out while you get ready for the day. Not far to cruise this morning, just three locks." With that statement, Alex unbolted the stern doors and Tess rushed out.

Fiona now dressed, prepared breakfast for all of us, cereal and crumpets for them, a pouch of fish for Lapsat and myself, and some sort of dry biscuit things for the dog, after which Alex fitted our harnesses and leads and allowed us freedom to roam and explore the immediate vicinity. I looked up at the dark red sandstone of the church clock tower which was now bathed in vibrant amber rays as the morning sun cast harsh black shadows from the gargoyles. Below on the old wharf was a hand operated crane that had been installed in 1912. This was all that remained of the wharf and accompanying warehouses from bygone days when the canal was a key form of transport in the locality.

"On 23rd June 1923, 26 tons of Brinton's carpet was despatched bound for Macy's department store in New York!" Alex, obviously proud of his historical knowledge, explained to Fiona. "Most of Weavers Wharf below the lock has been lost to the ring road and the retail park. Coal was delivered at the wharf, and every day, Kidderminster carpets dispatched using Shropshire Union flyboats enroute to Wolverhampton."

Boss-man started preparing for our departure and I casually strode back to the boat and took up my favoured position on the roof. Tess, who had been sniffing around the grass, was ready for the off and returned quickly, but Lapsat was having none of it and stubbornly refused to move. Eventually, Fiona picked her up with both hands and carried her back to the boat. "No doin' y'er own thing round 'ere," she grumbled to me.

"You'll need an anti-vandal key!" Alex shouted as Fiona strode off with the sole purpose for setting Kidderminster lock for our descent.

"What's that?" she called back.

"Anti-vandal handcuff key." Alex was waving a small metal cylinder with a short bar used for leverage at one end. "You will find you can't wind the paddles up until you release the locking mechanism. They are fitted to locks where there has been trouble with local youths tampering with the equipment and letting water run through the lock and draining the canal above."

Fiona set off again on her mission, this time with the required key. Apparently, the lock was in our favour and nearly full, hence within minutes we were on the move, sliding gently between the stone masonry of the lock walls.

Kidderminster lock was surrounded by a busy road junction where humans, obviously in a great hurry, were rushing in various directions. Lights went red, cars and vans stopped, Lights went green, vehicles moved. The sound of horns disturbed the serenity of canal life. The whole experience of this town lock was not a pleasant one for Lapsat or I, we longed for the wide-open spaces, where perhaps a mouse or two could be chased. Exiting the lock was not much of an improvement. We had descended below the level of the bypass, emerging into a manmade concrete coffin that closed in on us from all sides. Young artists had availed themselves of darkness to paint the walls with obnoxious colours from spray cans. I had the strong feeling that being unable to read was a distinct advantage for me at this point in time.

Once Fiona had closed the lock behind us, she rejoined the boat, and we sailed out of the darkness into the light and cast our eyes on the golden arches of the fast-food drive-through. An excited child in the rear of an Astra poked her head through the open window and shouted: "Look a cat on the boat! Hey mum, there's also a doggie on the back. Hello doggie," the girl shouted. Tess proudly looked up, while I, displaying a look of distain, turned my back on the whole performance.

We cruised through Kidderminster scraping the bottom of the boat on a shopping trolly and missing two others that had been pushed over the edge from the supermarket carpark. An old woman was feeding a flock of pigeons from the towpath, which as we approached, rose as one, circled above us and then bombed the narrowboat roof. "Missed me, you vermin!"

Caldwell Lock was perhaps the most benign and dull lock I have yet come across in my travels. Situated just below a busy road and pub, and alongside a dirty embankment with industrial units on show, it had no grace or charm. Being just over five feet deep we were through it quickly and on our way. There was one redeeming moment, however. As we approached, Fiona did her usual thing to prepare the empty chamber. As she wound up the paddle on the far side, which she was now accustomed to do with a rapid rotational motion, the air vent alongside her erupted, and a tall blast of water shot skyward depositing a considerable amount of canal over a very bemused female.

Alex, who observed the whole incident burst out laughing and even clapped his hands. "You rotten so-and-so. You knew it would do that didn't you! Why didn't you warn me!" was the vexed reply. No serious harm was done to the human partnership as I could see Fiona waving a fist in mock reprimand while a large grin adorned her face. She really does look charming when she smiles!

Falling Sands Lock is preceded by Falling Sands Bridge and the viaduct that carries the Severn Valley Railway from Kidderminster to Bridgnorth. After cautiously passing through the impressive brick viaduct and bridge hole, Alex moored the boat alongside the towpath.

"Why are we stopping here?" Fiona questioned, "are we not going on to Stourport for tonight?"

"I think a little pause in our travel is called for, and I have a special bottle of claret we could open."

We had only been stationary for a few minutes when a distant whistle could be heard. Upon the towering viaduct appeared a GWR Pannier Tank steam engine pulling a fleet of chocolate and cream liveried carriages. A plume of white smoke arose from the stack, and bursts of steam accompanied the chuffing sound of the pistons. At the same time a hire-boat in green and cream colours passed under Falling Sands bridge.

"Wow. Got it!" Fiona cried with delight as she briskly took a photograph with her mobile phone. "What a beautiful scene."

"Certainly is. I have to say it is rare to get train and boat in the picture at the same time. Worth mooring up for?" Alex asked as he took another sip from his wine glass.

"Most impressive. Did you know it was coming?"

"I have a good idea of the timetable, but you can never be certain. It's a heritage railway you know. Anyway, the hire crew on the boat have passed us now and that means the next lock will be against us."

Wine glasses empty, and we were on the move again. As predicted by Boss-man we had to wait while Fiona refilled the lock. I did not mind the wait as the surroundings were a delight. A wide sweeping bend allowed the narrowboat to swing ninety degrees to line up with the lock entrance. On the port side, broad open fields masked the Stour river that flowed alongside the canal. Starboard side was totally different, with a steep embankment of rich coloured sandstone rock.

Falling Sands turned out to be the last lock as we cruised majestically towards the town of Stourport as our destination for the rest of the day and the night ahead. We passed Pratt's Wharf, the former railway basin at Mitton, and Stourport Town Cemetery with its old and new inhabitants. In bygone days, according to Alex narrative to Fiona, the railway used to bring coal which was transhipped onto barges to feed the nearby power station which ceased working in 1984.

#

There were no flags or bunting to herald our arrival into Stourport, just an elderly couple walking the towpath who greeted us with a cheerful 'afternoon'. After the customary mooring of the boat with ropes for'ard and aft, of which Tess decided to assist by grabbing a rope in her mouth and pulling and swinging it from side to side, Fiona said: "Tess, you want to go walkies?" This was greeted enthusiastically by the mutt who jumped up and down, finally reaching her front paws on to her mistress, stretching full-length and wagging her tail with delight.

Fiona, after attaching a lead to Tess' harness, set off back up the towpath. Alex opened the rear doors on the boat and allowed Lapsat and I chance to wander the path, to the limit our tethered leads allowed, and generally make a nuisance of ourselves by getting in the way of passing locals.

Sometime had past when Fiona and Tess returned and the three of us animals were pushed unceremoniously inside the boat and the door locked from outside. Tess was not happy: "No, no, not again," she barked after them. The whining followed: "Please take me, don't leave me here with these stupid cats."

"Shut it dog!" Lapsat reprimanded. I think she was becoming annoyed by the animal's irritating manner. Lapsat choose to squat in the litter-tray, which Boss-man had kindly left under his office table, for our convenience. I may have mentioned before, we felines are private creatures, and so I choose to look away to avoid embarrassing my companion. Tess didn't! She just stared, and to make matters worse, after Lapsat had finished scrapping chippings over her deposit, she went across and sniffed. Unbelievable! How crass that dog is!

Our master and mistress were gone for some time, well into the evening as it happened, and upon their return it was obvious Fiona was just a little worse for wear. Our first indication of their return was, as usual, Tess who pricked her ears up and rushed to greet them at the stern doors. There was a thud, a grunt and 'Careful Fi' was heard from without. The door was unlocked, and Fiona was the first to make her way down the steps into the galley. The bottom step appeared to be a little troublesome as she stumbled and fell against the gas cooker. "Great evening, loved the Indian food."

"Yes, it was great, especially the chicken masala, but I think you had one too many Cobra beers."

"Um, that Cobra has a sting in the tail, or is it a bite?" she confirmed as she pushed her way pass Tess who was trying to smother her with affection. It was not long before Fiona said she was off to bed, and her trusty canine rushed passed her into the bedroom, to take up a recumbent position full length across the bed. I could hear the remonstrations of an incoherent Fiona encouraging the dog to move over.

Despite Tess' disagreeable nature, she was fun to have around, and I drifted to sleep that night wondering what fun and excitement the next day would bring in Stourport.

#

Lapsat and I had been left on our own again in the boat. Marvellous! At last, some peace and quiet so I can indulge in my favourite pastime of snoozing without interruption. Last night had been disturbed somewhat when two drunken louts noisily passed the boat, one of them falling against the side with a thump. All this had triggered Tess' automatic alarm system. In an instant she was awake and barking orders in her fiercest manner. The inebriated men soon departed on hearing the dog's reprimand, and while grateful for her protective instinct, it had disturbed our peaceful slumber, from which I found it hard to recover.

Next morning I awoke to the pitter-patter of gentle rain on the steel narrowboat roof. When by mid-morning the rain had eased off, the humans had taken Tess to reconnoitre the surrounding waterways and explore the High Street. As I drifted into a gentle doze, I couldn't help wondering what they were doing and if anything of interest lay beyond the canal basin.

#

"You should have been there, your Bossy-man was showing my mistress where the River Stour, which we have been following all the way down the canal, joins the River Severn." The peace had been shattered when Fiona returned Tess to the confines of the boat and went off again with Alex. Tess continued her narrative: "The River Severn is wide and fast flowing, and people in canoes, and a big bridge for vehicles from the town to cross the river, and a big river boat called the 'River King' with a party of revellers from upstream, and lots of locks, small and big, and ..."

"Tess, calm down," I pleaded, "take a breath, and tell us about the locks."

"Well, there are these two big, I mean huge, big, locks which Alex says are used for larger boats like some of the cruisers moored in the Upper Basin. He said that in 'the old days' Severn Trows would pass through these locks and tranship their goods onto narrowboats to continue the journey up canal towards Birmingham."

"What's a Severn Trow?" I asked innocently.

"Don't know! Anyway, there are these smaller locks, two doubles for boats like this one to go from the Clock Basin down onto the river. Bossy-man says you can go all the way to Gloucester, then on to Sharpness, and if you are brave, you can continue to Portishead or up the River Avon to Bristol floating harbour. But he said you need a pilot or something, whatever that is."

My interest in all things related to the inland waterways prompted my question: "Did you see any boats?"

"Lots of them, big and small, wide beam and narrow. There is a dry dock next to the narrow locks with a boat being painted black on its bottom, you could see the propeller and rudder and silvery metal things stuck on the sides."

"Anodes. You mean the sacrificial anodes welded on to the hull to help protect the steel from rusting."

"If you say so. Anyway, then we went to the funfair."

"Pardon, did you say funfair? We are not at the seaside you know."

"Well, it was a funfair. And this woman in a little hut gave us all some ice cream. Mine was vanilla in a little tub which I pushed my nose in and got it stuck. Then Fiona and Alex went on the dodgems, after tying me to a lamppost I have to say, and then they went on the waltzer, and then my mistress said she felt sick, must have been the ice-cream. Whilst tied to the lamppost I watched a little girl win a teddy bear at the coconut shy that looked just like me!

"After that we went to the town, and I sat outside the café tied to another lamppost, while they went inside to feast upon the appetising treats in the display window. Why I was not allowed inside I just cannot understand, can you?"

At this point Tess narrative was thankfully interrupted by the return of the humans. "Okay Fi, will take the boat down into the basin and do the services and get fuel, then back here to moor again for the night, then we will be ready for our return journey tomorrow."

The usual routine was enacted whereby Fiona set off, windlass in hand, to prepare the lock that would take us below York Street, while Alex cast off and raised the side-fenders. We drifted sedately towards the lock with the modern housing development on our starboard side where once stood the Staffordshire and Worcestershire Canal Company's maintenance depot and workshops. Adjacent to the lock is 'Ye Olde Tea Shoppe' from whence through its Georgian windows a limited number of patrons gazed at us and obviously made a comment or two about the dog and cats aboard the descending craft.

Our journey was brief as Boss-man pulled over to the port side and tied up again. Fiona joined him and together they filled the water tank, emptied the toilet cassette, and removed the rubbish bag. While doing this he was merrily chatting to Fiona about the Severn Trows.

"The upstream Trow would sail from Bristol to Gloucester or Stourport where it could be brought into the basin through the wide beam locks. However, they could not navigate the narrow channel to the Midlands, so a port town grew up here to transfer goods from the Trow to continue the journey on the narrow barges. The word Trow is thought to come from the old Saxon word 'trog' which means trough. They had sails to harness wind power but sometimes if the river level was low, before the river locks and weirs were introduced, bow hauliers would haul on ropes to drag the boats over the shallows."

"Sounds like hard work to me," Fiona observed.

"Right, so don't you go complaining when you have the next lock to do."

"Yes sir!" she replied with sarcasm.

"Now, to get diesel."

Alex with skill turned the boat around in the basin, careful to avoid bumping any of the moored boats. "That's why we don't call them barges, because we don't go barging into other boats!" he stated as he lined the bow up with the chandlery's pontoon. Alex supervised the taking onboard of red diesel while Fiona went to the chandlery's shop to 'take a peek at what is on offer.'

Diesel tank restocked and a new gas bottle installed, Fiona returned to the boat waving a small bag of swag. "Got some coasters with old canal scenes for the cottage and look!" triumphantly holding up a stove kettle painted in vivid canal colours and patterns, "for your stove, you can throw the old tatty one away now."

"But I like the old one, it has done me well for years."

"Not anymore, times, they are a changing."

The evening was spent back at the same mooring spot as the previous night, but this time, facing north ready for the journey back to base. Predictably, Alex and Fiona went out to dinner somewhere, but not until they had fed the three of us animals.

I am pleased to say Fiona was more restrained in her alcohol intake that evening, and we all enjoyed a peaceful and calm night on the still waters. I was lulled to sleep by the rhythmic drone of passing vehicles on the main road.

#

The following day started badly and got worse.

The previous night Alex had told Fiona, "We could make the journey back to Kinver in one day and be back in time for dinner at 'The Lock Inn', if we start early."

"Oh, great, you want me up early, I can't afford to lose my beauty sleep," she said with distain.

"Oh, I don't think you need worry about beauty sleep," was the swift riposte. Fiona looked perplexed at this comment, but she made no reply. I could tell she couldn't decide if it was a compliment or not. I also knew her reluctance to make the return journey so quickly was not so much about getting up early, but a sadness to see her time on the canal come to an end.

In the early hours of the morning, I had become aware of a storm brewing. Gentle raindrops gave way to squally showers which in turn became a full-blown gale by daybreak. When Alex opened the curtains, very little daylight penetrated the interior of the boat and my limited view of the sky above revealed dark menacing rainclouds with smaller soft fluffy grey clouds whipped along by a fierce south-westerly wind. It rained.

"Departure delayed!" announced Boss-man when Fiona appeared in the saloon doorway.

"Fair-weather boater, are we?"

"I see no point in getting soaked, and to be honest the boat will get blown around like a cork in wind like this. We can sit it out and leave later when it has eased off."

It eased off around mid-day, and thus we optimistically set about the return journey. We did not get far, in fact, we did not even make it to the first lock. The first indication there was a problem was when the engine was thrown suddenly into reverse, and we shuddered to a halt. Rushing up the steps to the stern I soon discovered the problem. "Tree down!" exclaimed Alex in an unnecessarily loud voice.

Ahead I could see Falling Sands Lock, but preventing our approach, straddling the width of the canal, was a fallen tree. No doubt the short but intense storm had been too much for the monster yew. From my vantage point I could see a rotten stump on the far bank with broken branches and green ivy strewn across the towpath. Having done his best to secure the boat to the uneven canal side, Alex called up the Canal and River Trust.

"They already know of the blockage, a walker phoned them earlier, but they cannot get a contractor out until sometime tomorrow." Boss-man stroked his chin thoughtfully for a few moments and then said: "I'll jump off and take a look at the situation."

Lapsat had joined me on the roof of the boat and Tess had taken up a lookout position on the stern seating. "Wasson?" Lapsat asked in her broad Devonian accent.

"Tree down, can't go on. Stuck here tonight."

We watched Boss-man walk up and down the towpath, looking at the problem from various angles and clambering over broken branches that hindered even the most determined dog walker.

"We could start by clearing the footpath, I have a bowsaw, then at least people and cyclists can pass. You stay here Fi."

"No, I am happy to help."

The narrowboat was not close into the bank due to the uneven ground, but a calculated jump found the humans back on dryland, while Tess paced up and down, eager to join them but unsure if it was possible to bridge the gap. Suddenly without warning she let out a loud bark: "I'm coming," and leapt onto the muddy path. Remaining to guard the boat, Lapsat and I watched with unbridled curiosity as the humans, hindered by the dog, attacked the rotten tree branches. Sawing, hacking and pulling, various pieces came away, mostly held together by ivy sinews, and were discarded over the embankment.

Some considerable time later and Alex stopped to review the situation. Returning to the boat he restarted the engine and pushed us up close to the fallen remnant of the tree. With dexterity he attached ropes to the broken end, throwing one to Fiona on the bank and one he attached to the boat. Slowly, very slowly, he reversed until the main rope became taut. With agonising creaking sounds, words of encouragement from Fiona and a steady hand at the tiller, the huge yew began to move. As it broke free it floated to the centre of the canal and with Fiona's efforts it drifted close to the towpath. Once more our journey could continue unhindered.

#

Together we ascended locks, passed under bridges, and waved at passing ramblers and cyclists. Due to the trials of the day, we were forced to spend an unexpected night back at Kidderminster, where Fiona cooked a lasagne on board the boat. The strong smell of garlic from the bread as it came out of the oven was overpowering, but the humans seemed to like it. Following dinner, and after taking Tess out for a walk, they sat in front of the television watching a long film of something they both found amusing.

The following day should have been a simple matter of a couple of hours cruising; however, nothing is simple with a narrowboat and especially one with a cockapoo on board.

We had not gone five minutes after Kidderminster when Alex announced: "Something wrong with the prop!"

Yet again the boat was brought to a stop at the side of the canal where Fiona grabbing the centre line held the boat against the Armco while Alex shut off the engine. There was a good deal of fussing as he opened the engine hatch and loosened the weed-hatch locking bolts. He rolled up his shirt sleeve and stuck his right arm into the watery pit. Each time he pulled his hand out he dragged debris with it. At first it was weed from around the propeller, but as he continued other items emerged. An old sock, remnants of a nylon washing line, a plastic shopping bag which had seen better days and finally with great effort wire from a long-lost shopping basket.

"Picked that lot up in Kidderminster I'll bet," Alex said as he replaced the hatch cover, ensuring it was firmly tightened.

After Wolverley Lock the canal twists and turns as it heads in a northerly direction. Fiona had set off to walk to Debdale and had taken Tess with her for company. Parts of the towpath edge were overgrown with nettles and grasses, which for an adult human caused no problem, but for a short-legged cockapoo it was a different story.

Tess is well known for her love of sniffing. Many a time I had observed her with a nose to the ground investigating the smells of nature. From my roof-top lookout I saw her lag behind her mistress who was striding out briskly to keep up with our boat. Suddenly, Tess looked up, could not see her mistress, panicked, saw the boat moving away from her, decided that is where she should be, took a short run and belly flopped into the canal!

A cry of: "She's fallen in the water!" rang out from Alex on the boat. There followed much anxious suspense from all parties except Lapsat and I. The dog started swimming towards the boat, but then when she heard her mistress on the bank calling, she doggy-paddled towards her. The problem with this was simple, the bank was too steep for her to climb out, and Fiona could not reach her. Alex shouted at the mutt: "Come here, Tess."

Finally, after much confusion, a very wet creature was hauled out of the canal by Alex onto the safety of the boat, where she, for the second time in recent days, shook herself, spaying us all with canal water!

We had just negotiated Debdale lock, and we were waiting to pick up Fiona when a hire boat with an inexperienced crew came into view. It really was most comical to watch as they failed completely to navigate the right-angle bend and shot at full speed into the far bank. There was the sound of breaking branches and a heavy thud, followed by some blue air from the stern of the boat. We waited patiently as the helmsman tried his best to pull back and extricate himself from the tangle of branches and roots. As we slipped passed him, he simply threw his arms in the air and said: "Messed that one up. I just don't understand why they can't build canals in straight lines?"

#

Last rope secured to the mooring ring and Fiona picked up her bag and called to Tess to follow as she walked back to Lockside Cottage. It had been a fun trip, and all of us, even Tess had enjoyed themselves. Now back at our base, Bossman unhooked the leads, and we were free to roam our old haunt again.

I had just returned from checking on Black Beauty and Dobbin in the field below when Fiona came rushing up to the boat, Tess following, both in a state of unease.

"Alex, hey Alex, I've been robbed!"

## 19 — AN UNINVITED VISITOR

Sniff, sniff. Excuse me, I am just checking out this broken padlock lying in the dirt next to the open shed door at the back of Fiona's cottage.

Following her exclamation of distress, Alex followed Fiona and Tess back to Lockside Cottage to investigate the matter and provide solace. I trotted along after them at a more relaxed pace, as I considered the damage had already been done, and thus no need for over-exertion.

I stepped back from the brass lock and considered carefully what was plainly obvious. It was not just broken, it had been deliberately cut with heavy duty bolt-cutters, no doubt. The shackle showed a tell-tale sharp edge and lay two feet away from the body. Having deduced the method of entry I cautiously moved toward the open shed door, which was swinging gently on creaky hinges. I peered inside and shuddered for a moment upon recollection that just a few days previous I had been incarcerated in this very shed for a longer period of time than was acceptable.

Certainly, the space within did not appear as cluttered with objects as it had done when I was imprisoned. Enlightenment stirred my memory as I realised that while trapped overnight, I had explored the shed with great eagerness to find an escape route, and in so doing had memorised many of the objects within.

Garden implements, such as shovels, forks and rakes were still hanging from well-established hooks. Boxes containing mysterious substances stood against the far wall, and amazingly the bag of peanuts and sunflower seeds which had provided me sustenance, and now apparently half full had been repaired and placed on the bench. Where was the garden mower, the strimmer and the green plastic carry box which had sported a picture of a battery powered drill?

I jumped up on to the bench to investigate further. No television, no radio, no alarm clock! Where were the photographs of the three boys and of the nurses in Africa? Something else was missing too, but what was it? I searched my simple brain for a indication. Looking around the shed I wondered if there was a clue as to the missing object? I saw nothing, but then I heard nothing either. Puzzling, what was it that nagged at my mind? Silence. That was it! Previously my solitude had been accompanied by the rhythmic ticking of the old carriage clock. It also was missing!

Jumping down from the bench I stepped outside and viewed the immediate surroundings with an abundance of caution. A distinctive footprint caused by a size ten work boot which I could not associate with either Fiona or Alex, had been left in the soft soil to the side of the shed, and upon further investigation I traced more prints leading in the direction of the stone wall at the end of the rear path of the cottage. The only escape route was over the wall towards the main road, where I had previously witnessed a disappearing shadowy figure. Could this have been the itinerant thief? If so, he must have struggled to get the spoils of his skulduggery over the far wall and away from the property.

With nothing more to be learned from outside I slipped into the cottage care of the downstairs toilet window as was my familiar custom. My first port of call was the lounge where I suspected the ever-present Tess might be warming herself in front of the open fire. I was correct. Sprawled out at full length with legs directed towards each point of the compass she lay with belly exposed. Revolting! Her eyes were closed but nevertheless I approached stealthily and sniffed at her underbelly. There was a warm musty smell of youthful dog, far from being repulsed I even considered resting my head on her soft fur and taking a nap. Afterall most of my feline companions, myself included, are happy to take any opportunity for some shut eye.

As I actively considered the proposal, Tess opened an eye and looked at me with the whites of her eyes showing. "Oh, er, hi there Tess. You okay then?"

In a docile manner she rolled onto her stomach and looked straight at me. "Doing good," she woofed, then added: "My mistress is not doing good. Very upset about the burglar affair. Seems he took a lot of stuff. Still, no doubt insured, so why worry."

"Perhaps it's the sentimental value rather than the money that has upset her. I'm going to see what they are talking about in the kitchen, you want to come with me?"

"Not likely. Leave this warm cosy fire! You go, tell me about it later."

I left her to continue roasting herself. After all I know some people like 'hot dogs!' I found Alex and Fiona in the kitchen as I had predicted. Alex was sat at the table nursing a hot chocolate drink while Fiona's cup, standing alone on the table, was going cold. Fiona was pacing the room as she spoke: "But it's the sentimental thing Alex. You know, I promised Brian he could have mother's pictures." She stopped pacing and picked up the saltshaker from the table, turned it in her hand and replaced it. As she picked up the pepper pot she continued: "The carriage clock! Alex, do you know what that is worth? I just can't believe it. I am so stupid, should never have put mother's things in the shed. What was I thinking." She replaced the pepper pot on the table and started pacing again.

"Fi, you are making me dizzy, why don't you sit down?"

"No, I don't want to sit down." She tapped the barometer that hung beside the window. "'Change!' Huh."

The kitchen table had two sturdy chairs pushed under it with just enough room for me to curl up on the seat. I choose the furthest from the door. From this location

I could see and hear well, but doubted I would be noticed, at least not until Fiona finally wanted to sit down."

"I need to sit down!" she exclaimed. Roughly she pulled back the chair and I took flight promptly. "That's your blessed cat, how does she get in here?"

"Toilet window is my guess," Boss-man informed her.

"What am I to tell Brian? Oh, I just don't know. Why did I put her things in the shed?"

I judged that Alex was becoming slightly annoyed by Fiona's self-castigation. "Let us stop and think for a minute. First the deed has been done and the items taken, so it is too late to stop that, but we can contact the police, they might have information that could help recover the clock and pictures, and we might have information that could help them find the culprit. Secondly, we could set up security to make it harder for a thief in the future."

"Like what exactly."

"Cameras, better locks, check the window catches around the house."

"No, no cameras, I really can't be had with that stuff about the place."

"What about some security lighting, you know this cottage is very dark at night. Perhaps a couple of lights on sensors at the front and around the back would be a deterrent. These roughnecks don't like to be illuminated."

"That sounds promising. We should contact the police; do I call 999?"

"No, it is not a crime in progress, but I do have inspector Blackwood's personal number, I think I should give him a ring. What time is it?" Alex looked at his wristwatch and answered his own question: "three-thirty. Good, he might be in the office."

With that Boss-man stepped outside the front door and made his call. Tess well toasted, sauntered into the kitchen and nuzzled up to her mistress' legs. Two human hands stretched down to caress the canine's large floppy ears. "Hello Tess, getting a bit warm for you in front of the fire?"

"What's happening?" Tess whispered to me.

"My master is calling the police."

Only a few moments past when Alex returned. "He's coming straight over now with a chap from forensics. Seems, there has been a spate of similar burglaries in Kinver over the past two nights, and he would like to search for any incriminating evidence left at the scene. He was most pleased I called him."

Fiona didn't reply. She seemed lost in melancholy as she shuffled the salt and pepper utensils back and forth on the tabletop.

#

The cockapoo suddenly lifted her head and tilted it slightly to the right. She was laying on the tiled kitchen floor, when something she heard outside the cottage aroused her keen sense of hearing and caused her to enter alert mode. Without warning she jumped up and barked: "Outside! Intruders coming! Full defence at the ready! I'll protect you, stay behind me people!"

"Shut up Tess." Commanded her irate mistress. Tess stopped barking, dropped her tail between her legs and wandered disconsolately into the lounge, where she lay flat on her belly, her head and pointed snout stretched out in front of her. While feigning rejection I could see she was not placated and remained on full alert, ready to intervene if the situation required action.

Alex was inviting the two police officers, who had parked their official vehicle in the drive next to Fiona's Mini Cooper, into the cottage. "Please come in gentlemen. Good to see you again DCI Blackwood, thank you so much for coming so quickly."

"Mr. Dewhurst. It is us who are thanking you for calling, as I mentioned on the phone, we have had a spate of burglaries over the past couple of nights in the area and are trying to collate information and forensics. Oh, and this is Scene of Crime Officer Marchant."

"How do you do sir?" the tall well-built officer said as he took Alex's hand and gave a firm shake.

"Officer Marchant, pleased to meet you. Please step in to the kitchen where I can introduce both of you to Fiona Fullerton."

I detected Fiona was just a little overawed by the presence of officialdom in her little kitchen. Alex eased the tension by continuing the conversation: "No hazmat suit Officer? Or is it in the van?"

"Nice to meet you good lady," he ingratiatingly greeted Fiona before replying to Alex's question: "ah, well, if you will pardon me, this is just a simple data gathering exercise, no one has died! Sorry, I didn't mean to minimize the seriousness of the incident to you. However, I will take photographs, look for clues and most important, fingerprints."

"Could we see the crime scene, the garden shed I think you said it was," Blackwood requested.

The four humans vacated the kitchen and as I was feeling a little exhausted from all the coming and goings, I looked for a place to nap a while. Back to the chair under the kitchen table, I felt sure no one would want to take a seat just yet.

"DCI Blackwood, why don't you take a seat?" Fiona invited as she pulled my chair out from under the table, noticed me curled up, tilted the chair, and gave me a firm push. I unceremoniously landed on the floor under the table, much annoyed. I had not expected them to return so quickly.

"Thank you, ma'am. Much obliged to you. Officer Marchant will be a while but assuming no one has touched or entered the crime scene he should be able to get some information for the records."

"No, we peered inside the shed of course, but we did not touch anything, not even the broken padlock," clarified Alex.

"Fingerprints are the key here. If we can lift some prints, they may matchup with someone on our database, that would be a good start."

Prints! I had been all over the crime scene. My paw prints would be everywhere! What if they suspect me. Surely, they do not think I could be a cat-burglar. I mean, how would I have carried the loot?

#

"Hello my favourite puss-cat. And how are we today?"

Two days had past since we had returned the boat to its permanent mooring above Kinver Lock. I had taken up a lookout position on the rear seating nearest the canal towpath and enjoyed watching all and sundry pass by. It was late afternoon, and the cheerful schoolgirl from Wayside Cottage was on her way home. As she patted and then stroked my head, I dipped my back encouraging her to run a small hand all the way to the base of my tail. Arching my tail in a semi-circle so that it came close to touching my head and making a full circle with my curved back, I miaowed profusely: "Oh, how nice to see you, what a kind girl you are, how was school today? Did you win any prizes?"

She seemed indifferent to my questions but rather continued to chat to me in enthusiastic tones: "You know puss-cat, we are getting a kitten this weekend. It's a little boy and he is going to live with us at Wayside."

I straightened my back, dropped my tail, and jumping onto the roof out of her reach I turned my back on her. Surly of me I know, but a kitten? A kitten becomes a cat! A cat, especially male, will dominate the cottage and surrounding area. Where will I go for my latrine now?

The young girl seemed unaffected by the sudden and abrupt change in my nature and bid me goodbye and went on her way home. I couldn't help noticing on her back was a very full and undoubtedly heavy backpack of books and stationery. Why humans load their offspring with heavy loads at the very age they are developing is beyond me. No wonder they suffer so much in later years from back related problems.

I was festering on the latest news from Wayside Cottage when Lapsat ambled passed. I told her, but she lacked interest in the matter. Something else, however, was activating her little mind. "Saw Chalky this mornin'."

"Oh," I indifferently replied, "So?"

"Seems 'e's not around public 'ouse much just now. Just thought I'd mention it as I plan to pay a visit tonight to see if there's any local gossip, ee want to come?"

"No. Thanks for the offer. Did he say why?"

"Wye what?"

"Why he is not around much?" that cat can be frustrating at times.

"Oh, yeh, 'e has new girlfriend. Some young flighty piece from up main road. Parson's Meadow, I think 'twas. Didn't get 'er name."

"That Chalky is going to get a girl in trouble one of these days, if he hasn't already," I remarked abrasively.

"Strange thing though, Chalky said while 'e was scouting 'round back of 'is girlfriend's 'ouse looking for mouse as gift, 'e noted shed full of stuff."

"Well, I guess most people around here have sheds full of stuff."

"Mmm. The only item 'e could see clearly through broken window was carriage clock that 'e says looked rather valuable. If anyone knows about carriage clocks, it's our Chalky."

Carriage clock? My mind was spinning. Time to go inside and take a nap to clear my head.

#

Next morning I was still brooding on the Wayside Cottage problem, while aware there was something else niggling at my mind. Something Lapsat had said. I couldn't think what, so decided to take a snooze after breakfast. This was well intentioned, but impossible. The moment I curled into a ball the noise started. It was a violent grinding sound which reverberated along the length of the whole boat and set my nerves on edge.

Exiting the boat through the bow doors, the furthest end from the racket, I discovered Boss-man, sat on a very small plastic stool with a battery powered angle-grinder attacking the hull of our boat. Madness! I moved a little closer, but only as close as I dared. Around him an assortment of tools, tins, brushes and cleaning materials lay scattered on the grass. The focus of his attention was a raised patch that had bubbled up under the paint and it became obvious was allowing rust to form and slowly eat away at the steel hull.

Certain the damaged area was fully exposed, he started cleaning, and then applying a red-oxide paint to the surface. I did not like the look of the finished patch, but as I considered the accompanying paint tins, I soon realised there were various under and over-coats to follow.

All the while, while working, Alex would stop and chat to walkers, cyclists and even an occasional dog that drew close enough to examine his handiwork.

First there was Chip the Sausage dog who just loves the sound of his own voice. "Well, I keep saying, she doesn't feed me right, too much starch, and all that jelly, I ask you. Then there's the weather, she insists I go out in all types, if it's raining or a little cold, there's this infernal coat thing I must wear." The incessant yapping continued even as his owner, the feisty lady, dragged him away.

Not many minutes past before another altogether fitter male approached. He was large, muscular and loaded with a huge rucksack, from the bottom of which was strapped a rolled-up ground mat. His very presence intimidated me, so I moved well out of the way to observe from the safety of the old oak. As he paused to speak with Boss-man, I looked him over. Here was a man on a mission: heavy leather hiking boots, sturdy but light weight trousers and bomber jacket and topped with a knitted beanie hat. Attached to his rucksack was a colourful board with some handwriting scrawled across it.

"How's it going?" Alex called out to garner his attention.

"Mighty fine, thank you."

"What's the challenge?"

"Walking the length of the Staffs and Worcester for charity."

"You seem to be making good progress. What's the worthy cause?"

"Cancer Centre at Queen Elizabeth Hospital. They cared for my mother. Cancer got her in the end of course, but they were very compassionate and professional."

"Cancer care. Yes. Something close to my heart that is. Can I give you something to support the cause."

"Sure, but online is good, I have a web site …" He withdrew a small yellow card from his pocket and passed it to a grateful Alex.

"I wish you well in your cause."

"Thanks man, have a good one." With that he strode off with a purpose.

My master is a kindly man, and I know he would be happy to support a commendable cause. It just so happened that another less-worthy cause was approaching us from the opposite direction.

You have never seen such a bedraggled and unkempt collection of hair and garments. Rather than marching along with a purposeful step as the previous visitor, this gentleman, I use the word inappropriately, was shuffling in his moth eaten worn and sorry excuse for shoes. A large oversized full-length coat which had seen better days mostly hid from view the tattered remains of yesteryear's fashion. His full, patchy grey beard needed a good grooming, and so did the long-matted hair. Behind him he half dragged a wheeled trolly with an assortment of canvas bags containing what must represent all his worldly possessions.

He stopped beside the narrowboat but did not look at it or at Alex. Alex however was eying him up and down. 'Oh, please just move on,' I was thinking to myself. Mortified I was when Boss-man spoke: "You alright there mate?"

"Huh!"

"You look like you are struggling, are the bags heavy?"

"Not heavy. No problem. Just my life! I'll be going."

"No, wait a minute," Alex stood up, "I've got something for you."

"This some sort of trick man, 'cause I don't want no trouble."

"No trick mate. You need something to eat?"

"Maybe."

"Sit there on the bench, I will be back in a moment." Alex disappeared inside the boat only to re-emerge some minutes later with a small plate of sandwiches, a packet of crisps, an apple and a hot drink, which I guessed was soup. Boss-man sat on the bench next to him without speaking while he ate the sandwiches and slurped the soup from the cup.

Finally, replete, the man spoke: "You're a kindly man. Not all people are so kind." Alex didn't reply, I guess he was waiting to see if there would be more enlightenment on the man's circumstances. There was: "Interesting how some poor judgments, a mistake or two, can set you on the wrong path, then how hard to recover."

"You know, a wash, barber's shop and a second-hand clothes shop would have a positive effect."

"Huh! Little money left so that's not happening."

"Well along the canal a few yards you will find a toilet block with handbasin and soap. If I get you a key and a towel, what do you think?" There was no reply, but Alex went back to the boat and returned with the facilities' key and an old grey towel. The man refusing to leave his trolly, dragged it behind as he shuffled along to attend to his ablutions.

"Well, that's the last you see of the towel or the key!" I said to Alex after he had left. Not that Boss-man was interested in my opinion.

I was wrong of course. When he returned, while still looking every part a vagabond, there was a marked improvement in his countenance. Just the simple process of a good wash had improved his spirits. "Do yourself a favour," Alex said to him as he passed a small white envelope into his clean right hand, "there is something in there, enough to get a haircut in the village. Also, there is a charity shop next to the barbers. And if you are careful, enough for a night's stay in the Travelodge at Kidderminster. You could get a meal and a good hot shower.

Was it my imagination or did the eyes of the outcast moisten. He took the packet with a simple 'thanks' and set off in the direction of the village.

The summer sun was starting to fade in the sky as the vagrant reappeared. I had not expected to see him again. Why? I felt sure he would have taken the money to the off-licence, bought beer and spirits, and wasted himself. No! Not so. He had clean, albeit second hand clothes, a tidy haircut and even his beard was trimmed and neat. He did not come to speak but raised two thumbs in our direction. I glanced up to see Alex face beaming, which I suspect reflected his warm heart.

#

"Are ee in there? Kippy, can ee 'ear me?" I was enjoying my afternoon siesta in the old wooden shed in the horse's field when I heard Lapsat calling to me.

"Uh, yes, I'm here. Wait will you." I pushed my way back through the rotten gap in the side panel and climbed the bank to the path where Lapsat was methodically washing a front paw. "What's the problem?"

"Oh, no problem. Just thought ee like to know Boss-man 'as gone to cottage, I thinks 'e is fitting security lights."

'And you disturbed my much-deserved rest just to tell me that?' I wanted to say. I didn't. Instead, I said: "Right, guess I should go and check out the workmanship."

By the time I arrived most of the work had been completed, with three new miniature floodlights installed. One facing the front of the cottage, one to illuminate the drive and one around the back where the shed is. The shed door had been repaired, albeit in a somewhat temporary manner, with additional wooden battening and a new and stronger lock. Our master had been busy! I located him inside with Fiona.

"So, if a light is triggered by the sensor, a small ping will be generated here," he pointed to a small box above the front door, "it should be loud enough to alert you to any visitor, but not so troublesome as to frighten you."

"Sounds good to me," said Fiona while looking less than convinced. Her mobile phone rang at that moment, and she answered it while Alex finished tacking the loose wire in place above the front door.

"Hello, Fiona speaking." There was a pause as someone was speaking to her.

"Afternoon Officer Marchant, good to hear your voice again." Alex looked up and then returned to his assignment.

"Oh, my pleasure, it was good to have you help us out two days ago. Always a pleasure to have a man about the house." Alex hit the small nail too hard, and it bent, he muttered an inappropriate word under his breath.

"You have? ... Oh, that's good. ... Yes ... Certainly."

"What does he want?" Alex mumbled just loud enough for Fiona to hear.

"Really! Yes, ... Yes ... No, Thank you, certainly I will tell Alex. Might see you again sometime. Goodbye and thanks for calling." She cancelled the call and looked up only to find Alex staring at her.

"Tell Alex what?" he demanded.

"Patience! That was Officer Marchant the Crime Scene ..."

"Yes, I know who it was."

"They have a match for the fingerprints. Not that they know for certain who it belongs to yet."

"You talk in riddles."

"The person who broke into the shed is the same person who tried to steal your car!"

"Wow! That is interesting."

A face flashed up in my mind. I knew the face behind the prints!

"They have confirmed he did at least one of the other local burglaries in the village that same night. Officer Marchant says they have strong evidence to link a known suspect, but he can't say who it is until they have completed further checks."

"Officer Marchant, you say."

"Yes, Richard."

"Richard now, is it? Seems to me you can be a right little flirt!"

"Oh, Alex, don't be so square. Besides I'm not exactly little!"

I slipped out of the front door and sat on the towpath watching a fiberglass cruiser drifting passed, its minimal crew having negotiated Kinver lock.

So, they can't say for sure who the suspect is. But I can!

## 20 — CLIFTON SQUIBB

"Just what have they done to you?" I said on seeing Tess.

Lapsat and I had wandered off in the direction of Wayside Cottage, as she wanted to look for the new kitten which should have arrived at few days ago. I did not think this was a good idea. Firstly, the occupants of the cottage were hardly likely to entertain a visiting moggy without an appointment and secondly, the new addition to the family would be kept indoors for some weeks. Who wants to see another kitten anyway? So, leaving Lapsat on her mission I returned to 'Rumah Saya' only to find Tess tethered to a mooring ring and Alex and Fiona deep in conversation sat at the stern of the boat.

"What has happened to you then?" I repeated.

"Been to the groomers."

"You've been butchered!"

"Quit your mockery you pesky feline."

"That's not your usual groomers, is it?"

"No, apparently, she has gone away for a few months and a temporary novice has stepped in. Nothing I can do about it."

It was not a successful cut. The overall coat was patchy, and the tail looked like a feather duster. Worse, however, was the poor cockapoo's face, it had become pointed and lacking substance.

"Don't worry, it will all grow back in a week or two," I said reassuringly.

Sat at the rear of the boat, our respective benefactors were sipping wine and eating cheese and nibbles. I considered this very civilised behaviour, Tess, on the other hand thought nothing of it.

Tess' mistress approached with a small piece of cheese for her, which she gently took from her hand after a quick sniff. Cheese is not good for me; I am not offered it and I would refuse it if it were offered. I was however, pleased to accept a couple of chewy treats from the hand of Fiona.

#

Later that evening Alex and Fiona walked over to 'The Lock Inn' for 'a spot of dinner' as Alex called it. I considered this a good opportunity to check out the new safety lighting at Fiona's cottage and spend a little time in the presence of the effervescent pooch who frequently provided an opportunity for a good laugh.

Approaching the cottage, I noted light emanating from the front living room window. Apart from this illumination the whole cottage stood in darkness, but this was as I expected. What I didn't expect was for the cottage to remain in darkness as I sauntered up the garden path. No glare of arc lights, no flashing neon signs, not even a candle bulb activated. So much for Boss-man's labours, not very effective it would seem.

I followed the usual route around the back, passed the well locked shed and the second sensor light, which also remained inactive, and in through the toilet window. I found Tess as predictable as ever sprawled out on the hearth rug in the living room. Without a word I entered the room, walked passed the animal, and sat upright in the far corner. "Lights don't work," I stated.

"They do."

"No, they don't. I just came in passed the sensors and nothing happened."

"You're a cat, stupid. It's not supposed to sense every cat, dog or fox that passes through the garden."

Well, for once I guess the dog was right, but as I am reluctant to admit an error, I chose to remain quiet for a period, following which we naturally both spoke at the same time: "Sorry, no you go ahead ..."

"You know where the humans have gone?"

"I saw them cross the canal in the direction of 'The Lock Inn', I guess they are eating in the pub tonight."

"You been fed?"

"Yes, and you?"

"Bully beef and vegetables mixed with gravy. Mistress made it up herself tonight."

"Sounds awful. I don't do vegetables."

All went quiet again for some time, and then without warning, Tess suddenly sat bolt upright and froze.

"What is it?" I demanded realising something was wrong.

"Shhh! Be quiet. Can you hear something?"

As the words escaped Tess' mouth a loud 'ping' was heard from the device above the front door, and a powerful light illuminated the front garden. We both heard a muffled curse word. The garden light went out, but almost instantaneously the light at the side of the cottage was activated. All this became too much for Tess who took to barking demands to 'cease and clear off' in no uncertain terms.

When, after some time, Tess stopped shouting all went very quiet and it seemed to me that the would-be intruder had left. Not so! The sound of breaking glass reverberated around the peaceful dwelling. The dog was on the move, out of the lounge, down the passage and entering the downstairs toilet. I followed with eagerness tempered with caution, always keeping two steps behind Tess. Just as well I did, as the intruder was forcing his way through the broken window and using his crowbar took a swing at Tess.

Tess reared up just in time for the blow to miss her but cause the assailant to lose his footing. He came crashing forward and half landed on top of the unfortunate canine. Taking the role of superdog personally, Tess set about the uninvited visitor with zeal, however the intruder managed to swing the crowbar which he still held in his right hand, just enough to score a blow on Tess' back.

"I've been hit!" yelped Tess. "Go, go get help Kippy."

I would have gone to get help without a question if only my feet were not routed to the spot. I found my fear caused me to lack movement. I watched in terrible fascination as Tess, now in pain and very much the underdog was pushed brutally into the small room while his assailant stepped into the hallway and slammed the door shut. Tess was trapped and I was next in line for a beating!

Sheer willpower unlocked my frozen legs and in a single leap I had reached the staircase, bounded two steps at a time to the relative safety of the upstairs landing and hid behind the wash basket. With relief I came quickly to realise he was not looking to attack me, which allowed me to take stock of the situation and catch my breath.

Alex and Fiona were at the pub and oblivious to the break in. The toilet window was shattered, and Tess lay injured among the broken glass, trapped and unable to protect her mistress property from this evil man in dark khaki trousers! I was hiding on the landing and listening to the disconsolate sounds from the front room. Nothing good would happen if I stayed hiding, so I bit the bullet and slipped quietly downstairs.

Around the open door I could see him gathering small ornaments and other easy to carry objects into a large plastic carrier bag he had brought with him. His eyes fell upon a jar of pound coins. Into his bag. The same fate befell the antique Chinaman figurine, and the pair of sterling silver and enamelled robins. Then his gaze fell on Fiona's second handbag which I knew contained monies put aside to pay veterinary bills.

Action was needed, but what? Charged with adrenalin and a strong sense of retribution I launched myself in his direction just as he struggled to get the handbag in his plastic shopping bag. Failure! In one easy movement he swiped at me, and while my claws tore at his neck, I felt myself easily thrust aside, landing heavily on the arm of the sofa. Instantaneously I had righted myself and made a speedy exit to the hallway, to avoid further humiliation.

No, I could not stop him on my own, I needed Tess to assist. I sat on my haunches for a moment, contemplating the door that held Tess prisoner. Almost without thought I leapt forward reaching high for the door handle. I felt it move slightly under my weight as I fell back, but nothing happened as I crashed to the ground in a heap.

"That you Kippy?" was a disembodied voice from behind the door, "it moved, try again." I wasted no energy in making a reply but simply moved slightly to the far side of the door and leapt again. This time, slightly higher and with more determination. I caught the handle full in my chest. My weight not only pulled the handle down but simultaneously pushed the door open. I crashed to the floor again, this time just as confirming his personal details tokhaki man was forcing an exit through the front door of the cottage.

Before I could stand, Tess was rushing passed me, "Great job old girl!" she barked as she flattened me against the ground again. I looked up from my prostrate position just in time to see khaki man fall flat on his face and spill some of the contents from his torn bag. I could not believe my eyes! Lapsat was right in front of the door, and as he attempted his getaway he stumbled headlong over my companion. Tess bounded through the open doorway and landed on the prostrate body pining him to the floor. I do believe the prone figure was busy swearing, but as he was also being suffocated to a large degree by the weight of Tess, whom I have to say, has gained a pound or two recently, his expletives were unclear.

"Get help you two," Tess pleaded. We both took off in the direction of the canal with the dog's pleading in our ears: "be quick, oh please be quick."

As we rushed through the garden gate, we stopped, looked around, saw no one walking and no boats in sight, thus, quickly we ran under the road bridge, where Lapsat caught sight of a dog walker and tried to arouse his attention. To no avail, he just looked vacantly at Lapsat and walked off. Lapsat then continued aiming directly towards our narrowboat home. I on the other hand made haste across the lock gate, round the pub car park and in through the saloon door.

It did not take long for Alex and Fiona to become aware of my presence as the first patron I encountered announced to the landlord that an agitated cat had made an entrance. All credit to the humans, they recognised my distress immediately and reacted by following me outside, their dinner only partially consumed.

Outside we crossed the main road, only to find Lapsat waiting for us at the top of the connecting path that led to the cottage. Bounding on ahead, Lapsat and I led the bemused humans towards our captive. On entering the garden, the floodlight activated, illuminating the tense scene.

"My cottage!" cried Fiona, "what has happened? Tess what have you done?" she said without a full comprehension of the scene being played out in her garden. Alex on the other hand knew instantly and wasted no time at all.

"Phone 999, get the police here immediately. Hold on Tess, I'm coming."

Lapsat and I watched bemused, as rather than running to help Tess, Boss-man charged into the cottage returning seconds later with a key. A key to the new lock on the garden shed! Moments later, having accessed the shed he returned with a pack of large plastic cable ties.

"Police please. Oh, yes, we need help, crime in progress. ... Yes, Mrs. Fiona Fullerton. ... Yes, Lockside Cottage, Kinver. ... That's right. Burglary. Suspect being held against his will in my garden. ... Oh, yes, thank you, as quickly as you can please."

"Grab his left hand, Fi."

Together they strapped khaki man's hands behind his back using the cable ties and then linked both legs in a similar fashion.

"Well done, Tess! That's my girl." Tess rolled off the prostrate man and sat panting, and obviously in some pain. Alex rolled the man over and looked him straight in the face.

"Yes, I know you! You tried to steal my car, you little scumbag." Alex looked around at the spilled contents of Fiona's home. "Your time is up buddy; we've got you now."

I strutted over and displayed a haughty air of superiority as I said to khaki man, "Yes and I also know you. Cracker! You it was who pushed 'Pinky' in the lock, so he died!" However, I don't think he or any of the other humans present understood what I said. Lapsat and Tess did!

#

It seemed an interminable time before the first wail of a siren could be heard in the distance off towards Stourton. As the incessant pulsing tone approached from the east a second siren became audible off towards the south in the direction of Cookley. Both police vehicles arrived simultaneously and rather than neatly parking off road, they chose to block the main road traffic as officers piled out and surrounded the little cottage. Irate motorists, when they encountered the flashing blue and red vehicles obstructing their route, had no choice but to multi-point turn in the road and return the way they came, seeking an alternative route in or out of the village.

"You Mrs. Fullerton?" the leading officer demanded upon seeing Fiona, who by this time, having never encountered such a spectacle in her life, was visibly shaking.

"Er, yes, I ..." but before she could confirm her identity the second policeman had stepped forward, grabbed at Cracker's shoulder, and staring him in the face said: "Well, well, look what we have here Sarg."

"I do declare it's Clifton Squibb. Had you before 'the beak' for that shoplifting misdemeanour, didn't we sunshine."

Clifton Squibb. So khaki man who I knew as Cracker is really Clifton Squibb. Whatever name he was known by, he was not letting on this evening to the Sergeant or any other individual. In fact, he was plain refusing to speak.

"This the guy you fellas caught robbing the cottage?" the Sergeant asked of Alex and Fiona.

"Well, it's a little more complicated than you imply, but the items next to him on the ground when we found him are definitely from the cottage," Alex said.

"Right," began the man of authority who at this point was looking somewhat confused. Another siren was wailing in the distance, somewhere on its way through the main street of Kinver and heading also in our direction.

Turning back to Cracker he stated: "You're under arrest for unlawful entry of Lockside Cottage and theft of said property's contents. You do not have to say anything. But it may harm your defence if you do not mention when questioned something which you later rely on in court. Anything you do say may be given in evidence. Understand Squibb?"

Young Mr. Squibb dipped his head slightly and then swore under his breath.

"Shall I write that down Sarg?"

"No Jackson, we are not that desperate!"

The third siren belonged to a police van, which when the rear doors were opened revealed a steel cage with lockable door. All of us watched as Cracker was shoved without dignity into the waiting van, the metal door slammed shut and locked securely followed by the outer doors. As the van moved away, two of the policemen, their job done also drove off.

The harsh glare of the floodlight illuminated Lockside Cottage simple garden. Surveying the crime scene, I saw Fiona leaning against the cottage wall looking drawn and despondent while Boss-man had a comforting hand resting on her shoulder. The two policemen were busy making notes, taking simple photographs, and getting a general perspective of the evening events. Strewn across the grass next to the path were the spoils that Cracker so nearly succeeded in removing from the property.

Beyond the open gate both Lapsat and Tess sat staring vacantly into the air. Tess looked weary and certainly in some pain following her encounter with Cracker, as she slumped down onto the front lawn and sighed.

The intense excitement of the previous events had left me physically drained; I needed recuperative rest and decided it was time to return to the warm comfort of our floating home. Before I turned my back on the gloomy scene, I looked into Tess' eyes and dipped my head. She in turn very slowly closed and then opened her big brown eyes. No words were exchanged, none were needed!

#

Time is a healer they tell me. In Tess' case, time and a brief visit with her mistress to the veterinary surgery to ensure no major injury had occurred. Many days had past since that eventful evening. Lapsat had followed me home that night, but neither of us spoke about the events for a couple of days. Alex went to visit Fiona and then Fiona with Tess came to visit us on the boat again. Fiona seemed even more affectionate towards us felines now, although neither human could fully understand what part we had all played in the capture of Cracker. It was on one of these visits by

Tess and her mistress that further information came to light about this person called Clifton Squibb.

Fiona and Tess invited themselves on to the boat, which in days past I might have viewed as inconsiderate, but I was more tolerant now. Tess simply said: "Hi girls," and deposited herself in a pile at the corner of the saloon. Fiona said: "Have you seen the local paper!" as she flung a copy in the direction of Boss-man, who sat in his favourite armchair, quietly minding his own business, and nursing a brandy. Without a word he placed the bulbous glass on the occasional table, lent back in his chair and opened the tabloid.

"'Anti-Social Local Man Caught!'" he read from the headlines. "Ah, good mug-shot of him on the cover."

"Go on, read it out."

Alex obliged: "'Local Kinver man arrested and charged with burglary, attempted auto theft and manslaughter.'"

"Police reckon he had something to do with the death of that young man Pinkerton Smith."

"It goes on: 'Arrested last week while attempting another break in at a residence in the village, Clifton Squibb, aged 23, a local man from Parsons Meadow, has been remanded in custody charged with numerous offenses and will be brought before Dudley Magistrates' court at a date to be set.' It goes on a bit about recent crimes in Kinver but without implying they are all his responsibility."

"Yes, but read the last paragraph."

To do this Alex had to turn to page five. "Um, right, here it is, 'Clifton Squibb is known locally by his nickname, Cracker. It appears he earned this unusual name while still in fourth form at Kinver High School. On one occasion he let off a few pyrotechnic devices behind the bicycle shed to amuse his mates. These fireworks included several Chinese firecrackers and one squib, a large firework attached to a cosh such as can be seen annually at the Bridgwater Carnival in Somerset. From this event Squibb earned the nickname 'Cracker'.'"

A break in the human conversation occurred while Fiona and Alex mentally digested the information found in the local rag. Fiona interrupted the silence: "You know, DCI Blackwood called me this morning? It seems they have located many of the items Cracker stole from the village over recent months in the garden shed and attic of his parents' home where he lived. He wants me to visit the station sometime to identify my property. Would you come with me Alex please."

"Oh, most certainly I will, shall we go tomorrow?"

#

There is one final detail to add to the account of Mr. Squibb. It occurred the next day when Fiona and Boss-man had gone to visit the local police station in Alex's Yaris. Lapsat pushed her way through the cat door and came calling me.

"Chalky 'as moved 'is girlfriend into pub!" announced Lapsat mockingly.

"Oh, so what?"

"She's pregnant!"

"Of course, we knew that was going to happen!"

"Yes, but ee see, Chalky found 'er undernourished 'nd weak at 'er 'ome in Parsons Meadow. It seems senior protectors are away for some extended period, world-cruise, or somethin', 'nd suddenly young man doesn't come 'ome. So, no one to feed 'er."

"And the publican landlord doesn't mind?"

"Well, Chalky is keeping 'er round back in gas bottle storage 'nd plans to bring 'er indoors only when she is due to produce kitts. By then, according to Chalky, landlord will be a pushover!"

## 21 — THE KEY TO A WINDLESS PATH

Roll over. Full stretch. Open eyes and glance at ceiling. Curl up into a ball and settle for another cat nap.

It was mid-afternoon, which seems as good a time as any to take a snooze. Something was niggling at my mind. I opened an eye and looked at the ceiling. Three sharp pinpricks of coloured light adorned the plain wood panelling of the boat ceiling. I closed my eyes, determined to have at least forty winks before any other residents of the boat disturbed me.

I opened my eyes again. Those specks of light should not be there! I sat up and observed the vibrant sunlight squeezing through a gap in the curtain and casting a defined warm line across the floor, up the chair and across Boss-man's desk in the corner of the saloon. Jumping down from the armchair I strode over to the desk, and in one simple leap landed on papers that were collated on Boss-man's desk.

Curious! A small royal blue felt box sat open in the middle of the desk. Poking up above the rim was a gold ring with coloured glass-like pieces embedded in a circle resting on the top. As the sunlight was striking the crystal shards, reflected light was projected onto the ceiling. The centre piece was a ruby red crystal-like stone with smaller clear but multi-faceted glass-like segments adorning the edges.

I cautiously extended a paw and touched the velvet receptacle. It moved a tiny distance but did not fight back. I pushed again; it moved a little closer to the edge of the desk, I was rather enjoying the power I could exert over this little object. Looking up I scanned the room, no one in sight. Quick push and over it went! I sat up with my most innocent expression as if to say: 'What happened? Not me!'

When I looked over the edge of the desk, I could see the box on its side laying on the floor, but the gold-coloured ring was missing. It was at this moment that Bossman, who had been fussing in the kitchen, decided to enter the saloon. "Kippy! What are you doing on the desk. You know you are not allowed up here. Oh, you have messed up my papers." Two huge hands reached under my shoulders, lifted me off the desk and deposited me on the floor. I sulked off to the far corner and sat watching him tidy the papers. Then he exploded: "The ring! Where's the ring?" A quick glance at the floor below the desk revealed the little box, and at first all seemed fine, until he discovered it was empty. "Oh, no. It must be here somewhere." But it wasn't! It seems to me, that when a human drops a nail or a screw it always runs away and finds somewhere to hide. The ring was hiding!

"Kippy, what have you done, where is the ring?" His searching was becoming ever more intense. After a quick hand sweep of the floor failed to spot the object, a light from his mobile phone was used to illuminate the area. Nothing! Ever more desperate, he widened his search until finally, success! Boss-man moved the wastebin and tucked behind it against the wall was the multi-coloured object. Alex returned it to its little box, closed the lid and pushed it into a safe place far back on the desk.

#

Stunning! I looked up at Fiona who had just entered the narrowboat to see her dressed in baby blue knee length summer dress with a round neck. It was topped off with matching blue and white waistcoat and patent black leather flat soled shoes.

The sound of the bedroom door opening drew my attention as Alex appeared in a royal blue dinner jacket, with black trim, black trousers, and white open neck dress-shirt. It was the powerful aroma of Old Spice that took my breath away. "Fiona Fullerton, you look glamorous tonight! Shall we go?"

I had no idea where they were going, but they were no doubt going to enjoy a special and perhaps formal evening together. I on the other hand had some sleep to catch up on, so I curled up on Boss-man's chair and slipped into unconsciousness.

#

Imagine my annoyance when, no sooner had I curled up than I heard car doors slam and voices outside. It was dark outside, so perhaps I had slept after all.

Alex and Fiona were chatting about their evening, which seemed to revolve around sirloin steak and béarnaise sauce. Alex slipped through to the bedroom to remove his jacket and upon return saw Fiona standing looking at the photograph of Brenda. "She was a lucky woman to have you!" she said with warmth in her voice.

At that moment I detected a serious atmosphere descend upon the interior of the little boat. Alex was fumbling with something in his right hand and looking intently at Fiona. Sensing his gaze, she turned and looked him directly in the eyes.

"You know I'm in love with you Fi?"

Following a brief silence Fiona replied: "Yes Alex I do."

Alex extended both hands towards her, and in them he proffered the small open box displaying the ring in all its glory. "Would you do me the honour of becoming Mrs. Alex Dewhurst?"

Now, I really don't think there was an audible response from Fiona, I certainly didn't hear one. What I did see was physical. Fiona reached for the ring, slipped it on her finger, reached out to Alex and wrapped her arms around his neck. Her answer came in the form of a long passionate kiss.

Disgusting!

Human displays of affection are just so nauseating. You don't see us felines carrying on in such a manner. I was so disturbed I made a quick exit through the cat door and sat meditatively under the mighty oak.

Life's path was twisting again. These two humans would no doubt live together. But where? On the narrowboat 'Rumah Saya'? Or would it be at Lockside Cottage. I have to say, while I love the boat, the cottage would be nice. However, being honest with you I am happy anywhere that has food and a place to sleep.

Just think. Lockside Cottage with Alex and Fiona, Lapsat and I. A happy family again. Oh no, I forgot … and Tess the cockapoo!

### THE END

## EPILOGUE — HALCYON DAYS

Fiona gripped Alex hand and together they moved away from the oak doors that facilitated entrance and exit of the registry office. With a beaming face and large brown envelope containing a copy of the marriage certificate in Alex's righthand they moved purposefully toward the waiting taxi. At their side Tess trotted in a dignified manner.

Under the mighty oak our two feline friends stood upright. Kippy moving with concentrated determination quickly made a direct line for Boss-man. Halfway across the green she stopped suddenly, poised for flight she eyed up Tess, but saw no mischief in her eyes and continued her amble. Fiona reached out and gently lifted the Persian into her arms, thus interrupting her planned attempt to rub her head against Boss-man's right leg. Under the tree Lapsat stood, stretched, and with slow dignity wandered in the same direction.

Fiona joyfully exclaimed to Alex: "Look Alex, they both waited for us, let us take our little family home."

"Quite right Fiona, together we will make a happy family."

Alex mind drifted over the past couple of troubled years. His path to renewed happiness had been stormy, but all along he had the two cats to provide an anchor to his soul. Now he also had a precious wife and her lovable dog. He was looking forward to walking a path of calmness and tranquillity. They both heard Kipepeo miaow audaciously.

"Hey, Lapsat, watch this!" Kippy expostulated.

"Oh no Kippy, not now!" But it was too late. Kipepeo leapt from Fiona's arms and rushed headlong towards the oak tree. This was just too much of a temptation for Tess who forgetting the seriousness of the occasion set off at high speed in pursuit. Once round the tree, up over the wooden bench, across the manicured lawn and finally Kippy ascended the trunk of the mighty oak. Tess came to a sudden halt below the tree and let out a full-powered bark.

"Just wait until we get home, you cheeky little minx, …" the sentence remained unfinished.

Alex and Fiona looked at each other with a frown on their faces, then burst into laughter. "A happy family indeed!" Alex concluded.

'The Windless Path' is a work of fiction. While much of the geography and locations are real, I have taken liberties to allow development of the narrative. All humans are figments of my imagination and bear no resemblance to any person living or deceased. The featured animals are however very real!

No animals were harmed in the making of this book.